RAID

Raid

Kristen Ashley

First ebook edition: February 27, 2013

First ebook edition: February 27, 2013
First print edition: 2013
Latest editions: July, 2015

ISBN-10: 0615766412
ISBN-13: 9780615766416

Discover other titles by Kristen Ashley at:
www.kristenashley.net

Commune with Kristen at:
www.facebook.com/kristenashleybooks
Twitter: KristenAshley68
Instagram: KristenAshleyBooks
Pinterest: kashley0155

DEDICATION

This book is dedicated to the memory of my Gramma, Mildred Moutaw.
She lived far away from me so I didn't know her all that well.
But what I knew, I loved.

Gramma, your afghan is still on my couch.
It's been to two countries, three cities.
It will always be with me.
And it's exactly what you intended it to be.
Home. Warmth. Comfort. Nurture.
Love.

1

RAIDEN

I sat in Rachelle's Café. Today's seat was facing the door.

I tried to switch it up so he wouldn't know.

If my back was to the door, maybe one day, if he noticed me, he wouldn't think I was looking for him, waiting, hoping for a glimpse.

Even though I was.

Raiden.

Raiden Ulysses Miller.

An amazing name for an amazing man.

The bell over the door rang, and having months of practice in not letting my hope and eagerness show, I slowly lifted my eyes to look, my heart skipping a beat.

It wasn't him.

I brought my coffee cup to my lips and took a sip, hiding my disappointment.

I'd started crushing on Raiden Miller when I was six and he came to Grams's annual picnic.

He was nine.

He was also beautiful.

Over time, he got more beautiful. He was just one of those boys who started out gorgeous and just got better.

So by the time I got to high school, a freshman to his senior, I was gone for him. He was the most popular boy in school. Tall. So tall. Six foot four. Broad.

Muscular. His hair a rich, dark brown, and even back then there were burnished highlights in his hair like he went to Betsy's Salon.

He didn't. It was natural and still the same. His sister Rachelle had the same hair. Everyone was jealous.

Even me.

Only of Rachelle.

As for Raiden, I just wanted to touch his hair, see if it was as thick and silky as it looked.

Just one touch and I'd be happy.

After high school, everyone thought it was so cool he went into the Marines. The perfect fit for him. Even as a boy, he was a man's man. His dad had taken off and after that everyone knew he'd taken care of his mom and sister. He kept their yard looking nice, fixed stuff at their house, and even though he played football in the fall and baseball in the spring he got jobs to help make ends meet.

He was a good kid, grew up fast because his dad was gone, and he easily took on that responsibility which made everyone like him. So the Marines were a natural choice, Raiden deciding to serve our country and doing it by joining the baddest of the badasses, as everyone knew the Marines were. Or maybe this was just me thinking Raiden was the baddest of the baddasses because he stepped up at a young age and looked after his family. But I think most everyone agreed.

What surprised folks was when he got out.

I'd heard people talking.

"Off the grid." I'd heard Paul Moyer, who owned the feed store, say. He'd gone on, "Suppose it's not a surprise, what with what went down over there, ole Raid losin' his buddies like he did. Gettin' that medal. What he had to do to get it. But still, sad to see a man like him…lost."

I knew what went down. His squad had been nearly annihilated. They'd lost almost everyone. Word was Raiden had almost singlehandedly saved the few who survived, and not only that, he'd made certain the bodies of his comrades went with them so the enemy couldn't get them.

I knew this because everybody talked, but also because it was such a big deal. It was all over the papers.

But the minute he could get out after that, he did.

Everyone thought he'd make a career of the Marines.

He didn't.

Then, six months ago, he came back to Willow.

The first time I saw him, having popped by Rachelle's to grab a coffee, I'd stopped breathing.

He was no less gorgeous, not after all these years, nearly fifteen of them. He was just as tall, but even more muscular. His shoulders so broad you could plant a tabletop on them and it would hold steady. Thick thighs. Sinewy, veined forearms. Big, rough hands.

Phenomenal.

And those eyes.

I'd studied them in the yearbook. So unusual, the way the green transformed from pupil to the edge of his iris.

They were better with him older, tan; his strong jaw always thickly stubbled, like he shaved once every week because he didn't have the time or inclination to bother with it, and further, he didn't care what people thought. Those lines radiating out the sides of his eyes which just made them more interesting.

His entire unbelievably handsome face and his thick, overlong hair seemed to exist in order to be a frame for those magnificent eyes.

It did a good job.

Excellent.

I could say this because I was an authority on this subject, as was nearly every available and not so available female in Willow, Colorado, our hometown.

But maybe I was the only one who crazily, creepily (it had to be said) semi-stalked him by hanging at out Rachelle's Café simply to catch a glimpse of him.

Okay, so maybe it was more than just to catch a glimpse of him.

It was silly, but I couldn't let go of the hope that one day he'd walk in, look at me, smile and maybe pop by my table to have a chat where I would boggle his mind with my brilliance. I'd charm him with my manner. He'd ask me out on a date. At the end of which, maybe, hopefully, I'd finally be able to touch his hair (amongst other things).

This never happened.

A couple of times, those beautiful eyes of his looked through me. Once, embarrassingly, I didn't move my gaze fast enough when he glanced through the café and he caught me studying him.

But he just gave me a chin lift and looked away.

That was it.

He did seem to have a lot on his mind. He never came to the café to hang out, eat lunch, anything like that. He usually moved through, always grinning at his sister if she was around, heading straight to the back room and disappearing.

This was, of course, intriguing; why he'd come to the café and disappear.

Then again, everything about Raiden Miller was intriguing.

It also meant that he didn't hang out to eat, and perchance, gaze about the room and fall madly in love with me.

And at that moment, I was realizing this was also not going to happen that day. I'd been there a while. It was getting late and I rarely saw him there late.

So I grabbed my purse and tossed down enough money to cover the check lying on the table, including a generous tip. Should a miracle occur and Raiden finally notice me, buttering up his sister with big tips wasn't a bad thing. She was a year ahead of me in high school. We'd known each other since forever and she already liked me, as I did her.

It also was earned. Her food and service were both stellar.

I grabbed my coat off the back of the chair, shrugged it on and looped my purse on my shoulder.

"Later Hanna!" Rachelle called as I moved toward the front door.

"Later!" I called back, throwing a smile her way and putting my hand to the door.

I pushed it open, went out onto the sidewalk, did a routine scan of the street and stopped dead.

Raiden was across the street standing beside his Jeep, making out with a very pretty, skinny-minnie, petite, big-haired, large-chested blonde.

My breath caught in my throat and my stomach churned.

She had high-heeled boots on, but still, she was so petite he was deeply bent into her. They were in a serious clinch. The only way I could see she had big breasts was because her clothes were skintight, her jacket was open and I could see one pushed out the side where it was pressed in his chest.

Oh God.

God!

She was skanky and I could tell this, too, what with the high-heeled boots (which weren't normal-person fashionable, they were skank fashionable), skintight clothes and big hair, but also, even in profile and across the street I could see she had on a lot of blusher and thick foundation.

But she was one of those skanky skanks who looked cool. Who worked her skankedness. Who made skankdom something you'd consider aspiring to.

Not to mention, her skankedness got her in a clinch with Raiden Ulysses Miller.

And he looked no less fabulous than he always looked. Tight-fitting long-sleeved thermal over cargo pants and boots, his shades pushed up into his amazing hair. No jacket, as if his level of testosterone was so high he didn't feel the cold.

God.

God!

I tore my eyes away, and blind, my stomach feeling hollow, I moved by rote to my SUV, swung in and luckily made it home without incident.

Though I didn't know how.

Because that hurt.

It *hurt.*

Oh God, why did it hurt so much?

Still battling what I knew was a self-inflicted wound, I got into my house and went directly to my girlie, frou-frou, countrified splendor living room. I sat cross-legged on my couch, stared at nothing and felt the pain.

Time passed by and finally it came to me.

I knew what it was.

I knew it was like when you crushed on an actor or some athlete and you found out he was single and you let yourself have crazy dreams that one day he'd run into you and fall head over heels.

Then you'd find out he got married, or got someone pregnant and then (maybe) got married, and your fantasy would die.

And it hurt when fantasies died.

A lot.

But that was exactly what it was.

The death of a fantasy.

Raiden Ulysses Miller was not a famous actor or athlete, but still.

He would never be mine.

I knew this because he was into women who could make skanky cool.

Big-haired, blonde, skinny-minnie, big-chested, *petite* women who could make skanky cool.

I had nice hair. It shone with health, it was thick and it was one shade up from blonde, but it wasn't big.

And I had an ample chest, but not *that* ample.

I was not skinny-minnie.

I was absolutely not skanky and could never be, no matter if it was cool and could get you Raiden Miller. I just knew I was the kind of girl who had no latent skank huddling deep inside, waiting for the makeup, hairspray and tight clothes that would let her out.

I was also not petite.

"*Chère*," my great-grandmother always stated (more than once), "thank the good Lord above He gave you those legs. Women the world over would die for your legs. They go on forever, precious girl, and trust your old biddy of a grand-mother, she knows, one day, you'll be glad for those legs."

That day, as much as I loved Grams and knew she was (almost) always right, was not today.

Slowly I pushed out of my couch and moved through the house to the bath-room. I switched on the light, stood in front of the basin, leaned in and looked in the mirror.

I'd had three boyfriends, and all of them, obviously, started with dates.

They also always went long-term.

Not one boy who asked me out didn't ask me again and again.

But they always broke up with me.

And staring into the mirror in the bathroom, just like I suddenly figured out why Raiden Ulysses Miller making out with a skanky (but cool) blonde hurt so much, I figured out why my boyfriends broke up with me.

Because I sat in cafés hoping for a glimpse of handsome guys and didn't *do* anything about it.

Because I didn't poof out my hair big.

Because when I was in high school I stayed home and studied. I didn't go out to parties. And when I wasn't studying, I was at the movies or reading. When I got older I didn't go to bars and do tequila shots and flirt over games of pool. I hung out with my ninety-seven-year-old great-grandmother, my friend KC, or again, went to the movies or read. I didn't take fabulous vacations where I could have ill-advised but delicious holiday flings that gave me good memories and better stories to tell. I went to my parents' house in Tucson, visited my brother in California or rented a cabin two hours away in the Colorado Mountains and, yes, you guessed it, I sat around and read.

I was living a narrow life and that narrow life made me uninteresting.

Boring.

Nothing.

I was twenty-eight years old and my great-grandmother, who had lived nearly a century, had a more active, fun-filled life than I did.

This was insane.

It was even more insane than falling in love from afar with a nine-year-old boy and hoping like heck I got picked for his tug of war team at my grams's annual picnic. Which I did, sickeningly gratifyingly, three years in a row, even though he never noticed me and thus didn't care. It was more insane than harboring that crush all through high school and even when he was away *for years*.

It was certifiable.

"And now it's done," I told my reflection.

Then I did what I never did.

I made a decision and acted on it.

I went to my kitchen, got a pad of paper and made a to-do list.

Once done, I immediately started on my list.

First up, I called Betsy at the salon and told her I needed a new style and she was in charge.

"Ohmigod, Hanna! I'm moving people around *right now*! You have to come in tomorrow! I...can't...*wait*!" she exclaimed.

I went in the next day and got a trim, flippy layers and highlights.

After that, I drove straight to Bob's car dealership and bought myself a pearl white Nissan Z.

It was awesome.

The next day I drove my new Z into town, walked into the travel agent and booked a vacation on a cruise ship.

After that I walked down the block. Something caught my eye at the bike shop, and, even though it wasn't on my list I turned and went right in.

I did not go back to Rachelle's except for the occasional coffee, but those were only flybys.

I did not see Raiden Ulysses Miller.

Not for five months.

What I didn't know was...

He saw me.

2

CAT FOOD

Five Months Later

"*Voilà!*" BODHI SHOUTED.

He shifted back. I saw the results of his ministrations, threw my head back and laughed before I looked back down at my girl. My pink and white daisy Schwinn now had opalescent white and pink streamers mixed with twirly silver ones streaming from the handlebars.

I looked at Bodhi, who had straightened away from my bike. I jumped up and down twice while clapping, and cried, "It's perfect!"

And it was. It was over the top, cutesie, girlie, *perfect*.

I *loved* it.

I loved it so much I rounded my girl, threw myself in Bodhi's arms and hugged him, exclaiming loudly, "I love it!"

Bodhi hugged me back, giving me a side to side shake.

Since the day I bought my Schwinn five months ago, Bodhi and I had become friends.

Good friends.

He was not like any of my other friends. He was a laidback cycling-slash-boarding dude (definitely a *dude*) who owned his own bike shop mostly so he could close it whenever he wanted and go biking or snowboarding whenever he wanted, which was often.

When he was working, it was not unusual to walk into his shop, shout his name and have him come out of the side office on a cloud of smoke and whiff of pot fumes. It was so blatant I honestly didn't know how he didn't get tagged by the Sheriff. But he didn't.

It had to be karma. No incarnation of Bodhi would hurt a fly, I didn't care how many times he thought he'd been reincarnated, and according to Bodhi, there were a lot.

That winter, Bodhi and his girlfriend, Heather, taught me how to board.

I knew how to ski, kind of. I'd been to the slopes with my parents and brother a lot in my life. When I got older, since I didn't enjoy it, I usually shopped or hung out at a lodge, drank cocoa and read while they hit the slopes.

But snowboarding was a blast. I loved it, and since Bodhi and Heather loved it a whole lot more than me, we had a ball.

So when the snow started melting and I could climb on board my Schwinn, Bodhi and Heather showed me the ropes of getting around. They also let me borrow a used trail bike from the shop and they took me out on trails.

It was amazing. I'd lived in Willow, thus Colorado, all my life but I had never seen the fabulous places and beautiful vistas I saw with Bodhi and Heather.

Mostly because I hadn't gone out and looked.

Now I did, all the time. Even when Bodhi and Heather weren't with me, I'd rent a bike from Bodhi and hit the trails.

Heaven.

The last five months I'd also worked hard to expand my business so I could enjoy my new lifestyle that included living, but also included such things as lift tickets, board gear, bike racks and insurance on two vehicles.

Thankfully, my expansion efforts worked so when I needed help with packing and shipping, I'd hired Heather.

She was as laidback as her boyfriend and she took me up on the offer. It was a good fit for both of us. She worked when there was work to do. It could be two hours a week, it could be twenty. She was up for anything and I needed someone who was flexible.

Heather definitely was that.

So I spent a lot of time with them, and Bodhi was helping me trick out my bike. I had a lighted, woven daisy basket. I had a hot pink, retro bike bell. I had a bright headlight and flashing taillight.

And now I had cutesie, girlie streamers on my handlebars.

I had it all.

Bodhi, arms still around me, suddenly whispered in my ear, "Dudette, GI Joe checkin' you out. Three o'clock."

It was such a bizarre thing to say, I leaned back in his arms. My face split in a huge smile, and I looked in his eyes.

"What?" I asked.

"Total GI Joe. As in GI Joe, *whoa*," he muttered, and we both were wearing shades so he had to jerk his head to his left to indicate what he was referring to.

I looked right.

And saw Raiden Miller standing outside his Jeep, wearing a skintight army green tee that was straining so much at his biceps it looked in danger of ripping. He also had on tan cargo pants, boots, and unbelievably cool gold-rimmed aviator sunglasses which did, indeed, seem to be trained on me.

I felt my breath start burning in my lungs as I mentally rewound the hit-the-town-for-errands preparations I'd done that morning.

Light makeup.

Blown out hair.

Pink, cuffed short-shorts and a white cutesie top that had a little ruffle around the collar and capped sleeves. On my feet were pearlescent pink slim-strapped Havaianas.

Oh God, I matched my bike.

No! I matched my bike!

Thank God I'd worn my own fabulous shades, pink on the inside of the arms, black on the outside, but the frames were silver and shaped like cop glasses. They rocked.

"Seriously, they should update the doll to look like him," Bodhi went on, and I looked back at him to see he was still eyeing Raiden. "Every kid in America would buy that doll." He turned to me. "Boys *and* girls."

He was absolutely not wrong.

I pulled out of his arms, lifting a hand to tuck my hair behind my ear, acutely aware that Raiden Miller might be watching these movements.

In the last five months I'd let my hair grow, and Betsy said if I kept it up with just trims to the flippy layers she'd cut into it that it would be down to my bra strap by the 4th of July. This was because it grew so fast. Now it was halfway there.

Long, thick with highlights and lowlights in it that Betsy said, "gives it lift and personality."

It definitely had that. With its natural health and shine and my being in the sun all the time making the blonde even blonder, even I thought it looked pretty great.

Still, it wasn't big hair, like Raiden's cool, pretty skank.

I put Raiden out of my head (kind of) and opened my mouth to ask Bodhi how much for the streamers so I could get the heck out of there when Bodhi kept talking.

"I'm a dude, so even though he's wearin' shades, I can tell you, as a dude, you in those shorts, his eyes are aimed at your legs."

At his words, I wondered if legs could blush. If they could, mine would have done just that, even though it was just coming on June and they were already tan since I was on a bike so much.

"I also know this seein' as he's lookin' down...*at your legs*," Bodhi finished.

Okay, definitely, legs could blush. I knew this when I felt the heat hit them.

"How much do I owe you?" I asked, taking Bodhi off the subject of Raiden and my legs. Moving to my basket, I was wishing for the first time I didn't have a daisy basket that any six-year-old girl would be in throes of ecstasy over, but, suddenly I was realizing, any twenty-nine-year-old woman should think twice about.

"Was fifteen, seein' as they're custom-made by Heatherita, but since you gave me a hug, and I give discounts for hugs, we'll call it square at ten," Bodhi answered.

I grabbed my wallet. A long, Coach slimline pocket wallet that was made of a silvery champagne leather that I *had to have* the minute I saw it, but right then I worried was glitzy and ostentatious. I pulled out a ten and a five and extended the bills to Bodhi.

"Girl, I said ten," he told me, but I shook my head and my hand.

"Take it," I urged.

He had a bike shop to keep open, a pot habit, expensive hobbies and a questionable work ethic.

He needed the five bucks.

His shades held mine, then he took the money because he knew better than me that he needed it.

"You rock," he said quietly.

"So do these." I ran my finger through the streamers, something else I now had second thoughts about. Then I thought…forget it. I liked them. So Raiden saw me on a cutesie, girlie bike wearing a cutesie, girlie outfit that matched it.

I had my cop glasses.

I had a groovy friend who made me laugh and taught me to snowboard.

And I probably wouldn't see Raiden for another five months.

So what did I care?

I mounted the bike, wishing I was pedaling home instead of pedaling further into town to run some errands for Grams. Raiden was parked, and thus obviously in town for a reason, and that reason might mean I'd run into him again. I turned around to face town.

"We goin' out on the trails this weekend?" Bodhi asked, and I threw him a bright smile over my shoulder.

"Absolutely," I answered.

He grinned back.

I dipped my chin to look at my feet and again tucked my hair behind my ear as I pushed up the kickstand and put feet to the pedals. I also looked out the corner of my eye Raiden's way.

Just to check.

I felt heat hit every inch of my body making it tingle when I saw that now he was leaning back against his Jeep, arms crossed on his massive chest, shades, it appeared, still on me.

He had a sexy smile playing about his mouth and he looked settled in, like he was enjoying a show.

What on earth?

Okay. Whatever. It wasn't every day a guy saw a twenty-something woman on a six-year-old's dream bike wearing an outfit that matched her bike. So he had a show.

Again, whatever.

This was what I thought.

What I felt was idiotic.

I had to let it go, but more, I had to get out of there, so I took off, shouting to Bodhi, "Later!"

"Later, girl!" Bodhi shouted back.

I pedaled away and felt funny, hot and strange while picking up Grams's meds from the pharmacy and grabbing cat food for Grams's cat, Spot, at the pet store.

These feelings only died down when I was paying for Spot's food.

The meds were important, of course. But although Spot couldn't see the cupboard where Grams kept the tins of his food, he could sense when they were getting low and he got antsy.

Grams and I had learned the hard way that when Spot got antsy, something needed to be done about it.

I could have picked up the meds the next day when I usually did Grams's big shop for the week. But since Spot only accepted two different flavors of a special brand of cat food that had to be bought at the pet store and Grams was running low, I'd pedaled into town, and unintentionally made a fool of myself the first time Raiden Miller's attention turned to me.

I loved that cat, no matter how ornery.

But at that moment I cursed him to perdition.

I'd bought the food and was heading out of the store when Krista, the owner of the store, called after me. "Is it still cool if I go over to Miss Mildred's on Saturday to learn how to make her biscuits?"

Grams was known for her cooking. She was from Louisiana. Full-on Cajun, full-on Southern, and she'd brought to Colorado all the knowledge she'd learned from home.

She was also generous with it.

I kept heading toward the door as I looked over my shoulder at Krista, smiled and called, "Absolutely!"

Her head jerked, her eyes went up and she cried, "Hanna!" two seconds before I hit wall.

This shocked me since I'd been in that pet store more than once in my life, a lot more, and I knew where the walls were, even if I wasn't looking right at them.

And no walls were there.

Walls also didn't have fingers that could curl around your upper arms, which, by the time I'd swung my head around, had happened.

I saw army green tee and I tipped my head back, back, *back* and stared straight into Raiden Ulysses Miller's eyes.

Close up.

I'd seen them in his yearbook picture, of course, dozens (okay, maybe hundreds) of times.

He'd even run them through me when I'd been at Rachelle's.

But I'd never seen them that close when he was right there, alive, breathing, with his fingers wrapped around my arms, so close I could feel his body heat.

"You okay?" His deep voice rumbled through me.

He had a phenomenal voice, but all I could do was stare in his eyes.

They were a weird light brown/green with a yellow tint at the pupil, but as it radiated out to the edge of the iris it went pure light green.

Startling.

Amazing.

Gorgeous.

I dropped my bag of kitty food.

The crash was loud. The tins overflowed and started rolling everywhere, and all this helped me jerk myself out of my stupor.

I also jerked myself out of his hold and immediately went into a crouch to rescue the cans.

Unfortunately, so did Raiden, and our heads smacked together with a painful thud that sent me falling back, right on my behind. It also sent my sunglasses, which were on top of my head, flying.

I slowly lifted my hand to my head where it slammed into his, thinking, *Someone kill me. Please. Right now. Kill me.*

"Hey, are you okay?" he asked. He was in a crouch, leaning toward me, his hand coming up, fingers wrapping around my wrist.

They burned the instant they touched skin.

I lifted my eyes to his.

Startling.

Amazing.

Gorgeous.

With effort, I found my voice, but when I did, it came out high.

"Are you...uh, okay?"

"Got a hard head," he replied. "I'm good. You got knocked on your ass."

That I did.

God!

"I'm good...fine, fine...just, uh, fine and, well...good," I murmured.

And babbling! I thought, right before I realized there were cans everywhere, and I realized this mostly because a kid went running toward the door, kicking some and they went flying.

Not thinking and freaking way the heck *out*, I pulled my hand free from his, shifted to my hands and knees and started crawling around on the floor of the pet store (gah!), gathering up stupid cat food tins.

Seriously, Spot was lucky I loved him or I'd kill him.

I stopped doing this when I felt a tingle shift along the small of my back. I turned my head and saw Raiden had hold of my bag in one hand. He had four tins of cat food clamped in his other, but his body was still and his eyes were locked on my upturned booty.

Oh *God*.

I was a klutz and a dork.

I was a dorky klutz!

Quickly, I shifted to just my feet, still gathering tins, piling them in my arm, snatching up my glasses, shoving them on my head and not wanting to, but having to move toward Raiden, who had my bag.

"How 'bout we take this in turns. You go up first," Raiden suggested.

I forced myself to look at him and saw he was grinning at me.

I'd seen that grin. It was beautiful. I'd seen him smile. That was even more beautiful. Way back in the day, I'd heard his lush, rumbling laughter. Sublime.

But he'd obviously never grinned *at me*.

I was right. It was beautiful.

Beyond beautiful.

Life altering.

I froze.

Entirely.

Every inch of me.

And I stared.

"Everything okay here?" Krista asked, coming curiously late to this harrowing incident I knew I'd play over and over in my head, wanting to do every second differently and kicking myself that I didn't.

I forced myself to speak, and this time it wasn't high. It was squeaky.

"Me first?" I asked Raiden.

His grin got bigger. My insides melted and he jerked up his chin.

I straightened to standing.

"Here's another can, Hanna," Mrs. Bartholomew said as Raiden rose to his full height. In other words, towering over all of us.

I turned to her and took the can she was offering. "Thanks, Mrs. B."

She gave me a smile then looked up at Raiden. "Raid, tell your mom I said hi."

"Will do," he mumbled.

She grinned at him and took off.

Raiden opened the plastic bag, indicating to me I should divest myself of my pile of cat food tins, and I had to lean forward to dump in all the cans I had clutched to my chest. This I did, excruciatingly aware that he could see right down my shirt.

That was when I thanked God I'd tossed all my crappy underwear five months ago and loaded up on the good stuff during my now-not-infrequent trips to Denver.

"I think you got them all," Krista shared, and I looked to her, lifting a hand, tucking my hair behind my ear and wishing I was anywhere but there.

And I meant *anywhere.*

A sweatshop in China. At a phone making marketing calls to people who hated marketing calls and thus would abuse me before they hung up on me.

Anywhere.

Krista was scanning the floor for cans then she looked between Raiden and me. "You guys conked noggins pretty hard. You good?"

"I am, but Hanna seems a bit dazed," Raiden answered and I stopped breathing.

He said my name.

He said my name!

I looked up at him, my lips parted.

Then I realized he thought I'd been dazed by our head knock and that was not good.

I had to get myself together.

I pulled in a breath, and on the exhale I reached out and gently took the bag from him, and assured them both in my normal voice (thank God), "I'm fine. Just...I have a lot on my mind. But I'm okay." I looked up at Raiden. "I'm also klutzy. I'm sorry."

"Don't apologize, honey. You didn't run into me, I wouldn't have a chance to smell your perfume. Made my day," he replied, and I blinked.

Oh cripes. He called me honey in that rumbling voice.

And he was being (could it be?) kind of flirty.

God!

I had to keep it together.

I did this (just barely), then I ran through my morning again, seeing as I was a perfume whore. I had at least twenty bottles of it. It could be anything.

I settled on a morning memory, realizing it was Agent Provocateur, and deciding the minute I got home I was ordering another bottle (or seven).

"I best get back to work," Krista mumbled.

I tore my eyes from Raiden to look at her and saw she was looking at the floor, grinning like an idiot.

She took off.

Raiden spoke again.

"You Miss Mildred's grandkid?" he asked.

"Sorry?" I asked back.

"Krista said she was goin' to Miss Mildred's this weekend. Heard her grand-kid was takin' care of her. You her?"

He didn't know who I was.

I'd lived for twenty-three years convinced I was in love with him, no matter how totally crazy that was, and he didn't know who I was.

He heard Krista say my name.

He had no clue.

"Great-grandkid," I told him.

"You lookin' after her?" he asked.

I nodded, still coping with the devastation that we'd played tug of war together at Grams's picnic and he'd been on my team three years running, and he didn't know me.

"How's she doin'?" Raiden went on.

"Great. Ninety-eight going on twenty," I replied, and he awarded me another smile.

I must have been getting better with practice seeing as that one only made my scalp and kneecaps tingle.

"Least that doesn't change," he murmured.

He was right about that. Mildred Boudreaux never changed. Even acts of God couldn't change her. I knew this because, when Grams was sixteen she got struck by lightning, wandered home, clothes still smoking (or that was how the story was told, incidentally, by Grams) and asked her mother what was for dinner.

"Listen, I need to go," I stated and his head tipped slightly to the side, which I wished he hadn't done. Because it was just a head tip, but being his handsome head, his fabulous hair, his amazing eyes, his attention on me, it seemed both cool and hot and I wanted to ask him to do it over and over again just so I could watch.

I pulled myself together (again) and kept talking.

"I'm really sorry about bumping into you and, well…then banging heads."

"I'm good, long's you're okay," he replied.

"Peachy," I muttered and forced a smile. "Sorry again and…later."

I immediately took off, hoofing it by him and walking fast to my bike.

I dumped the cat food bag in my cutesie, girlie basket, mounted the saddle, put my feet to the pedals and took off, heading straight to Grams's and not looking back at the pet store.

This was good, seeing as if I did I would have seen Raiden Miller, arms crossed on his chest, sexy smile playing at his mouth, watching me go.

3

SWEET TEA

One Week, One Day Later

I OPENED THE door to Grams's place and shouted, "Hey, Grams! I'm here!"

To this I got shouted back, "I'm on the back porch, precious. Soakin' in sun and drinkin' sweet tea. Bring the pitcher, I'm low!"

I grinned at the hardwood floors and lugged in the bags of groceries, stopping when Spot came into my vision.

He sat on his ample booty in the hall and stared up at me.

He was white with big splotches of gray. He was one of the prettiest cats I'd ever seen. He was also the orneriest. And the fattest.

He wasn't just fat, he was *solid*. Twenty-two pounds of compacted cat held in by soft white and gray fur.

It was good he was beautiful because he was a pain in the patoot.

Like when he got in a lovable mood no matter how infrequent that was and you were lying on your back on the couch and he jumped up on you and settled in, there was a good possibility he could crush you.

You didn't move him, though.

There were two reasons for this.

One, he could turn at any time. I'd had to have his front claws lasered since he kept clawing Grams and breaking skin.

Two, he was so pretty that when he was lovey you took advantage.

"Meow," he said.

"Meow right back at 'cha, buddy," I replied.

Luckily, that worked for him, and instead of complaining, hissing and attacking my ankles, he turned and waddled toward the back door.

I went to the kitchen, dumped the groceries, grabbed the pitcher of sweet tea out of the fridge and headed out back.

Grams used to be my height, but she'd shrunk. And on top of that, she was stooped so now she seemed tiny. She was also wrinkles from head-to-toe. This was partly because she was old as dirt. This was mostly because she was a sun fiend. I'd had to buy her one of those outdoor heaters, because, even in the winter, if it was sunny she'd grab afghans, put on slippers, sit outside and stare at the sun glinting off the snow, wrapped up in wool.

Mildred Boudreaux loved everything, everyone and every moment of her life (except when her husband died, of course, and when her son, my granddad, died, and when her three other children died, obviously).

She was just that kind of person.

But she loved some things and some moments better.

And any moment that included sun, she was all for.

I pushed open the back screen door and turned, mouth open to tell her I had more groceries in the car to bring in, when I stopped dead.

This was because Grams was sitting in her cute grandma dress, her blue hair newly set, because Sharon from Betsy's came out every Thursday morning to give her a wash and set, and it was Thursday. Her feet were up, red painted toenails wriggling in the afternoon sun that was peeking under the roof of the porch. And Raiden Ulysses Miller was sitting in the loveseat kitty-corner to her. His arm wide, resting on the back of the seat, long, strong, masculine fingers wrapped around a glass of sweet tea.

What on *earth*?

"Look here, precious girl, I got a gentleman caller," Grams announced, and Raiden's eyes, already on me, smiled.

My stomach dropped.

"Well, *chère*, you gonna say hey?" Grams prompted.

"Uh…hey," I mumbled to Raiden.

"Hey," he didn't mumble back.

"You didn't bring yourself a glass," Grams noted, staring at the pitcher.

I tore my eyes from Raiden's gorgeousness lounged on Grams's back porch loveseat and looked at my beloved great-grandmother.

"I don't like sweet tea, Grams," I reminded her.

"I didn't say you had to fill it with tea, precious. But you gotta have a cold one, you sit in the sun," she replied.

"I have groceries to bring in," I told her, and she looked to Raiden.

"Son, do us ladies a favor, bring in the groceries," she said, and my body lurched even as Raiden leaned forward to put his glass on the coffee table.

"It's only a couple of bags. I'm good," I announced, and Grams looked at me.

"Get yourself a cold drink, Hanna, sit down. Let the menfolk help you take a load off," she said then tipped her head way back to look up at a now standing Raiden. "Hanna, my precious girl, she runs herself ragged takin' care of this old biddy. You help out, it'd help me out."

"Not a problem," he rumbled and moved to round the coffee table.

Grams kept talking. "Now, she's sure to have brought me some ice cream. You get that in, child, you put it in the freezer. You hear?"

Raiden was closing in on me, his eyes on me, mine glued to him, and he winked at me as he replied to Grams, "Yes, ma'am."

I found it miraculous that, at the wink, I didn't melt into a puddle.

He disappeared.

Grams prompted, "Hanna. Fill me up and get yourself a cool drink."

I jerked out of my daze, and lightning fast I filled her tea, filled Raiden's glass and rushed to the kitchen in hopes I got my "cool drink" before Raiden got in with the last of the groceries.

This was foiled as he walked in while I was walking out with a bottle of diet root beer.

Therefore, since his huge frame filled the doorway, blocking my escape, I was stuck in the kitchen with him.

"Sweet ride," he said, eyes on me.

I looked to his chest. "Sorry?"

He dumped the groceries on the counter. "The Z. Sweet."

Oh God.

My car.

And I was wearing white jeans and a white, fitted, scoop-necked tee.

The last time, I matched my bike.

This time, I matched my car.

I matched my car!

Luckily, I had a slim black belt and a pair of black gladiator sandals on so at least that was something.

Seeing as his eyes were on me even as his hands were in the bag, I felt it necessary to respond.

"Yeah."

Yes, that was all I could get out.

He looked down at the bags, muttering, "She drives a Z and all she can do is agree it's sweet."

"I got her because she's pretty," I informed him, sounding like an idiot, but also telling the truth.

It was just the idiotic truth.

Raiden pulled out the carton of ice cream and shot another smile my way. My legs went weak and he headed to the freezer, talking.

And, incidentally, rocking my world by calling me honey again.

"Honey, the wheels on her, I'd *give* you my Jeep just to drive on those wheels. Smart upgrade, the sports package."

"Sorry?"

He shoved the ice cream in the freezer and turned to me. "You got the sports package."

"I did?"

His head cocked to the side and again it was sexy as all blooming heck. His brows snapped together. They were as lush as his hair, which made the whole maneuver *seriously* sexy as all blooming heck.

"You didn't know you got the sports package?"

"The sports package?"

"Yeah, on the Z. You didn't know you had that upgrade?"

"Is that, um…more?" I asked.

"As in, more money?" he asked back.

"Yes," I whispered, definitely feeling like an idiot.

Raiden wasn't looking at me like I was an idiot.

He looked weirdly angry.

"Yeah, Hanna. It's more money. Like, a fuckuva lot more money. The dealership didn't tell you that?"

"No," I told him, and his head jerked to straight again.

"Where'd you go?" he asked.

"Bob's," I answered.

"You go alone?" he pressed.

"As in, by myself," I asked (yes, idiotically!).

"Yeah, a woman alone buyin' a car. Did you go by yourself?"

"Yeah," I told him.

His mouth got tight and he walked back to the bags, muttering, "Bob just got scratched on my to-do list."

What did that mean?

Before I could ask, he spoke again.

"Any of this need to go in the fridge?"

"You can go back out, finish your tea. I'll do it," I said, and he turned his head to me.

"You do everything for her?"

"Everything?"

Yes, *still* being an idiot.

He flipped his hand out to the groceries. "Yeah, everything."

"She still cooks but I, uh…get her groceries in every Thursday and I clean her house. And I take her to church Sunday morning and we have breakfast together after. Oh, and I take her out to dinner every Tuesday night. And, of course, to mah jongg every Monday morning. But mostly, she does her own thing."

Raiden turned to me. "Don't you have a brother?"

"He lives in California."

"Folks?" he pushed.

"They're in Arizona," I replied.

"They all left her with just you?"

"Well, yeah. I mean, no, but yeah," I babbled. "What I'm saying is," I carried on in an attempt to make sense (for once). "Mom and Dad wanted her to go to Arizona with them, but she refused to go. But Mom got in a really bad car accident about two years before they moved. It was snowy and she never really liked driving in snow. That just capped it. She became terrified. Dad got a transfer offer to Tucson and they wanted to take it, go down there, Dad working until retirement, Mom getting a part-time job. Kind of semi-retirement. Grams, well, she's old, but she's still good on her own. She's busy. She has a lot of callers. Someone is by every day, not just me. And Grams and I are close so I'm good with, uh…popping by and seeing to things. So I talked them into going and Grams was right there with me. She didn't want to delay their retirement preparations since she's convinced she's never going to die and daily proves that she's right so, uh…they went."

Raiden stared at me.

I inwardly squirmed.

Finally he again spoke.

"How 'bout you give it a rest for today and let me deal with this shit?"

I blinked.

"You mean, put away the groceries?" I asked.

"Yeah," he answered.

"You don't know where anything goes," I told him.

"I'll find my way around."

It struck me that if I let him do this I could quit talking to him and therefore quit acting like an idiot. So I decided to let him do this.

"Okay, but," I started to warn, "if Spot shows, and he's feeling less than lovable and attacks your ankles, just ignore him. He doesn't have any claws and he doesn't ever bite too hard."

It was Raiden's turn to blink.

Then he asked, "Are you talking about that fat cat?"

"Yes," I replied, and a slow grin spread on his face.

Magnificent.

"Miss Mildred named her cat Spot?" he asked.

Oh boy.

I was going to have to show my idiocy again.

"Actually, she couldn't come up with a name, so I named him Spot."

His features shifted with the warm amusement that flowed through them.

I was wrong before.

That was magnificent.

"You named a fat cat Spot," Raiden stated.

"Yes," I whispered.

His amazing eyes dropped my mouth.

I forgot my name.

"He wasn't a fat cat then," I stupidly went on. "Seeing as, back then, he was just a little kitty."

His eyes came back to mine.

"You name a dog Spot," he informed me.

"Okay," I agreed (again, stupidly).

"Unless you're cute. Then you name a cat Spot."

I had no reply to that, mostly because there wasn't one, but partly because he kind of said I was cute, so I was having trouble breathing.

He jerked his head to the door. "Go. Take a load off. I'll be out when I'm done with this."

"Righty ho," I muttered.

His grin came back, I decided to check online for a hairshirt so I could wear it and torture myself for my idiocy (I mean, "righty ho?"), and I scuttled out.

Grams was snoozing in the sun, but she came to when I threw myself in the cushioned Adirondack chair kitty-corner to her and across from the loveseat Raiden had been sitting in.

"Where's our handsome company?" she asked, searching behind me with not a small amount of obvious excitement, looking for Raiden.

Seriously, I was so totally of her loins, except I wasn't funny and interesting.

"Putting away the groceries," I answered, and she gave me a big smile.

"Coulda knocked me over with a feather, the front bell went and I opened the door to that tall drink of cool water," she remarked, settling back into her chair and closing her eyes. "Woke up and I knew it was a good day. Felt it in my bones. Opened the door to him, glad I was right."

I wasn't.

"Grew up good and strong, that one did," Grams kept talking. "Coulda called it. You asked me thirty years ago, would Raiden Miller be a fine, tall, strong, handsome man? I woulda said, 'You *betcha*.'"

I sucked back root beer, wishing it was vodka, sat back and lifted my feet up to the coffee table, saying, "You're rarely wrong, Grams."

"Damn tootin'," she replied. "And, get this," she started, so I looked at her to see her eyes open and her head turned to me. "He asked if there was anything he could do around here. Says his momma sent him to check on me, make sure I was okay and that the house was in tiptop shape. I told him I had to pay that Crane boy twenty dollars a week to mow my lawn and cut back my bushes. He said he'd be out every Friday to see that's done and won't charge me a penny. I took him up on that, you better believe it."

Seriously?

What was going on?

Years, Raiden Miller didn't know I existed. He took off, was gone for years more. He came back and for months he still didn't know I existed. And suddenly he was everywhere I was?

I straightened, taking my feet from the coffee table and began, "Grams—"

She waved a hand at me. "Don't take away my fun." She smiled and leaned my way. "Every Friday, him in my yard, sweatin' and mowin' my lawn. Even old women need a thrill." She settled back and closed her eyes. "That right there's gonna be mine."

If I didn't act like a klutzy, dorky idiot every time I was around him, I would be there every Friday to watch Raiden mow the lawn, too.

Instead, I would do my best to be in Bangladesh.

I put my feet back up on the coffee table and sucked back more root beer. I knew it would be useless to argue with Grams, tell her favors never came for free, explain what my dad reminded me of time and again. You paid for it, like Dad did, sending up money for Grams to pay the Crane kid, or you did it in the family.

You didn't owe anybody.

And I was thinking, even for a ninety-eight-year-old woman, you *really* didn't owe Raiden Ulysses Miller.

On this thought, Grams straightened like a shot two seconds before Raiden showed on the porch.

Ninety-eight or not, she had the hearing of a German shepherd. Always did.

"Good! You're back!" she cried then snapped her fingers at me. "Hanna, go get your afghans. The taupe one. And the cream."

I couldn't see me, but I was relatively certain my eyes bugged out, and I was relatively certain because I could *feel* them protruding from my head.

"Raiden, child, sit. Let Hanna show you her handiwork." She threw a bony, wrinkled hand toward the loveseat then leaned that way over the arm of her chair to get closer to Raiden, who was folding himself in and grabbing his tea. "My precious Hanna, she not only makes, but *designs* the most *divine* afghans you'll ever see *and* feel," she bragged.

"Grams—" I tried to cut in.

"I know this not only because I have *three*, but also because she sends them everywhere, even all the way to *New York City*, and not one of them sells for less than two hundred and *fifty* dollars." She nodded as if Raiden had cried, "No!" (which he didn't) and kept babbling. "Some of 'em, the better ones, are worth *five hundred dollars*."

"Grams!" I snapped.

"This I gotta see," Raiden drawled, and my eyes shot to him.

"Get 'em, precious," Grams ordered. "All of 'em. The pink one too."

I tore my eyes from an amused Raiden and looked at my grandmother.

"Grams, he's a guy. He doesn't care about afghans," I told her.

"He cares about five hundred dollar ones. Any fool would wanna see a five hundred dollar afghan," Grams shot back. She looked to Raiden. "All three of mine would cost that in one of those fancy shops Hanna ships them to, and let me tell you they're worth every penny. I sit out here, dead of winter, one of Hanna's afghans around me, snug as a bug. Like it's August in Looseeanna, but without the humidity. I'm not joking." Grams turned a proud smile to me. "That and her preserves, makes her livin', and it's a good one." She looked back to Raiden. "Now tell me, how many folks can say they make a livin' off knittin', crotchetin' and cookin' fruit? Don't answer. I'll tell you. Not many. To pull that off, you gotta have sheer talent, like my Hanna."

Again, her head turned my way.

"Well, you gonna get those afghans or what?"

I wanted to say, "Or what."

Instead, I put my root beer down, hauled my behind out of the chair and went into the house.

Spot was on the pink afghan. He was not pleased with me moving him and therefore hissed and batted me with a paw.

"Don't complain to me, buddy. It's the old biddy who sent me on this errand," I muttered.

Spot was not mollified and he shared this by hissing at me again while trying to sink his teeth into my wrist.

I escaped the Spot Attack, found the other two afghans and headed out.

"Look at those!" Grams cried like I just unveiled three masterpiece works of art. "Decadence in blanket form!"

I tossed them over the back of the chair I'd been sitting in and smoothed them out.

Truthfully, I was proud of my afghans, and Grams didn't lie. They cost that much because the wool cost a fortune. It was the best of the best. And they were pretty; loose weave, tight weave, patterned. I was proud of them.

Even so, my eyes moved very slowly toward Raiden.

His eyes were aimed at the blankets, but he must have felt my gaze because they lifted to me.

"Gorgeous," he said quietly, and he sounded like he meant it.

Warmth suffused my body.

"Thanks," I replied just as quietly.

"Told you," Grams stated. "Now you should try her preserves."

Oh no.

I'd had enough.

"Actually, I have to get to work cleaning the house," I said quickly.

"And I gotta get back into town," Raiden said on the heels of my statement, and he did this while standing. He looked down at Grams. "You call Crane, Miss Mildred. Tell him you got a new lawn service. I'll be here next Friday."

"I'll do that, child," she replied and turned to me. "Walk our caller to his car, will you, *chère?*"

This just never ended.

Before I could do it or find an excuse not to, Raiden spoke.

"No need. Don't have a car since I walked here. I can find my way, and I'm sure Hanna wants to finish up so she can sit back and enjoy her visit."

He'd made it around me, but moved in to lean down and touch his lips to Gram's creased, paper-thin cheek.

"Next Friday, Miss Mildred," he murmured while lifting up. "Thanks for the tea."

"Look forward to it, son." Grams twinkled up at him. "And you're more than welcome anytime."

Raiden turned and looked down at me. "Later, Hanna."

"'Bye," I mumbled.

His lips twitched, then his body moved and I watched him walk away.

It was a good show.

From where I stood I could see all the way to the front of the house, so I enjoyed the show until the front door closed on him.

"He's the cat's pajamas," Grams declared, and I looked down at her to see she'd twisted so she was curled around her chair so she could watch the show, too.

"Time to clean toilets!" I declared brightly, purposely trying to break the mood.

I sallied forth into the house to do just that, avoiding Grams's eyes, which I knew would hold rebuke.

Fifteen minutes later, I found something that cured thoughts of Raiden Miller, how beautiful he was and how much of an idiot I acted around him.

Cleaning toilets.

I could not do this every moment of my life, however.

Therefore, if he kept popping up, I was in trouble.

4

CHICK FLICK

That Evening

"SERIOUSLY?" MY BEST friend KC asked in my ear.

"Seriously," I replied.

"*Seriously?*" she shrieked.

We were on the phone. I was lounging sideways on the swing on my front porch, a half-finished afghan on my lap, a glass of white wine on the table beside me.

I'd just told her about Raiden's visit to Grams. I'd already told her days before about me bumping into him at the pet store.

Now she was freaking. Like me.

I had not, however, told her I'd gone to Rachelle's a mortifying number of times to catch a glimpse of him.

That said, KC and I had been best friends since seventh grade, so she, along with me, had a crush on him while growing up. Somehow, both of us sharing this crush and both of us crushing huge did not destroy our relationship. It could happen to girls of that age, regardless of the fact that neither of us had even the remotest shot of that particular dream coming true.

This was how close we were.

I adored her.

She gave that back to me.

Now she was married, had a daughter and another one on the way.

I thought her husband Mark was a jackass, but no matter how close we were, I did not share this with KC. At least not openly.

She thought he walked on water.

My thoughts on this subject were that this mostly had to do with him being particularly talented in the bedroom, something which she shared, in detail, even if it meant I had to become really good at fighting my lip from curling in disgust. A feat I bested, and now I was a practiced hand, seeing as they had sex. A lot.

I didn't want to think this of my bestie, but it could also have to do with him making a very decent living.

She said he was a lot sweeter when people weren't around.

I hoped that was true.

Now she was freaking with me about Raiden, who I had not (outside of when I was cleaning toilets, vacuuming, dusting, doing laundry and changing sheets) been able to get out of my head.

So I was making an afghan that would eventually make me a silly huge amount of money, drinking wine and letting KC and my home work their magic.

I grew up in my house and bought it from my parents when they moved, thus I got a screaming sweet deal.

At my behest, they'd sold all the stuff inside before they moved so I could make it my own.

And that I did, going to every antique shop from Denver to Cheyenne to Albuquerque. I wallpapered. I painted. I refinished. I restored. And I made my childhood home all about me.

Countrified splendor with a healthy dose of quirk and a hint here and there of edge to knock off some of the pretty, cutesie and girlie.

It was fabulous.

Like my front porch with its white posts and railings, latticework at the edges of the posts where they met the porch roof, its swing and wicker furniture with mismatched cushions and pillows that said what my grandmother's porch furniture said.

You're welcome here, so sit back and stay awhile.

I lived there, and again, like my grandmother, when it was warm I was out on my porch in my swing, sitting back and staying awhile.

Like now.

"What do you think this means?" KC asked in my ear.

"I think it means Mrs. Miller told her son to check on Grams, and he's a good guy so he's going to mow her lawn," I answered.

"It does not," she returned and I smiled.

"It does, KC."

"How about this scenario?" she began. "He got a load of you being cute and goofy and he's into that, so he popped by your grams on a day when every-freaking-body knows you go over there to get another fix of Hanna-Style Cute and Goofy."

I burst out laughing, and after I did this for a bit, still laughing, I told her, "Seriously, I'm not his type."

Silence then, "You know his type?'

I had also not shared that I saw him with the pretty, cool skank. That had been too painful to share, and further, I adored KC, and even though she was married that didn't mean she couldn't crush, and I didn't want to pollute her fantasy either.

Now, however, was the time to share.

Forcing nonchalance, I answered, "Yeah. I saw him making out with someone a while back. Lots of hair. Lots of chest. Lots of tight clothes. Skinny-minnie and short."

More silence then, "That's damned disappointing."

It was.

But whatever.

"Anyway, half of Willow troops to Grams's and offers to help out. It was a Miller's turn," I told her.

"I prefer to think Raiden Ulysses Miller is into cute and goofy, not skinny, short, big-boobed and big-haired," she retorted.

I preferred to think that, too.

Incidentally, like every girl who knew him way back then, KC thought of him *with* his middle name. That made a cool name doubly cool, and thus we frequently referred to him as such in spoken conversations.

Like now.

"Well yeah, but he isn't and whatever," I said. "Helping Grams out is just a cool thing for him to do. Now Grams can pocket Dad's yard money and blow it on mah jongg."

"She's got an extra twenty bucks to bet, she's going to own half the town. *My* gram says she's kills at mah jongg."

I blinked at my wool. "She tells me she's always losing."

I could hear KC's laughter in her next words. "She lies."

I then heard a car approach and I looked from my wool to the drive.

I lived in a wooded area about a five-minute drive from town that looked half-Colorado, half-someplace else. This was because my dad planted a bunch of trees all around, so we had conifers, we had aspen and we had everything else under the sun that would take in the arid climate. We also, which meant that now *I* also, owned an acre all around.

So with trees and land, my two-story, three bedroom, two and a half bath farmhouse was cozy, isolated and quiet.

Exactly the way I liked it.

Except for right then as I was sitting on a porch swing, having taken off my white going-into-town outfit. I'd put on a pair of red knit shorts that said "USC" in yellow across the butt (my brother's alma mater) and a shelf-bra camisole that left little to the imagination. My face was clean of makeup. My hair was in a messy knot on top of my head. And my wits were partially washed away as I was well into my third glass of wine.

But I was going to need them.

And I was going to need them because a hunter green Jeep was approaching my house.

"Holy Moses, KC," I whispered into the phone. "I'm watching a green Jeep drive up to my house."

"No shit?" she whispered back.

She knew what this meant. Every girl in town, I figured, knew that Jeep.

"None at all." I was still whispering.

"Ohmigod, is it him?" she asked.

The Jeep stopped close to my front walk.

I could see through the windshield.

This meant I stopped breathing, so I had to wheeze out my, "Yeah."

"Holy fuck!" she shouted.

Raiden swung out of the Jeep.

My heart flipped over.

"I think I gotta go," I told KC.

"You think?" she asked.

I didn't answer.

I couldn't.

Raiden Ulysses Miller and his big gorgeous body were walking up to my house.

"Report back the minute he leaves," KC ordered.

"Righty ho," I muttered the instant his boot hit the first step up to my porch.

I beeped the phone off and watched him climb the next four steps. Then I watched him saunter five paces to me where he stopped.

He did not speak.

I didn't either.

His eyes moved from my hair to my feet to my hair again.

My eyes stayed glued to his eyes.

He turned his head around a bit and took in the porch.

I kept my head stationary and took in him.

His eyes came to mine. "Are you shittin' me?"

I blinked.

"Sorry?" I asked.

He crossed his arms on his chest, making the muscles in his biceps bulge and the veins in his forearms pop. I was concentrating on taking in all this fabulousness so I might have missed the full orgasm, but I was relatively certain I had a mini one.

Then he smiled.

There it was.

The full orgasm.

It was a wonder I didn't moan.

"Honey, you look straight out of a chick flick," he remarked.

Again, I blinked.

Then, again, I asked, "Sorry?"

"Cute outfit. Glass of wine. Sexy, messy hair. Cute house that looks out of a magazine. Not a lick of makeup and you look prettier than any woman I've seen for over a year. Gabbin' on the phone like you look this good, in a place that looks this good every day when that shit's impossible." He paused before he concluded, "Chick flick."

Did he say sexy, messy hair?

And that I looked prettier than any woman he'd seen for over a year?

"Sorry?" I repeated yet again.

"Say that again, I'll kiss you."

Oh my God!

Did he say *say that again, I'll kiss you?*

Kiss me?

I stared and swallowed.

What I did not do was speak.

Raiden was silent. So was I.

When this went on an uncomfortable while, I broke it.

"Can I ask at this juncture what you're doing here?"

His lips twitched and he answered, "Yeah, baby, at this juncture, you can ask that."

He said no more.

But he called me baby.

I didn't look to confirm, and I was glad he didn't either, seeing as I was relatively certain my nipples were now hard.

Cripes!

When he remained silent, I asked, "What are you doing here?"

"You doin' anything for your grandmother tomorrow night?" he asked back.

"Uh...no," I answered.

"You hangin' with that pothead and his pothead girlfriend?"

My head jerked at the way he referred to Bodhi and Heather, not to mention his knowledge of them and me spending time with them, but I replied, "No."

"Then you're free to go out to dinner with me."

My chest compressed like Spot was lying on it and my lips parted.

Raiden's eyes dropped to my mouth and his lips muttered, "I'll take that as a yes."

"Uh..." I mumbled, then stopped mumbling.

"I'll take that as a yes, too," he declared.

"I—" I started to say something. I had no clue what, but got no more out.

"I'll be here tomorrow, six thirty. Not fuckin' around with all the cute that's you, we're goin' to a steak place, so you'll wanna dress nice."

All the cute that was me?

"I would request that white blouse you crawled around the pet store in," he went on, and I felt my face start to heat at the reminder of my idiocy, which, clearly, Raiden didn't recall as idiotic. "But everything I've seen you in since then is far from disappointing," his eyes swept my chest and legs before coming back to my face, "so I'm lookin' forward to the surprise."

Was I asleep?

Was I dreaming?

How was this happening?

I said nothing because I feared, if I did I'd wake up, and I most certainly did not want to wake up.

His head cocked to the side. "You gonna be ready for me at six thirty?"

That required a response so I tested the waters.

"Yes."

His eyes got lazy, my heart did a somersault and he murmured a rumbling, "Good."

He turned, sauntered down my porch, my steps and to his Jeep.

He swung in, reversed at an angle and drove away.

I stared into the trees where I last saw him for minutes that seemed to last for hours.

Then I lifted the phone still in my hand, hit redial and put it to my ear.

Five minutes later, KC shrieked, *"Seriously?"*

I burst out laughing.

Giddy laughing.

Excited laughing.

Freaked laughing.

And even laughing, thank God, I didn't wake up.

5

CLUELESS

The Next Evening

THE DOORBELL RANG.

I was in my bathroom upstairs, staring at myself in the mirror, but I'd been ready for twenty minutes.

Now I was hyperventilating.

I drew in deep breaths, turned toward the door and hit the light. I forced my mind to go over my appearance, which at that point I had memorized.

KC and I had gone into Denver so I could get a new outfit. A blue jersey dress that was great with my eyes, showed just enough but not too much cleavage and clung at all the right places. It was a miracle dress that gave me a miracle body, and as such cost a miraculous price that I charged.

I also bought a pair of strappy, high spike-heeled sandals that were to die for. They were made up of blue snakeskin straps interspersed with green snakeskin straps and they made my feet—and my brand new pedicure (with a design on my big toenails that included a little crystal; this was Raiden Ulysses Miller, I was going for the gusto)—look fabulous.

They also cost a mint.

I charged them, too, and I didn't care.

It all had to be right. Perfect.

And it was.

KC convinced me to wear my hair down, and I did my face with an edge toward drama. But not too much, because I didn't want to go over the top and overshadow the dress and shoes, both of which packed a punch.

So after a busy day of shopping, pedicure and manicure then nervously getting ready, the time had come.

It was six thirty-three.

Raiden was here.

I turned out the light by my bed. I grabbed my clutch and walked out of the room, down the stairs and to the door. I pulled in another deep breath then opened the door.

Raiden stood there in all his glory. It was more glorious seeing as he wasn't wearing cargo pants and a skintight tee (which were always awesome), but a nice, dark pair of jeans, a deep green shirt with a subtle pattern in it that looked good with his skin, hair and eyes, and a black belt and black boots (which were awesom*er*).

Delicious.

"Hey," I greeted and it came out breathy.

He didn't reply.

His eyes were moving down and they were taking their time. After they hit my shoes, they stayed there awhile. Then, just as slowly, they came back up.

They hit mine and the look in them made my heart, already beating like a jackhammer, go into overdrive.

"Hey," he rumbled.

I'd practiced this while doing my makeup (and hair) so I was able to take a slight step back, motion inside with my hand and ask, "Do we have time for you to come in for a drink?"

"You don't want me comin' in for a drink," was his reply, and I felt my brows draw together.

"I don't?"

"You, that dress, those shoes, that hair, beverages and furniture you can get horizontal on would not be a good combination."

"Oh," I whispered, and with his words it hit me like a shot that he was into me.

The date kind of said that, but his words stated clearly he wasn't just into me.

Raiden Ulysses Miller was *into me*.

I felt that warmth settle in, digging deep, as he kept talking.

"Not to mention, we got a reservation and I'm hungry." He leaned in and grabbed my hand. "Let's go."

He drew me out onto the porch, and I had just enough presence of mind to grab the door handle and pull it to as he did. I started across the porch, but stopped when his hand tightened in mine.

I turned back.

"You gonna lock it?" he asked.

I stared at him, moved my stare to the door then brought it back to him.

"Sorry?"

He shifted closer and my breath went faster. "You gonna lock the door?"

"Um...I never lock the door."

It was Raiden's turn to stare at me.

Then his hand gave mine a squeeze and he ordered, "Get your keys."

"My keys?"

"Your keys," he stated firmly.

He was hungry, and I had a feeling this discussion could go all night (with me losing), so I nodded, hustled to the door, went through and scurried to the kitchen. Since I never locked up (seeing as I didn't have to; neither did Mom and Dad, we lived in the boonies for goodness sakes—unless they knew we were out there, no one came around) it took some doing, but I found a set of house keys and hurried back, walked through the door, closed and locked it.

I turned to him. "Ready."

"While you were in there, you lock the back?" he asked.

I blinked.

He grinned.

I blinked again.

He leaned in to me, tugged the keys from of my fingers and unlocked the door. He opened it, sauntered through and disappeared, then came back, locked the door, pocketed the keys and grabbed my hand.

"Let's go," he murmured.

We went, Raiden holding my hand as we walked across the porch and down the steps. He let me go, but only to swing his arm around my shoulders and pull me into his side as we moved to his Jeep.

Nice.

Nicer still, he walked me to the passenger side and opened the door for me.

Three boyfriends; not one opened *any* door for me.

Already phenomenal, Raiden Miller just kept getting better.

His hand cupped my elbow as I climbed in then he closed the door.

Definitely kept getting better.

I was buckled up when he swung in the other side. He started up, reversed at an angle and we took off.

"Talk to your grandmother today?" he asked, and I turned to him.

Holy Moses.

I was sitting next to Raiden in his Jeep.

I couldn't believe it.

Beautiful. Him. The moment. Everything.

I didn't have time to let that settle as deep as I wanted. I had to respond or he'd think I was a freak, staring at him silently but reverently.

"Yeah, I talk to her every day," I answered.

"How's she doin'?" he asked.

"Busy, seeing as she's been calling everyone in town and half of her family in Louisiana to tell them she has a new yard boy."

I watched him smile.

Yes.

Beautiful.

"Took half a year for her to open the door when I rang yesterday, another half followin' her as she walked from the front to the back, slow as molasses. But the woman's fingers work just fine," Raiden said. "Had four people stop me today to say they thought it was cool I was seein' to Miss Mildred's yard."

"She's generous," I shared. "Something exciting happens, she passes that love around."

I watched his smile get bigger. Being there with him in his Jeep, going to dinner, knowing he thought I was cute and he was into me, living a dream I never thought I'd have, my nerves smoothed out and I looked forward.

"Where are we going?" I asked.

"Chilton's," Raiden answered.

My nerves came back.

Even though Chilton's opened a town over ten years ago, I'd only been there once, the year before when my brother came from San Diego for a visit and brought his new fiancée with him.

The menu was *à la carte*. The cheapest steak was fifty dollars.

I didn't know what Raiden did for a living, but I did know that even with twenty new boutiques I was shipping my afghans to, Chilton's once every ten years was about as much as many people could afford. Including me.

So I wondered what he did for a living, and therefore wondered if he could afford Chilton's. I also wondered what I should order since there was no way I was ordering *à la carte*, building on the foundation of a fifty dollar steak if I didn't know how deep that would cut into his wallet.

"Mood in the Jeep suddenly veered south," he remarked.

I looked at him. "Sorry?"

"You don't seem fired up about Chilton's," he noted.

"Um, I am, of course. I've been there once before. It's really nice but it's…" What did I say? "Not exactly cheap."

"You bought me a sexy dress, least I can do."

I stared, my mouth dropping open.

I snapped it shut to ask, "How did you know this is a new dress?"

He glanced at me, back at the road, then his lips turned up. "Didn't. Guessed. Now I do."

I was totally an idiot.

I proved this more when I looked forward again, mumbling stupidly (but he probably figured it out already), "I also bought new shoes."

My entire body went hot when he briefly touched the skin below my skirt at my knee and rumbled, "Appreciated, honey."

Okay, maybe I wasn't an idiot, and at that moment I knew without a doubt that regardless of how expensive they were the dress and shoes were worth every penny.

"Don't worry about dinner," he stated.

"Okay," I replied.

"Order what you want," he went on.

"Righty ho."

Raiden chuckled.

At the rumbling, masculine sound, the area between my legs got wet.

We lapsed into silence, which was both uncomfortable and oddly a relief, seeing as I would have been more uncomfortable if I had further opportunities to make a fool of myself.

We hit Chilton's and the valet helped me out of the car. Raiden rounded the Jeep, gave the valet his keys and then claimed me by grabbing my hand

Holding hands, I walked into Chilton's with Raiden Miller.

The date was twenty minutes old, if that, and it already had crazily veering ups and downs for me emotionally, but we hit an extreme up when we walked into Chilton's.

Or, for me, it was walking into Chilton's hand in hand with Raiden Miller.

The place, no matter how expensive, was packed. I saw two people I knew at whom I smiled.

But best of all, they saw me. They saw me hand in hand with Raiden.

My other three boyfriends, obviously, I'd liked. I thought they were attractive. I enjoyed spending time with them.

But never was I overwhelmingly proud to be at their side anywhere like I was right then with Raiden.

We were seated at a two top with Raiden at my side rather than across from me. We also ordered drinks, got them and ordered our meals, all this without incident.

So my nerves were again smoothing out as I took a sip of red wine and felt Raiden's eyes on me.

I looked at him and the instant my eyes hit his, he asked, "You know my name?"

That was such a strange question, I felt my head give a slight jerk and I asked back, "Do I know your name?"

"Yeah, honey. Been around you now a few times, you've not once said my name."

"You're Raiden Miller, Rachelle's big brother," I told him and, for some bizarre reason, that made him burst out laughing.

It was gorgeous, lush. It warmed me through and through, and I smiled while he did it, but I didn't understand it.

When it started waning, I said, "I don't get it. Why are you laughing?"

He trained his amazing eyes on me. "Rache would love that. She's always been Raiden's little sister."

My smile died and I leaned toward him. "I'm sorry. I didn't mean to be offensive."

He leaned toward me. "Me laughin', baby, how could you mistake that for me takin' offense?"

Again, I was an idiot.

"I can sometimes be an idiot," I offered as an understatement.

"Don't know about an idiot. Do know you can more than sometimes be all kinds of cute."

I bit my lip.

I liked that.

His eyes dropped to my mouth and he rumbled, "Like now."

I liked that, too.

I let my lip go.

"Girls prefer to be sexy and hot and, maybe, mysterious," I informed him, and his eyes came back to mine.

"You got the first two down, Hanna. And I don't know about other men, but I've played games, and in the end found out what I won wasn't worth the trouble of winning. Prefer to be with a woman who's cute and shy and obviously into me. Means I can save time and get straight to shit that matters."

What he said was nice, way nice, especially the first part, but still, I felt heat hit my face. My head jerked down and I adjusted my napkin in my lap, murmuring, "This is kind of embarrassing."

"What?" he asked, and I forced myself to look at him.

"You knowing I'm into you. That's embarrassing. I suppose it's obvious, but it's still embarrassing."

He reached toward my hand, engulfed it in his big one and brought them up to rest our clasped hands on the table.

"Honey, get me," he said gently, his eyes moving over my face, my hair, my chest then back to mine when he finished, "I wouldn't have said it if I thought you'd be embarrassed about it, but bottom line, you got not one thing to be embarrassed about."

I hoped he was right.

"Okay," I whispered.

"Afghans," he stated and I blinked.

"Sorry?"

"Those things were gorgeous, I did not lie, but Hanna, how the fuck do you make a living outta knittin' afghans?"

He was changing the subject.

That was nice.

Yes, he got better and better.

"I sell in two hundred and twenty-three shops all over the US and export to some boutiques in Canada."

His brows went up before he asked, "No shit?"

I shook my head.

"Fucking hell," he muttered.

I nodded my head and continued.

"It was less, but earlier this year I stepped things up. Now I have a girl. I think you might know her, Heather. She helps me out, packs them for shipping. I used to do it, but with the new shops I need more time to make them, so she does it for me. I have a kind of warehouse slash kitchen over the gift shop in town. My inventory is there, she does the packing there, and when fruit is in season I make my preserves there. She hasn't been with me very long, but she says she's going to help with the preserves when I do them. They're kind of…" I struggled for a word that wouldn't make me sound like I was bragging and settled on, "exclusive. I only do them when fruit is in season so they aren't on the shelves all the time. It ratchets up the prices and they don't stay in stock for long seeing as most people buy them in bulk so they have them all year."

His face got a strange funny look when I mentioned Heather, but he quickly rearranged it. He sat back while I kept talking, but did it continuing to hold my hand.

"Impressive," he remarked when I went quiet.

"It's preserves and blankets," I replied.

"You live in a cute house, drive a sweet ride, ride a cute bike and wear great clothes. You do all that outta preserves and blankets, over two hundred shops in two countries. Honey, that's impressive."

"Okay," I decided to agree, and he grinned at me.

The waiter came with bread. Raiden unfortunately let my hand go and reached for the basket.

He offered it to me (totally getting better and better, I mean, hot, cool and a gentleman!).

I took a roll as he asked, "Why did you step things up?"

I shrugged, broke my roll to butter it, and explained evasively (because I certainly wasn't going to tell him the real reason), "I don't know. Just one day it hit me. My life was kind of narrow. I enjoyed it, but I wanted more." I spread butter on my bread and looked at him. "To get more, go on vacation, learn to snowboard, you need money. I was doing okay, but I needed to do better. So I worked harder." I tipped my head to the side. "Now I do better."

"So your girl, she does all your shipping for you?"

I nodded. "I haven't been to my place in town in, gosh, I don't know. Weeks now, at least. She even comes out to the house to pick up the afghans I've done and takes them into town. She's a huge help. Especially with more orders, helping out Grams and all."

I took a bite of my buttered roll.

Delicious.

I chewed, swallowed and watched Raiden take a sip from his beer. I liked how his throat worked when he did that, so I decided more conversation was in order so I didn't obsess about how beautiful his throat was, or more accurately what that throat might taste like.

I just didn't know what conversation to make.

I wanted to ask what he did for a living, but I was too nervous. It seemed pushy and intrusive, regardless of the fact he asked about my business. I just felt that for a man, and a man like him especially, it was something he needed to share in his way at his time.

I also wanted to ask about something else that had been kind of bugging me since he mentioned it. I didn't think it was a safer topic, but I did think it was the safer of the two.

Still, I went in cautiously.

"Can I ask you something?"

He put his beer down and trained his eyes to me. "Yeah."

I put my roll on my bread plate and looked at him. "I'm guessing you know Heather and Bodhi since you mentioned them."

"Small town and two characters like that don't go unnoticed," he replied.

I nodded, thinking his statement was a little weird of the not-good variety, but I pushed myself to keep going.

"If I'm not wrong, you were referring to them when you called them potheads."

"You're not wrong because they are potheads," Raiden responded.

They were.

Still.

"That's kind of, uh…" I cast my mind for a word, couldn't find one so I went for it, "*mean*."

He leaned in to me and wrapped his hand around mine that was sitting on the table.

"Pot is legal in Colorado," he stated and I tilted my head.

"It is?"

He stared at me a second then grinned. "Yeah, baby, it is."

God, I liked it when he called me baby.

"Don't you vote?" he asked.

"Well, yeah," I answered.

"Straight ticket?" he guessed.

"Well, no," I told him. "But all the referendums freak me out. I used to try to understand them, then one year I voted for one and found out after that I voted the wrong way because they made the language purposefully confusing so you thought you were voting for one thing and you weren't. I went back and read and reread it and there was no way I knew what I was voting for. That's dirty business, so I decided that I should vote only on things I totally understood instead of making another mistake like that because, well, you know, these things affect people's lives and you shouldn't screw up something that important. As none of the referendums make a lick of sense to me, I concentrate on the candidates and hope they'll take care of the referendums."

"Makes sense. Whacked sense but it makes it," he murmured.

"What does pot being legal have to do with Bodhi and Heather?" I asked, though I had to admit, this was good news and nice to know why the Sherriff didn't get into Bodhi's business.

"I voted against legalizing pot," Raiden declared, and I got it.

"Oh," I replied.

"I'm good with live and let live, but shit like that bleeds into bigger shit, and no one needs that."

"I don't smoke it, but I know both Bodhi and Heather and they're really nice people. And I'm not sure something like that bleeds. It's a personal choice and it isn't like crystal meth or stuff like that that destroys lives."

"It is when it bleeds," he returned.

His eyes were now weirdly sharp, so much so it was uncomfortable, and I squirmed in my chair.

"Okay," I gave in. "I'm guessing you know more about this than I do."

"Unfortunately, I do," Raiden replied.

I bit my lip again, intrigued if a little frightened.

I carefully tugged my hand from his and looked to the corner of the table.

"Hanna," he called and I turned my gaze to him.

"Bodhi and Heather are my friends," I told him.

"I know," he replied.

"Well, I, uh…spend time with them."

"I know."

"How do you know?" I asked.

"Saw you with the guy. Wasn't hard to read you were tight. And, again, small town. A couple of questions, links you to the girl too."

Links me to the girl?

What a weird way to put it.

I shook that off and pressed on, "Well, this is a, um, *date*, and if this goes, uh…*well*, then…"

"This goes further, I will not hang with them," he declared firmly, and I stared.

"You don't like people that much who smoke pot?" I asked.

"Not that. Got friends who smoke. Don't give a shit. Don't like it, but it doesn't say anything about them except they're into something I'm not into. Just don't got a good feeling about those two."

"They're kind and funny."

He leaned toward me. "They give me a bad feeling, Hanna. They don't give you that same feeling, cool. But this date goes well, we go further, I will not hang with them. Straight up. No bullshit. You're into me, I'm into you, but that does not mean I gotta be into all your friends and the same goes for you."

I had to admit, that was fair.

"Okay," I agreed.

"And I'm not sayin' that shit knowin' how into me you are, layin' down the law. I mean it. You connect with my people, you aren't into them, same goes for you."

That was nice.

"Okay," I stated more resolutely, then asked (yes, stupidly), "How into you do you think I am?"

"Honey, you crawled around on all fours in a pet store, totally unable to cope with bein' in my space. You're seriously into me."

This was true and this should have mortified me.

It didn't.

For some reason, it annoyed me.

I narrowed my eyes at him. "It's kind of annoying you figured that out, and more annoying you keep bringing it up."

To this he threw his handsome head back, burst out laughing and held my hand tight for a second.

His hold loosened and he lifted our hands so our elbows were on the table, our hands up between us, but he again leaned in to me.

This time super-close.

Which meant he was pressing my hand into his hard chest.

I held my breath.

"Open book," he said quietly. "Like I said, it's cute. It's also refreshing, baby."

"I'm glad you think so," I whispered, no longer annoyed. With him that close and my hand pressed to his chest I was back to nervous.

"I do," he confirmed.

Okay then, he thought it was cute and refreshing, so I felt it safe to give him more.

Therefore I did.

"Just so you know, I find you extremely attractive and I'd really like this date to go well because I'd like another one, and not as an excuse to buy another dress and killer pair of shoes."

I did it, but felt no relief when something weird and a little alarming flashed in his eyes. His fingers squeezed mine before he hid that look, let my hand go and sat back.

"For a guy, that question is answered at the end of the date."

Fabulous.

Something to be *more* nervous about.

He grinned at me.

I licked my lips.

His grin faded and his eyes dropped to my mouth.

I stopped breathing.

The waiter showed with our appetizers.

Thank God.

"BE BACK, YEAH?" Raiden asked as the waiter swept away our dessert plates.

I nodded to him while he stood

When he was up, he reached out a hand and tucked my hair behind my ear. My scalp tingled, the tingle shooting straight down my spine, and I wished I could touch his hair or that he'd do that again (and again) while he walked away.

I watched him go while internally shivering through the remnants of the hair tuck maneuver.

Once he was out of sight, my mind turned to the date.

I wasn't certain how it started, but once we were over the Bodhi and Heather thing and the how into him I was thing, Raiden steered conversation to safer subjects. People in town we both knew. How great Rachelle's café was doing. Grams. How I did up my house.

I thought, in the end, it was going well.

Conversation was easy. It flowed. There were smiles, some laughs for him and for me, the food was delicious and I'd loosened up because of my company, not to mention three glasses of wine.

The one thing that was weird was that Raiden shared zilch about himself, outside talking a bit about his mom and more about his sister, both of whom, when he spoke of them, it was clear he cared a lot about.

But he didn't tell me about his house when I was talking about mine. He didn't share about what he did for work. He didn't talk about the time he was away. In fact, it was him that led the conversation and I followed its flow, sharing generously without getting but a hint of anything personal back.

It was on this thought I realized I had to use the restroom, and this thought led to the fact I should have told Raiden that before he left. I figured he'd know where I was when he got back and saw me gone. A bonus, it would save me having to give him that information and the nerve-wracking moment of walking away while he was watching.

So I grabbed my bag, moved from the table and headed in the direction of the restroom.

I got to the ladies in the back hall and put my hand on the door, but stopped dead when I heard Raiden's voice coming from around the corner that was at the end of the hall.

"She's clueless," he stated.

I stared at my hand at the door, my mind going blank.

"Totally," Raiden went on. "Hanna has no idea those two assholes are transporting ice with her afghans."

My breath clogged in my throat.

Ice?

As in methamphetamine?

"Yeah, it's completely escaped her," Raiden continued. "She thinks the girl is helpin' her out. Hanna's got no part in it. I end this with her tonight, we'll meet, plan the takedown."

I end this with her tonight.

Oh my God.

What?

How?

What?

"She trusts them. Whacked," Raiden carried on. "Motherfuckers are using her. Thinks they're her friends. She's got no fuckin' clue."

I pushed the door and hurried inside. I somehow had the presence of mind to tiptoe in because the bathroom was tile, the hallway carpeted, muting my footfalls and he obviously didn't know I was there.

The door swung closed behind me. I put my back to the wall beside it and deep-breathed.

Holy Moses, Bodhi and Heather were using my shipments to transport drugs.

Holy Moses! How would they even *do* that?

And why?

And…

And…

For some reason, Raiden was out with me to ascertain my part in this hideous scenario.

He wasn't into me.

He was using me.

Like Bodhi and Heather.

My friends who I rode trails with, snowboarded with, laughed with.

Using me.

"Oh my God," I breathed, pain searing through me, the heat white-hot, leaving devastation in its wake.

I wasn't an idiot. I was…

I didn't know what I was.

A moron.

A loser.

I shoved my bag under my arm so I could put my hands over my face and I pulled in huge, broken breaths to control the tears clawing at the backs of my eyes.

A new dress.

Excited laughter with my best friend.

Shoes that I'd have to knit five afghans to pay for.

And all because I was a moron.

Thoughts assaulting my brain, it took everything I had to pull myself together.

Raiden couldn't know I knew. I had to pretend. I had to finish this stupid, *stupid* date.

Then *I* would end things tonight.

And *I* would take care of business.

Then *I* would learn my stupid lesson.

A narrow life was better.

Books. Movies. Friends I'd had since junior high who I could trust. A great-grandmother who adored me. An ornery cat who liked me occasionally. A job I enjoyed that was free of the drug trade.

That was it.

The rest of it…

No.

I had no idea I'd been smart before. I had no idea I'd been living the right life.

I had no idea.

Now I did.

"Shit," I whispered.

I rushed into a stall, took care of business then left the restroom carefully. Checking the back hall, which was empty, I stealthily moved out and saw Raiden at our table. I skirted the main area of the restaurant, walked outside and took in huge lung-fulls of crisp, mountain air, coming up with a plan while doing so.

The wine had gone to my head. I was a bit tipsy and more headachy.

I needed to go home.

I squared my shoulders and swallowed my tears. I turned to the front door, walked in and moved to the table, Raiden's head coming up when he saw me, his brows snapping together at my direction.

God, he was gorgeous.

Amazing.

Phenomenal.

Using me.

"You okay?" he asked as I sat.

I drew in one more breath.

Then I turned to him. I took him in and felt my dream take its final, shuddering breath before it died...

And I lied.

6

LAST CHANCE

THE DRIVE HOME was silent. The whole time I looked out the side window.

That wasn't strictly true.

The drive home was silent, except once we were in the Jeep on our way home, Raiden asked, "This happen often, headaches comin' on this fast?"

"Yes," I lied.

Raiden left it at that.

I spent my energies holding myself together.

This took a lot of my energies.

Therefore, by the time we got to my house, I was exhausted.

Raiden parked, and as he was shutting the Jeep down, I swiftly unbuckled my seatbelt, threw open the door and climbed out as gracefully as I could.

I was hoofing it double time to the front door when my efforts were foiled by Raiden's hand closing around mine.

He slowed my dash and dug into his jeans pocket, got out my keys, stopped us at the door and let us in.

I took two wide steps inside, unfortunately dragging him with me. I tugged my hand free of his and turned on him, hand up.

"Thanks for letting us in. I'll take those now."

I avoided his eyes as he deposited my keys in my hand, my fingers closing around them instantly, and my hand dropped.

"Hanna, you gonna be okay?"

I looked up at him.

Raiden Miller in my foyer.

A dream come true then turning straight into a nightmare.

"I'll take some ibuprofen and I'll be fine," I lied.

I wouldn't be fine. Not for ever and ever.

"Can you hang on a second?" I went on to ask. "Before you go, I want to give you something."

"Sure, honey," he replied gently.

Raiden Miller calling me honey.

Gently.

Total nightmare.

I looked to my feet, tucked my hair behind my ear and hurried to the stairs. "I'll just be a sec."

I rushed up the stairs on the toes of my sandals.

I'd had the idea on the way home. It didn't make sense at all, but the instant I had it I knew I had to do it. And I never knew I had to do anything the instant I had the idea, so I decided I was going to go with it.

I ran to my bedroom door and tossed my clutch and the keys across the room to the bed. Then I dashed to the spare bedroom where I kept my finished afghans and found the one I was looking for. A fluffy, black, loose weave cashmere already tied in a wide, dove gray satin ribbon with my signature tag on it. Heavy cream cardstock, and on it, in black, handwritten in the calligraphy I taught myself from a book after painstaking hours of copying, *Made special...by Hanna.*

I hastened down the hall, slowed my step at the stairs and again avoided looking at Raiden while I descended.

But I walked right up to him and held out the throw.

"I want you to have this."

"Jesus, baby," he murmured, his voice deeper than normal, and I looked up at him.

He was staring down at the afghan, his face strange.

He looked stunned, moved, pleased.

Really.

He was an amazing actor.

His eyes came to mine. "I can't take this."

I jerked it toward him. "Take it."

He lifted a hand then dropped it and held my eyes. "It looks like a five hundred dollar one."

"It's a seven hundred and fifty dollar one."

He did a slow blink. "Come again?"

"Cashmere," I explained and jerked it at him again. "Please take it."

"Hanna—"

"Take it."

"Honey—"

"Please," I whispered, my voice suddenly husky, "take it."

He studied me closely as he took it then abruptly his head jerked down, and, as if he didn't know his mouth was saying the words, he stated, "Fuck me, it feels like heaven."

"Cashmere," I repeated and his eyes came back to mine. "I had a nice night," I continued, moving directly to the door, opening it then standing wide so he had plenty of room to get through. "Thank you."

He looked at my feet then out the open door and finally at me.

He hesitated what seemed like days before he walked to me and stopped close. Too close. I had to tip my head way back (even in four inch heels!) and he had to dip his chin way down.

"Outside the headache, you okay?" he asked low.

"Outside the headache, peachy," I lied and quickly concluded, "Thanks again for a nice night."

Raiden didn't move.

My heart kept breaking.

"I'll call you tomorrow," he told me.

Right.

"Okay," I replied, though I didn't know how he'd do that since he didn't have my number. He also wouldn't be able to do that because I was no way, no how picking up any call from an unknown number. And last, he simply wasn't going to do that because he was totally lying.

"We'll go to a movie," he stated.

"Great. I like movies." At least that wasn't a lie.

He moved into me.

I moved back.

He stopped, his brows snapping together. "You sure you're okay?"

"I should never drink red wine," I shared.

Another lie. I loved red wine and it loved me, though in abundance it could make me maudlin, but I was three whole glasses away from maudlin.

Something else was making me maudlin.

"It always does a number on me," I kept lying when Raiden didn't move or speak. "But I just can't seem to eat a steak without it."

"Next time, beer," he said.

Like there'd be a next time.

Raiden still didn't move.

I didn't either.

This lasted some time.

God! He wanted to "end this?" Why didn't he end it?

"I should probably get some ibuprofen," I told him on a prompt for him to leave.

"Doesn't feel good, leavin' you alone and feelin' like shit," he replied, and seriously, *seriously*, what *was* it with him?

He could just go.

Why didn't he just go?

"I'll be fine." More lying.

"All right, baby," he murmured.

I closed my eyes.

Baby.

"Hanna?"

I opened them. "Goodnight."

He held my eyes and his were searching. Then he lifted a hand and tucked my hair behind my ear.

I felt his sweet touch in my scalp, down my spine and the tingles it caused exploded along the small of my back.

And there he was, Raiden Ulysses Miller, in my foyer, tucking my hair behind my ear, faking concern about my fake headache and faking that he was into me.

He wanted to fake it?

Fine.

He could fake it.

I'd give him a doozy of a chance to fake it.

And at the same time, I was going to take my shot, my last chance, the only one I'd ever have.

And I was going to go for the gusto.

I lifted my hand, wrapped my fingers around his bicep, leaned in and went up on my toes.

I pressed my lips to his.

They felt *great*.

So great, I couldn't take more. That was all I could do. That took all the courage I had left. I didn't want to know how good it could be and never have it again, even if it was fake.

So that was it.

But Raiden...

He was good at faking.

The master.

I knew this when his arm instantly sliced along my lower back. He hauled me into his hard body and his mouth opened over mine. Mine automatically opened under his and his tongue slid inside.

His tongue felt better, tasted divine, and I pressed into him, tangling mine with his.

My last chance.

He was giving it to me.

Suddenly, I didn't care if it was fake.

Suddenly, I didn't care if I'd never have it again.

I had it now.

I was going for it.

I tilted my head and offered him everything.

He slanted his. I heard the soft *flunf* of the afghan falling to the floor and his free hand drove into my hair, fisting. I felt pain that should have felt bad but felt oh-so-good spike across my scalp and I pressed deeper into him, giving more.

He took it.

My hands slid up his arms, his shoulders and finally, finally, I had his hair sliding through my fingers.

It *was* thick.

It *was* silky.

It was *perfect*.

He shuffled me back. I hit the door, the door hit the wall and he pressed in.

I pressed up, held on and kept giving.

Raiden kept taking.

It was the best kiss of my life.

It could have been the best kiss in history.

It took superhuman effort to remember it wasn't real. To tear my mouth from his, wrench myself out of his arms and step out of reach.

Lost momentarily, I lifted my hand to touch my mouth, my breathing heavy. Then I lifted my eyes to see his head turned toward me, his eyes on me burning in a way that made *me* burn, *everywhere.*

Really, a *great* actor.

Tactical error, taking my last chance.

Now I had to get this done.

I rounded him, crouched where he dropped the afghan, picked it up and moved to stand at the other side of the door, holding it out to him.

"Drive safe home," I said and he stared at me.

"Come again?" he whispered and there was something sinister in that whisper that scared the heck out of me.

But I ignored my fear, jiggled the afghan at him and repeated, "Drive safe home."

He approached me and I felt my body stiffen from head-to-toe.

Raiden didn't miss it. I knew it when his frame jerked to a wooden halt and his eyes bored into mine.

"Talk to me," he ordered, his voice now low and rumbling, but also strangely rough and commanding.

"I'll talk to you tomorrow when you call. Now I really need to get some medication and lie down."

He lifted a hand and curled it around the side of my neck, dipping his face close to mine.

"Now isn't the time to start playing games, Hanna," he warned quietly.

Was he serious?

He was saying that *to me?*

I looked him straight in the eye and declared, "No games, Raiden. It's just a headache." More like heartache. "With me, you get what you see, that's it. No mystery. No nothing. Just me."

"You aren't you," he told me.

"You don't know me," I returned.

Raiden went silent, but he didn't move away.

Then he murmured, "Fair enough."

Thank God.

He slid his hand to the back of my neck, pulling me close as his head lifted up and he spoke, "You kiss like that when you got a headache, honey," he touched his lips to my forehead and they moved there as he finished, "lookin' forward to havin' your mouth when you don't."

Liar.

Liar.

Liar.

I decided not to respond.

I also decided not to allow myself to think about how wonderful it felt to have Raiden Miller kiss my forehead.

His hand slid to my jaw and his chin tipped so he could catch my eyes.

"'Night, Hanna," he said softly.

"Good-bye, Raiden," I replied.

His eyes flashed at my words, but his face moved in. He touched his lips to mine, moved back, took the afghan from me and sauntered out the door.

Keeping up appearances, I stood in it, and when he swung in his Jeep I waved.

Raiden did not wave back.

I closed the door and locked it. I switched the outside lights off and turned off the lights that I'd left on in the foyer. That done, I dashed up the stairs as best I could because I was also tugging at the buckles and straps of my sandals to get them off while I went.

I hit the bedroom, tossed my shoes on the bed and turned on the lamp on my nightstand.

Only then did I hear the Jeep pull away.

He waited until I'd made it upstairs and he knew I was settling, getting ready for bed before he drove away.

That was sweet.

God, I wished he was real.

I dashed back down the stairs and grabbed the phone in the hall. I ran through the dining room into the kitchen, snapped on the light and found the phonebook.

I flipped through it and found the number for the Sherriff's Police.

Then I called it.

7

REWARD

Raid

R AID WALKED DOWN the sidewalk to the shiny, black SUV parked on the side of the road in town. He pulled open the door and angled in.

Blue and red lights flashed into the cab as they did the same outside, illuminating the street.

"You hear the police band?" Tucker Creed asked.

Raid kept his eyes to the three squad cars and one K-9 SUV all angled in around Bodhi's bike shop. Then he shifted his gaze down the street where, at a distance of a little over a block, two more squads and another K-9 unit were angled outside the gift shop.

"Raid, you hear me?" Creed asked, and Raid cut his eyes to his partner.

"I heard it," he growled.

"She called it in," Creed told him something he already knew.

"I said I heard it," Raid repeated.

"You know how she knew to call it in? You said she was clueless," Creed asked, and Raid's eyes moved back to the flashing squads.

He knew.

She'd played him.

Sweet, shy, cute, goofy Hanna Boudreaux didn't go out for a breath of fresh air to clear her head and try to get rid of a burgeoning headache like she told him she had.

She'd been the one he heard open the ladies room door.

She'd overheard him.

She'd covered it, came back looking freaked, lied that it was a headache and then spent the next thirty minutes acting jacked because she was freaked that her friends were fucking her over.

Then, minutes after he left her at her house, she'd made a call and blown their whole fucking, eleven month operation.

"This lead's dead," Creed declared, and Raid looked back at him. "They got both that Bodhi kid and his girl in custody. May luck out and they'll flip for the police, but this guy pullin' the strings, doubt those two goofballs got the breadcrumbs to lay that trail so they'll probably only give the cops shit we already got."

None of this was wrong.

Creed kept going, "Headin' back down to Phoenix. Sylvie's already pissed I've been up here this long. Says I need to haul my ass back to the valley and play daddy to Jesse, and next time it's her turn to try and track down drug supplying whackjobs."

Tucker Creed had been coming up, on and off, a day here, a week there when things got hot, for the last eleven months.

Whenever it got hot it eventually fizzled out, so he went home to his family.

Raid had met Creed's wife once. She was a relatively new wife, a new mom, but like her husband, she was a seasoned private investigator and ass kicker.

She was the ballsiest bitch he'd ever met in his life.

He'd liked her immediately.

Sylvie Creed had a baby boy named Jesse who she didn't like leaving, but she also didn't like her husband leaving. Further, they strangely, considering both of them were badass, consummate professionals and skilled, really hated being apart in a way you could almost taste how much they hated it.

Therefore, the longer this operation went, the more trips Creed took north, the more impatient Sylvie became.

And she was getting antsy down in Phoenix looking after a kid when she'd prefer to be in Colorado cracking heads with her husband, and she wasn't all fired up about the fact that Creed got to have all the fun.

"You gonna call this shit in to Knight or you want me to do it?" Raid asked.

"You do it," Creed answered, and his lips twitched. "You gonna wait until tomorrow to lay into your new babe for jacking up our action or are you headin' there now?"

"She overheard me talkin'. We didn't say much. She has no clue about the operation."

Creed smiled. "So you gonna wait until tomorrow to lay your new babe or are you headin' there now?"

Oh, he was heading there now.

It was fucking uncool she overheard him, came to the table, lied her ass off then pulled that tease shit at her house—whatever the fuck that was about—and called the Sherriff.

He had no idea what was in her head.

He was fucking going to find out.

Then he was going to drag her ass to her bedroom, which he hoped to God was as appealing as the porch and foyer of her house, and "lay his new babe."

Thoroughly.

She deserved a spanking for this shit.

But they were new. He had to break her into that.

Raid didn't answer Creed's question.

Instead, he asked, "You headin' to DIA now?"

"Hotel, book a flight, then I'm out."

"I'll call it in to Knight, then I'm goin' to Hanna's. I'll update you if we get a new lead and we need you or Sylvie to come back up. Though, advice. I'd throw your wife a bone. Knight says she's threatening, we don't find this asshole, then she's gonna come up and do it on her own so she can stop livin' the life of a woman without her baby daddy."

"Right," Creed grunted, his lips curved up.

"Later," Raid said.

"Later," Creed replied.

Raid threw open the door and knifed out. He walked the three blocks to his Jeep, swung in and headed to Hanna's house.

He did this trying to control his temper, and insanely, he did that by thinking about Hanna.

And he did this because, for weeks, he couldn't get her out of his head.

And this was because, over the last week and a half, he'd come to understand Hanna Boudreaux was his reward.

He'd thought it the second he saw her in front of Bodhi's bike shop, looking adorable, jumping around on those long, tanned legs, clapping and crying out excitedly wearing short-shorts and a little white top.

He'd suspected it when she crawled around gathering cat food tins, that sweet ass of hers in the air, making him fight his dick getting hard and giving him ideas for their future.

It came clearer when it just plain came clear that she was one of those women that needed a man. Taking care of her grandmother on her own. Paying her mortgage by knitting fucking afghans. Getting fucked over at a car dealership. Getting taken by her friends.

But he knew it the minute she timidly tossed her afghans over the back of her grandmother's porch chair and smoothed her hand down the soft wool, yards of nothing that, at her hands, looked like everything. Home. Warmth. Comfort. Nurture. Love.

And if he didn't know it then, it was cemented when she opened that mouth of hers under his and let him take everything he wanted.

His reward for his sweat.

His blood.

Their blood.

His goddamned nightmares.

Other than visits to his mother and sister, he had no idea that when he came back to Willow—something he never intended to do—that he'd find it there.

Her there.

What he'd earned.

What was *his*.

What he knew was months ago they'd traced the shipments to Bodhi and his girlfriend in Raid's own damned town.

That was why Knight had called him in.

That was why Raid came home.

They never got a lock on the supplier. He always sent his minions with the dope, but Bodhi and Heather used the bike shop as a front, shipping it with the bike business as a cover.

Bodhi and Heather were relatively harmless, cogs in a wheel, low-level players they needed to watch and work and hope they led the team to the puppetmaster.

By the time the team was done dicking around with those two and ready to close in on them to try to squeeze them for information, strong arm or blackmail them into a maneuver that might out the big man, Bodhi and Heather got smart with protecting the bike shop and moved the business to Hanna's shipments.

A local. A third generation Willowite.

Thus a complication.

At that time Raid had no clue who Hanna Boudreaux was. He knew Miss Mildred. Everyone did. He also knew Hanna's older brother, Jeremy, who was a year behind him in school. All he remembered of the guy was that he was a decent wide receiver and he'd bragged overtly, and nauseatingly frequently, when he'd tapped Lori Kowslowski's ass.

But he didn't know Hanna.

Once word got out Bodhi and Heather had moved their operation and involved a local—a local linked to the town's most beloved citizen, a ninety-eight-year-old fixture of their society—he'd had no choice but to ask around about Hanna.

He'd heard nothing but good things. She looked after her grandmother. She went to church. She was a quiet girl. She read a lot. She liked to go to the movies. She was sweet. Loyal. Funny. Loving.

An easy mark for those two assholes.

Even though Raid never saw her there, his sister Rachelle told him she came into café all the time.

"But haven't seen her for a while, bro. You see her, though, you'll know. Fantastic figure. Pretty smile. Great legs, but uber-mousy, you get what I'm saying? Has no clue, if she put in a teeny-weeny bit of effort she'd be *all that*," Rache had said.

But sweet, shy, mousy, reads-a-lot Hanna, who everyone knew and everyone said was always around, had disappeared.

By the time spring hit Willow and Raid first laid eyes on Hanna Boudreaux, weeks before he saw her at the bike shop and took his shot to follow her and "run into her" at the pet store, he didn't know what the fuck his sister was on about.

Hanna Boudreaux was not mousy.

She was standing with one of her hands on the handlebars of that ridiculous bike of hers, talking to Paul Moyer.

No.

Laughing with him. Her shining blonde head thrown back, her pretty face lit up, her body shaking, her other hand clutching Paul's arm like she had to hold herself up with the hilarity of it all.

Paul had been watching her tits while she laughed.

Raid had wanted to land a fist in his face.

He held back.

They needed to know if Hanna was clean, then they needed to be *certain* Hanna was clean, then they could extricate her from the scenario and carry on with the operation.

And after Raid had finally caught sight of her he had decided that he would personally be extricating her because Hanna would be in his bed, under his protection and she'd feel none of that shit.

Fortunately, it took about a nanosecond to figure out that Hanna was being taken.

Unfortunately, before he could get her in his bed, she'd overheard him and blown the operation, so now they had nothing.

No one to lead them to the supplier who fucked with Raid and Creed's buddy, Knight, who lived in Denver, had a successful nightclub, a questionable side business and a shitload of money with which he could use to throw at problems he wanted solved.

Something he didn't hesitate doing.

So Knight contracted with Raid, Raid's crew and Creed to solve it.

Now they had nothing.

Knight was going to be pissed.

Raid already was.

He turned onto the single lane road that led to three houses, the last one being Hanna's, and pulled over. He yanked out his phone and made his call to Knight.

He was right. Knight was pissed.

He ended the call, pulled back into the lane and headed to Hanna's house.

The light, upstairs right, was on.

Her bedroom.

So was the light, downstairs left.

The living room.

This meant she was up.

Excellent.

He threw open his door and folded out. He prowled to the front door, put his hand right to the knob and turned.

Fuck.

Now she locked it.

He hit the bell.

Nothing.

He looked to his left.

The lights were on, curtains drawn. He could see no movement.

He hit the bell again then pounded.

He stopped.

Still nothing.

"What the fuck?" he clipped.

He turned and prowled to his car. He opened his glove compartment, got his kit and prowled right back. He squatted by the doorknob, pulled out his tools, and in about five seconds picked her shitty, going-to-be-replaced-tomorrow lock.

He shoved his tools in his back pocket, opened the door and saw her instantly, standing in the foyer, staring at him, her big, pretty blue eyes huge.

He slammed the door behind him.

Hanna jumped.

She was very lucky that she'd changed into an adorable pair of very short drawstring pajama shorts and a skintight ribbed tank, both that left little to the imagination, both in colors that highlighted the golden tan that shimmered on every inch of her skin. She was also lucky she had her hair up in another messy knot his fucking hand fucking *itched* to yank out or he wouldn't have had the patience to draw in the breath he needed to calm down.

But he drew in the breath he needed to calm down.

In that time she whispered, "Oh my God. You picked my lock."

"How's your headache?" he asked.

Her eyes, which had moved to the doorknob, shot to his.

She started backing up.

"Smart," he murmured as he advanced.

"Raiden—"

"You heard me on the phone."

She visibly swallowed. Her shoulder hit the doorway to the back hall and she shifted sideways.

Raid followed her. "You came to the table and lied through your teeth, right to my face."

"I—"

"You told me you had a goddamned headache, which worried me, then you pressed tight to me, giving me your mouth and takin' it away, a bullshit bitch tease move I didn't know you had it in you to execute."

She stopped dead. "I wasn't teasing you."

"What was that shit then?"

She stared into his eyes and announced, "A good-bye kiss."

It was at that Raid stopped dead. "What?"

"Raiden, the gig is up," she declared, and Raid closed his eyes.

Jesus, how could the woman be so infuriating and so fucking cute all at once?

He opened his eyes and asked, "The gig is up?"

She leaned in to him and hissed, "Yes."

Fuck, he wanted to kiss her.

He also wanted to shake her.

"Baby, it's *jig*," he corrected, and her head jerked, which made that mess of hair on her head jerk, which reminded him he wanted his hands in that hair.

Then elsewhere.

He needed to speed this shit up.

"Sorry?" she asked, sounding confused, and he looked from her hair to her eyes and saw she was, in fact, confused.

Yeah. Infuriating. And fucking cute.

"The jig is up, not the gig," he told her.

Her eyes narrowed. "Seriously? You're correcting my street lingo?"

"Think that street lingo was the street lingo about eight decades ago, Hanna. So now it's just lingo."

Hanna threw up her hands. "Now you're giving me a street lingo history lesson?"

Raid found what he thought was the impossible happening.

He lost patience with Hanna Boudreaux being cute.

"Why are we talkin' about this shit?" he asked.

"I don't know. Why are you here at all?" she shot back.

"I'm here 'cause I wanna know why you lied to me. I wanna know why you didn't come to the table and talk to me about what you heard so I could explain it and shit would not right now be totally fucked."

"I'm sorry, did I mess with your plans, Raiden? Were there more ways you could use me like Bodhi and Heather used me before you threw me away?"

At her words, Raid went completely still.

Then he asked, dangerously quietly, "Come again?"

She missed the danger, but she didn't miss his words. "You used me and now you're here acting like a jerk. Why?"

"How did I use you?" he asked.

"I don't know. I didn't go to the table, tell you I overheard, allow you to explain the intricacies of your plan of pretending you were into me so you could ascertain if I was in on my oh so very *ex*-friends' fiendish plot to use my *afghans* as cover for transporting *drugs*. So I don't know all the ways you used me. I just know you, like them, *used me*."

"Pretending I was into you?" Raid whispered, and she threw up her hands.

"Raiden, *I know*," she snapped.

"You don't know shit," he clipped.

"Really? So, you don't notice me for months—no, *for years*—then suddenly you're everywhere I am and how I'm," she lifted up her hands and did air quotation marks, "*linked* to drug dealers or transporters or, uh…whatever you call them."

"Yeah, babe, for years I didn't notice you, then I did when two pieces of shit used a kind, trusting woman as cover for transporting dope."

"Right, then, now that we have that cleared up, you can leave," she announced.

Jesus.

"I'm not leaving," he returned.

"Why?" she cried. "It's over. You know I have no part in it. I don't know your part in it. I don't *want* to know your part in it. But my part is done. This is over. You don't have to pretend anymore. Why can't you just *go*?"

"I'm not pretending *jack*," Raid bit out.

"God!" she yelled. "This is *insane*!"

Then she made a big mistake.

Huge.

She impatiently shoved her hand in her hair, not remembering it was up in a knot. She encountered whatever was holding it up, yanked it out and her hair tumbled in a shining mess around her face and down her shoulders.

Raid watched it, lost it, and advanced.

Hanna retreated, slamming into the wall at the side of the stairs.

Raid caged her in, putting one hand to her hip, fingers spread, pads digging in, one hand to the wall at the side of her head and he bent low so his face was in hers.

She'd quit breathing, which was good.

That meant she couldn't spout more bullshit.

He forced his voice to gentle when he said, "I get you're tweaked about this shit. I get you're hurt that your friends fucked you over and how they did it, which is huge. What you need to get, honey, is that I'm not using you. I'm not pretending jack. I *am* into you."

"Stop it," she whispered.

Fuck him.

"Do not transfer the pain you feel that two people you let into your life and your heart fucked you to me, Hanna," he warned.

He thought he had the upper hand. He thought if he could get her to calm down and see reason, they'd get past this.

So he was unprepared for Hanna Boudreaux rocking his world.

"I've crushed on you since I was six. We were on the same tug of war team three years in a row at Grams's picnics. We were both out of class and alone in the hall at the same time second semester my freshman year, your senior year. Your locker was nowhere near mine. I don't know what you were doing in that hallway but I'd gone to the nurse because I had flu and was getting my stuff to go home. You walked by me, looked at me and said, 'hey'. I said 'hey' back, but I don't think you heard me because you kept walking and didn't look back. Until the pet store, that was the only word you ever said to me. 'Hey.'"

Fucking shit.

"Hanna—"

"You left Willow then you came home and I went to Rachelle's once a week, twice, three times just to catch a glimpse of you. You looked through me, dozens of times. Once you caught me looking at you and you jerked up your chin. You looked right at me and jerked up your chin. Then you looked away. Months later, I run into you in the pet store and it was like you'd never seen me before."

Christ.

"I don't remember that at the café," Raid said softly.

"I know," she replied. "When you met me, you didn't know me at all, but I've been around for years."

"Baby, me not remembering you doesn't mean dick."

"It does to me."

He could see that. He knew she was that into him before she told him all that. No woman got that flustered around a man who she wasn't extremely attracted to. And he'd liked it a fuck of a lot. From the minute she first tucked her hair behind her ear, hiding she was glancing at him to be sure he was still checking her out when she was with Bodhi and her bike.

And he liked it more than a fuck of a lot that she knew she was on his tug of war team when he was fucking eleven or whatever and remembered them walking by each other in the hall in high school years ago.

It was cute. It was sweet.

It was her.

He just didn't understand the history of it, but Hanna explaining the length and extent of her crush on him explained a lot about her behavior the last week and a half. Raid could see that his not noticing her would cut deep.

He moved his hand from the wall to wrap it around the side of her neck. She tried to jerk away, but he dug his fingers in and pushed closer. This had the desired effect. She quit moving.

"A buddy of mine has some issues in Denver," Raid explained. "Those issues leaked to Willow. He called me in, contracting me to find the supplier who's been shifting drugs through Willow. This asshole is slippery. Every lead we got led to shit. He's got soldiers everywhere, but he's a ghost. Honey, you might have been at Rache's, I might have seen you, but I had a lot of shit on my mind."

"You thought I was involved with drug people and investigated me. You got involved with me to investigate me."

"I got involved with you to get involved with you, but I also had to clear you of that shit so we could move on and get his fuckin' guy."

"Raiden, can't you see how *I* can't see that I've been around, you've even looked right at me and didn't *see* me and now, all of a sudden, you're into me, and how I can't believe you're actually, well…*into me?*"

"How the fuck can you make something that makes no sense make sense?" he asked back.

"So you understand what I'm saying?"

"I do and it might make sense, honey, but it's still whacked."

Her eyes rolled to the ceiling.

"Hanna, look at me," he ordered.

Her eyes rolled back.

"I'm into you," he told her.

"I don't believe you," she told him.

"Why the fuck not?" he asked.

"I just don't," she answered.

"Christ, honest to God, you think I'm a man who comes back to his hometown, a town his mother and sister still live in, takes the town's beloved native daughter—who also happens to be the great-granddaughter of the town's matriarch —out to dinner in order to play her, and I'd do that shit at Chilton's where everyone can see?"

She blinked.

She hadn't thought of that.

Thank fuck, he was getting somewhere.

Raid kept going.

"And you think I'm a man who lays out bullshit lines to cute, sweet, pretty women and keeps at it after a job is fucked just for shits and grins?"

She pulled one side of her lips between her teeth.

Yeah, getting somewhere.

Raid kept at it.

"And serious as fuck, Hanna, you think that kiss was pretend?"

She stared into his eyes and her little white teeth appeared to bite her lip. She let it go and whispered, "That kiss *was* really good."

Raid's eyes didn't go to the ceiling. His head dropped and he contemplated his boots.

He also saw she had fucking sequins glued to her toenails that looked varnished with black polish, but had some kind of white flower design painted around the sequin.

Christ, she was adorably ridiculous.

A sequin stuck to her fucking *toe*.

He couldn't help it, and didn't try. He started laughing.

"Are you laughing?" He heard her ask.

"You got goddamned sequins on your toes," he said, his words trembling.

"They're pretty," she returned, and he lifted his head to look at her, no longer laughing.

His reward.

"Yeah," he agreed. He wasn't talking about sequins and he knew she knew it when he heard her sharp intake of breath. "Are we done with this idiotic conversation about me not being into you?"

"Uh…I think so."

"So you get I'm into you," he pushed to confirm.

She pressed her lips together and thought on it awhile.

Raid used the last of his patience to let her.

Then she nodded.

"Thank Christ," he muttered and finally relaxed.

"So, uh…when you said you were going to call me tomorrow, which is today, incidentally, you actually meant it?"

Raid heard the growl roll up his throat before he rumbled after it, "Yeah, Hanna. I meant it."

Her eyes lit. She liked that, didn't hide it and he liked both.

Again, he wanted to kiss her.

"Cool," she whispered.

"Honey, tell me you see the absurdity of me callin' you tomorrow, which is today, incidentally, askin' you to a movie, only so after the movie I can maneuver you to my house, then my bed, when I'm right here in your house with your bed upstairs?"

Her eyes rounded and she again stopped breathing.

Fuck yeah, he wanted to kiss her.

"Well, I can see the absurdity of you calling me when we can make plans for a movie right now," she allowed.

Goddamned ridiculous.

And cute.

Fuck it, he was just going to kiss her.

So he did.

It was a repeat of the one before. Hot. Wet. She slid her fingers in his hair and pressed her warm, sweet, soft body to his, opened herself up and gave him everything.

He fought back the near overwhelming urge to drop her to the floor and take her in her foyer when what she said penetrated.

He ended the kiss, slid his lips to the skin under her ear and felt the soft puffs of her quick breaths against his neck.

"I'm sensing you wanna slow this down," he noted, his voice rough.

"We've only had one date," she replied softly. Then, quieter. "I'm not that that type of girl."

She wasn't. Hanna Boudreaux absolutely wasn't that type of girl.

Fuck.

His reward.

He lifted his head and looked down at her to see her face soft, eyes bright and heated, lips swollen.

Fantastic.

"Movie. Tomorrow night. You pick. Text me," he stated.

"I don't have your number," she told him.

"Where's your phone? I'll program it in," he offered.

"It's upstairs." She made to move, mumbling, "I'll get it."

Raid locked his arms around her and her eyes shot back to his.

"Unh-unh." He shook his head. "Already watched you run up those stairs in a sexy dress and heels tonight. Not gonna watch you do it in your sweet pajamas. Only so much a man can take."

"Oh," she breathed.

Fuck.

His reward.

"I'll be here, six o'clock. Pick a movie that works with that time, but I wanna take you out to eat before so plan accordingly."

"Okay," she agreed.

"We need to go earlier, call Rachelle at her café. She can give you my number."

"Okay," she repeated.

"Now, I gotta go."

She licked her lips and again said, "Okay."

Raid made a move, but her arms tightened around him.

Suddenly, she dipped her chin and planted her forehead in his chest.

"I know you think I'm an idiot and this is ridiculous and I understand why you were angry I didn't discuss things with you when I overheard you talking. But I heard you say I was clueless and you were going to end this tonight. I obviously mistook what you said, but what you said didn't sound good," she explained in a hesitant, hushed voice.

He pulled her closer and dropped his lips to the top of her hair.

Finally, he got it.

She hadn't heard it all.

Not even most of it.

Just the part she could misinterpret.

"You missed the part when my partner was givin' me shit about my new babe takin' my mind off the job, how I needed to get my head back in the game and how you were distracting me from doing that."

"Oh," she whispered into his chest, her arms around him going even tighter. She dropped her head back and he lifted his up to catch her eyes. "I should have told you I overheard. Let you explain. I'm sorry."

Straight up apology.

It took balls to do shit like that, even for sweet, cute, shy women.

His *fucking* reward.

"It's done, baby," he told her.

Hanna nodded, then again tipped her chin down and planted her forehead in his chest.

"Do you think I'm a crazy, creepy stalker lady, hanging at Rachelle's just to see you walk in?"

"Absolutely not," he replied immediately, his voice steely, and her head jerked back so her eyes could scan his face to ascertain the veracity of his words.

He let his expression do the talking because he didn't think her crush was crazy or creepy.

It was like everything about her, sweet and cute.

He just wished like fuck he'd been paying more attention, so instead of spending the next however long it took coaxing her into his bed she'd already be there.

Finally, she said, "I think I actually believe you."

Raid smiled. "Good, 'cause I'm not lyin'."

Hanna's body melted into his and she gave him a smile back.

Fuck, he had to get out of there.

"Now let me go unless you want me to stay," he ordered.

He was gratified at the lengthy hesitation before she let him go.

He leaned in, kissed her forehead and moved to the door.

He had it open when something occurred to him and he turned back.

"You thought you were ending this earlier," he noted. She tipped her head to the side, but then righted it and nodded. "So why did you give me the afghan?"

Her brows drew together in confusion, he sensed not at his question, but at her actions. Then she laid it out honestly.

"I don't know. Maybe I was being my usual idiot and wanted to give you something to remember me. Maybe, even with what I thought you were doing, I knew you were a partial good guy, what with offering to take care of Grams's yard and all, and I wanted to give something back. The only thing I had to give. Something that would keep you warm. But really, I don't know. I just…" she shrugged, "did it."

"Glad you did, honey," he replied.

"Me too," she said.

He gave her a grin. Hers was shy, but she returned it.

"Lock this after me," he commanded.

Hanna nodded and he jerked up his chin.

He walked out the door, closing it behind him. He was on the steps when he heard it lock.

Raid sat in his Jeep and didn't pull away until the downstairs lights were off and he saw her shadow moving behind the filmy curtains of her bedroom.

He drove to his place. He tagged the afghan and walked up the side stairs, unlocked his door and moved in.

He pulled off his clothes, yanked the comforter off his mattress, untied the satin ribbons around the afghan and threw it out on his bed.

Then he climbed under it.

He'd been right when he first touched it.

She'd been right when she said it would keep him warm.

Heaven.

Then Raiden Miller fell asleep under the warmth of Hanna's cashmere, and for the first time in a long time he didn't have a nightmare.

Not even one.

8

DOUBLE FEATURE

The Next Evening

"LEAVE IT TO you, when I'm lookin' forward to my plans for after the fuckin' movie, you find a double feature," Raiden grumbled.

I threw a nervous smile over my shoulder at Raiden, who was carrying a big bucket of popcorn in the crook of his arm and two huge sodas in his hands. He was following me down the aisle of the Willow Deluxe, our theater in town that, against the odds of competition from the huge cineplexes only forty-five minutes away in Denver, stayed in business.

This was mostly because the town liked it. Then again, the citizens of Willow just liked Willow.

Our town was one of those strange exceptions to every rule. We had not gone the way of one-stop convenience and bulk buying economy.

We had a butcher. We had a fruit and veggie shop. We had a non-chain hardware store. We had a grocery store that everyone went to that was family owned and had been for over fifty years. We had a florist, a craft shop, three gift shops, a coffee house, Rachelle's Café, a pizza joint that did great Italian on the whole, a biker bar, a cowboy bar, a Broncos fans only bar and more.

Including the Deluxe, which was a not-for-profit and stayed in business as well as continued renovations due to the generosity of a town that wanted to keep its old-fashioned, hometown feel.

I loved the Deluxe.

I loved my town.

But my smile was nervous because of what I suspected Raiden's plans were for after the movie, not because I was still worried and wondering if he was really into me.

No, even if last night, or more accurately, super-early this morning he had not made that very clear, earlier that evening he'd made it even clearer.

Needless to say, Raiden's idea of "slowing this down" clashed with mine.

In other words, before the movie he took me to Rachelle's for dinner, and even before that, he'd told me to call *his sister* to get *his number*, which, of course, I did not.

He had to know, since Rachelle was at the café a lot even in the evenings, that she might be there and see us together.

And she'd been there.

I'd been at that café a lot and never seen Raiden there with a woman.

Making out with one outside, yes.

Inside, never.

And neither had anyone else, like KC or my other friends, all of whom followed Raiden's actions like, well, what we were: crazy, creepy Raiden Ulysses Miller stalkers.

So it was not lost on Rachelle (or me) what Raiden taking me to her café meant.

However, this was the least of my worries, when, after she saw us together and her eyes bugged right out of her head, she came rushing to us, exclaiming, "Ohmigod! Hanna! I haven't seen you in *forever*! Look at your hair! I love those highlights! They look *great*! And it's so *long*! I barely recognized you."

Raiden gave me a brows raised look as he pulled out my seat, and I belatedly avoided his eyes as I sat.

"And you're so *tan*!" Rachelle went on, stopping at our table. She put two fingers to her cheek, tilted her head and gave me a once over before enquiring, "Have you lost weight?" Then she answered her own question, "No. But definitely toned up. I am *so* getting my own Schwinn if that's what it can do."

I tucked my hair behind my ear and chanced a glance at Raiden to see his lips quirking and his eyes on me.

Rachelle seemed not to notice the looks Raiden and I were giving each other or the fact that neither of us spoke.

Instead, she cried, "Don't order! You're both getting the special. Tonight's special *kicks ass*, if I do say so myself." She turned to her brother. "Beer for you, bro." She turned to me. "Hanna, white wine or diet root beer?"

"Root beer," I answered.

"On its way," she replied.

She then bounced off, Raiden's burnished highlights shining in her long, swinging, brunette hair.

Unfortunately, albeit a gentleman (at times, when he wasn't cursing or angry and backing me up against walls), Raiden didn't let this pass.

"So I didn't notice you or I didn't recognize you?"

"Whatever," I mumbled to my knife and fork, which were rolled in a pink paper napkin and rounded with a sticky tabbed slip of paper in robin's egg blue; one of Rachelle's Café's many signatures.

Raiden roared with laughter.

I quit avoiding him, lifted my head to watch and my discomfiture fled because I enjoyed the show. So much I ended up grinning at him.

He ended his laughter with his face getting soft when he saw my grin, his lips ordering, "Come here," but his body not giving me the chance to comply (or not).

He stretched a long arm across the table and hooked me at the back of the neck. He pulled me across, met me halfway and touched his lips to mine before he let me go.

This was not lost on the many patrons or Raiden's sister. I felt it *and* saw it.

So much for going slow.

That was the only thing uncomfortable about dinner, except Raiden told me he'd share about the "job" he was working in town "later," and he did this in a way I didn't question at the time, but made me slightly troubled.

Mostly we talked about what went down with Bodhi and Heather. Or more to the point, Raiden quizzed me about my less-than-stress-free day after the police arrested my friends and raided my kitchen warehouse, a large part of that day being taken up with the police escorting me through my warehouse and asking me questions then taking me to the station to ask more and giving me updates in return.

"They found ice?" Raiden asked, his mouth still full of Rachelle's delicious (she was not wrong) grilled turkey and swiss sandwich with a thin coating of French dressing and chili oil infused cream cheese.

I nodded. "Apparently lots of it. Though, they didn't share how much."

"And Joe was cool with you?"

Joe was Sherriff Joe who had been Sherriff Joe since I was about twelve.

I nodded again. "He asked me not to leave town, but he told me he knows I'm not involved."

"Did he explain the operation?" Raiden went on.

Another nod from me.

"He said the dogs found little baggies of crystal meth at both the bike shop and my place, most of it at my place hidden under the floorboards, but apparently they bagged the drugs at the bike shop. Evidently, Heather packed it with my afghans and shipped it to drug people that were around my boutiques. They got their drugs and hand delivered my shipments to the local shops so no one would be the wiser. Though if the USPS sniffed it out, which thank God they didn't, they'd trace it back to me and I'd have uncomfortable questions to answer, but Heather and Bodhi would be long gone. Sherriff Joe said Bodhi told the police all this when they interrogated him. They shipped it everywhere, all over the country. Some of my shipments were drug free because they didn't have a dealer to ship to in that area, but a lot of them were tainted. "

None of this made me happy, most especially my friends duping me and putting me in danger of being arrested for a felony I had no knowledge of, but also me being such an idiot. Heck, I actually *paid* Heather to do it. But there was nothing I could do about it except feel relief it was over.

The other part of my day was spent calling the boutique owners that were in the areas the police suspected the drugs were shipped to and, luckily, Bodhi was right. None of them were the wiser. They had no idea and Sherriff Joe advised me not to tell them.

"What's done is done and unless they read the *Willow Chronicle*, they'll never know and don't need to know."

I decided to take him up on his advice.

For some reason, Bodhi had used his one phone call to call me, and when I picked up he said, "Banana." Banana was his what-I-once-thought-was-sweet, now-I-thought-was-unoriginal-and-grating, nickname for me. "Please don't hang up. Heather and I wanna ex—"

I'd hung up.

I also told Raiden about this call.

He seemed less happy about it than I was.

"Any more attempts at contact, honey, you disconnect and call me immediately. I'll shut that shit down," he'd ordered and the way he did, in his rough and commanding voice edged with more than a hint of anger, I just nodded.

Close to the end of the meal, Raiden had asked, "How's Miss Mildred about all this shit?"

This was another part of my day I didn't like, and it was the part I didn't like most of all.

"She was shocked," I answered, a quaver in my voice. I cleared my throat to wash it away. "Upset for me. Worried in general about the state of the world. Rocked that something like this could happen in Willow. Shaken that it happened, and that it happened to me." I locked eyes with him and concluded, "Not good."

"Church tomorrow?" he asked, and I nodded again. "She got someone with her tonight?"

"Eunice, her widowed neighbor, is over. They're watching movies."

"Good," he muttered.

"I'm going to keep a closer eye on her for a while," I told him. "She acts eighty, which everyone knows is the new sixty-five, but she's not and I can't forget that. I did manage to talk her into not calling my folks or Jeremy."

At that, Raiden's brows shot together before he asked, "Why the fuck did you do that?"

"Uh, sweetheart, Grams freaked. You think I want my parents to freak?" His chin weirdly jolted back when I said the word "sweetheart," but I ignored that and kept going. "Like Sherriff Joe said, it's over and they don't need to know, which, for them, means they don't need to worry."

"Baby, not sure that's a good plan," Raiden noted gently.

"Sat with Grams and saw her face, Raiden, her hands shaking," I replied and finished firmly, "It might not be good, but it's my plan."

He let it go for which I was grateful.

Now we were at the Deluxe after he'd paid for dinner and tipped his sister. He paid for the tickets and paid for movie refreshments we did not need after a big sandwich and Rachelle's Colorado-wide famous seasoned shoestring fries.

I knew without worrying even a second about it that this date, without a doubt, was going well, and after our two kisses I was nervous, but excited, about what came after the movies.

But first, I got two movies.

I slid down the aisle and did it babbling, "Film noir night. My favorite night of the year at the Deluxe. And best of all, this year, *Sunset Boulevard* and *Chinatown*."

I sat, immediately tossed my purse in the empty seat beside me and shifted up the armrest—after a huge fundraising drive, the Deluxe had updated their seats two years before. They rocked. They reclined. You could lift up the armrests. They had cupholders. They were *awesome*.

I reached up to Raiden and divested him of my drink and slid it in my cupholder. As he folded into his seat I relieved him of the popcorn and plonked it down in the area between us that was freed by the raised armrest.

Perfect for both of us to get to.

I also kept blabbing.

"My two favorite noirs, though *Touch of Evil* and *Double Indemnity* are up there, and *Chinatown* is a little creepy, you know, considering the whole Faye Dunaway-John Huston thing, which is gross. I won't ruin it if you haven't seen it but... serious ick. I mean, it also isn't classic noir because it was released in the seventies, but it still kicks noir booty. And *Sunset Boulevard* is otherwise known as *noir lush*, this, obviously, according to me. But Billy Wilder may be my favorite director and screenwriter of all time. *Sunset Boulevard. Double Indemnity. Sabrina. The Apartment. Some Like It Hot.* Noir. Romance. Comedy. He was the master of it all. Seriously, sheer talent."

Suddenly, Raiden yanked the popcorn from between us and kernels flew everywhere. His arm went around my shoulders. He tugged me into his side and dumped the bucket in my lap. He then lifted his hand to my jaw, tipped my head back and laid a hot, heavy, wet, *long* kiss on me right in the Deluxe that was not even half filled, but *still*.

He came up for air, which luckily gave me the chance to suck some in at the same time I was trying to control my rapidly beating heart and the pulse throbbing between my legs.

"Not pissed about the double feature anymore, seein' as you're so fired up about it," he murmured.

"Okay, well…good," I replied, my voice breathy. I got control of the breathy before I went on to inform him inanely, "You got popcorn everywhere."

"Don't fuckin' care."

There was no reply to that so I made none.

"I'm gettin' you really like movies," he noted.

"Yeah," I confirmed.

His hand, still at my jaw, slid back into my hair. "Then live it up, honey."

He tipped my head down and kissed my forehead before his hand slid out of my hair, taking its time, traveling the entire length. He curled away from me, but held me close with his arm still around my shoulders.

I focused on regulating my breath, and, as the lights went down, I said, "I hope you like the movies."

"I'll like 'em," he replied, and I twisted my neck to look up at him.

"You like noir?" I asked tardily, and continued, "Have you already seen these films?"

"Not a movie person, or never was. Haven't seen either. But bein' in the dark with you close, givin' you something you like to do, don't give a fuck what it is. Just glad to be doing it."

God.

That was nice.

"You're very sweet," I blurted as the commercials rolled on the screen.

"No, I'm not," he returned. "I'm selfish and goal-oriented. This shit is multi-tasking. Got you close, smell your perfume, feel your warmth, and later you'll be in a good mood. All that works for me."

To that, being an idiot, I couldn't stop it.

I kept blurting.

"You might want to try to stop being so sexy and hot and cool or you'll give me a heart attack and then your plans for later will be completely derailed."

I heard the smile in his voice even over the loud commercials. "Then I better shut up."

"That would be wise."

His arm drew me nearer and I felt the light shakes of his body, denoting his silent laughter.

I liked the feel and memorized it as I turned my attention to the screen.

I'd been to movies with my other boyfriends and none of them held me tucked tight throughout one movie, much less two.

To be fair, the Deluxe didn't have those killer seats back then so it would be uncomfortable if they tried.

Still, they didn't try.

If they did, I might have attempted to be less uninteresting.

Because it was amazing.

Or maybe it was just Raiden who was amazing.

Halfway through *Sunset Boulevard*, when he set aside the popcorn, I put my head to his shoulder. I cuddled closer, he let me and decided it was Raiden.

All Raiden.

Amazing.

9

NOT THAT KIND OF GIRL

AFTER TWO MOVIES with a fifteen-minute intermission it was late when Raiden, his arm around my shoulders holding me close, my arm around his waist doing the same, walked us four blocks down to the car park at the edge of town.

When he'd come to my house to pick me up I'd suggested we take my car since he'd said he wanted to drive it.

He took me up on this offer, and although no one but me had been in the driver's seat, I liked sitting beside him in my girl.

I liked more the way he handled my car. The ride was smooth; the car maneuvered unbelievably, but I wasn't exactly a daredevil. I'd never explored the limits of her functionality.

Raiden was not so hesitant.

He drove her faster than I'd ever risk, testing her handling on the winding roads that led from my place to Willow.

This normally would frighten me, but he operated the car with a natural confidence, like he drove her every day, or like he drove NASCAR for a living. So I wasn't frightened.

I was exhilarated.

And thus looking forward to the ride home.

We approached her, he beeped the locks and I saw the kick butt "Z" at the side illuminate in a flash when he did.

I loved my girl.

And, Bodhi and Heather notwithstanding, I was back to glad I made my decision months ago to broaden the horizons of my life.

Case in point: Raiden Miller walking me to my car at midnight on a Saturday night.

He moved me to the passenger side, but I turned my back to the car, blocking the door and looked up at him.

"You said at intermission that you thought *Sunset Boulevard* kicked ass. How did you feel about *Chinatown?*"

"You were right, that Dunaway-Huston gig was freaky, but it was a fucking good movie," he answered.

He liked noir. For some reason, this thrilled me.

Yes, he just kept getting better and better.

Therefore, I blurted, "In case I forget, I'll say it now to be sure you know. I had an amazing night, Raiden Miller."

At my words, one of his hands moved to span my hip, the other one cupped my jaw. He shifted close and dipped his face to mine.

"Good to know, Hanna Boudreaux," he rumbled through smiling lips.

I smiled back and shared, "I'm glad I didn't eavesdrop and ruin the night by freaking out and being stupid."

"I'm glad I didn't leave a pretty woman at a table and make a poorly timed phone call," he returned.

My smile got bigger. "I'm also glad nothing world rocking happened, like learning my best friend since forever, KC, was the evil mastermind behind a dire plot to take over the world, Homeland Security raided her house and hauled me in as a possible accomplice due to our copious phone conversations and pedicure appointments."

His body was shaking as were his words when he replied, "Reason to rejoice."

I was laughing softly when I finished, "So thank you."

"You're welcome, baby."

Baby.

I *loved* that.

So much I rolled up to my toes and kissed him.

Again, I was going for a quick peck. I was looking forward to making out with him on my porch (or wherever) when he took me home, but just then I was going to do what he did.

A brush of lips against lips.

Raiden, as I was learning anytime this happened, had other ideas.

Except this time, without reason, when Raiden's arms locked around me, crushing me to him and his tongue slid into my mouth, the world exploded.

The other kisses were phenomenal.

Even though this one was not executed in the privacy of my farmhouse at the end of a single track lane that was surrounded only by trees, but instead in a public parking lot in our hometown after a movie just let out, the kiss detonated.

Maybe it was because I wasn't freaking out, heartbroken and being stupid.

Maybe it was because we hadn't just finished exchanging heated words or heartfelt confessions.

Maybe it was because my dream *actually* was coming true, bigger and better than I expected. I was in Raiden's arms and he wanted me there.

Maybe it was just because it was the end of a really good date.

Whatever it was, it was like nothing I'd ever experienced. Nothing I even knew existed.

And something I wanted never to end.

It was huge. Consuming. The world melted away and there was just Raiden, his arms, his big, hard body, his mouth and his tongue.

I couldn't get enough. I couldn't give enough.

And Raiden felt exactly the same.

I knew this when he arched me into the car, pressing close, hips, chest, lips.

I knew it more when his hands slid down over my bottom and he jerked me up.

I had my hands in his hair and I held on even as my legs automatically circled his hips. He shifted down the car, planted my booty on the hood and bent into me so my back was to the Z, my legs circling his hips, his groin pressed deep to me and his tongue ravaging my mouth.

I was so lost in the kiss, in Raiden, I would have been happy for it to go on forever and more, even in the parking lot. No kidding, I would have been happy for it to escalate to bigger and better things.

But suddenly, my surprised cry drowned down his throat, he yanked me up and set me on my feet with a jarring thud.

I barely got myself steady before his hand clamped around mine. He dragged me the short distance down the car, wrenched open the door and shoved me inside.

He slammed the door after me. Out of habit I dumped my purse on the floor in front of me and I was trying to get my wits together, come to terms with the drastic and unwelcome turn of events, and, with shaking hands, get my belt around me when he angled in the other side.

"No belt," his voice growled at me and my head snapped to look at him as he tossed the key in the cupholder, hit the button to start the car and shifted into reverse before the automatic ignition fully engaged.

We reversed out of our spot so fast, my body swayed with the movements. Then he rocketed out of the car park and through town, picking up speed quickly. My breath caught and I didn't notice he was going in the wrong direction.

I didn't notice this mostly because we left town behind in a blink, and we no sooner did that when his hand wrapped around the back of my neck and he roughly yanked me his way. Shoving my face in his neck, his other hand quickly captured my wrist and pulled it to him, then smoothed my hand over his hard crotch.

It was so hot, so forbidden, so dangerous; it felt like fireworks exploded in the car, their sparks landing everywhere, all over me, dazzling me at the same time making me burn.

I pressed my hand deeper, moaning into his neck, my tongue gliding out, tasting his skin.

His hand left mine. The car sped wherever he was taking us as I felt and heard his gruff, rumbled, "Fuck me."

My body molten, my mind dazed, everything that was me was about everything that was him. I touched the tip of my tongue to his earlobe and whispered a desperate, "Hurry."

My girl revved, Raiden shifted and my hand curled tighter around his crotch.

I trailed my lips along his neck, his jaw and reversed my path, using my tongue. I shoved my face deep into his skin, loving his taste, his smell, the feel of his stubble, the whisper of his hair against my forehead so much, I uncurled my hand and rubbed my palm hard down the length of him.

Raiden grunted and we came to an abrupt stop. He hit the button and the car turned off, but he already had his door open, knifing out. He dragged me over the driver's seat, taking me with him.

I didn't know where we were. I didn't even look.

I didn't care.

I got my feet under me and ran to keep up with his long strides as, hand in mine, he towed me to a building I noticed vaguely looked like stables. We went up a flight of open backed steps at the side. Raiden wasted no time unlocking the door and pulling me in. He slammed the door, flipped the latch then he stalked across a room, dragging me with him.

I took nothing in and kept taking nothing in when he stopped, picked me up and suddenly I was flying through the air.

I landed on mattress.

Raiden landed on a knee beside me, his hands at the belt on my jeans.

"Condoms, baby, floor by the bed. Get one. Now," he muttered, then my zipper was down and my jeans were being yanked off.

As best as I could I twisted, noticing we were on a mattress on the floor, but not noticing much about this because my fingers closed around one of a half dozen packets of condoms by the bed. I didn't notice much about this because my flip-flops flew off with my jeans and my panties were now being dragged down my legs.

I twisted back just as Raiden's hand slid between my legs.

That felt so good, all my concentration centered on that feeling. I dropped the condom and my back left the bed as my lips parted on a silent moan.

"Thank fuck, soaked," Raiden growled. I forced myself to right my head and look at him. "Spread, baby."

I didn't hesitate.

I spread.

His hand kept toying between my legs, creating beauty even as he tugged at his pants. He pulled himself free, used his teeth to open the condom packet he somehow got hold of and dropped his hand to roll it on.

I pushed up and shoved my hands up his tee, my movements fevered, even frenzied, taking in his hard muscles; the angles, the plains, the ridges.

Amazing.

I shoved my face in his midriff, breathing deep, taking him in, all this time his fingers creating bliss between my legs.

Then they were gone.

For less than a second, because Raiden, using one arm to lift me, pulled me out of the bed and plastered me to him. My legs circled his hips. His other hand was between us, guiding him in.

He jerked me down on his cock, filling me.

I drove my hands in his lush hair, my head falling back on a whimpered, "Ohmigod."

And I was back to bed and Raiden was pounding inside me, his arm still around me, driving me down with each upward thrust.

"Ohmigod," I repeated, one of my hands fisting in his hair, the other one trailing down his back.

I'd never had this.

This was...

It was...

It didn't exist. It couldn't.

This was only for Raiden and me.

I felt it building. My hand dipped under his tee, my head jerked up. It was going to be so huge it was going destroy me.

"Raiden," I gasped, my voice harsh with passion and edged with fear.

"Give in, baby," he grunted, still driving me down as he thrust up.

"Sweetheart, it's—"

His mouth came to mine. "Give into it, honey."

I gave in. I had no choice. And when I did, my fingernails dug into his back, scoring up; his hips ground deep into mine as his back arched. A hot, amazing groan rolled up his throat and he came with me.

It lasted forever, an eternity. I gasped, then moaned, then panted through it, and finally wrapped my arm around Raiden and held on because the world was gone. There was nothing but that feeling.

Nothing but Raiden and me.

The eternity passed, and when I came back to reality Raiden's arm was still tight around me, his cock still buried inside me and his face was in my neck. His other hand was laced in mine and he'd tucked them to our sides so I had most of his weight.

It was glorious.

Right before it was mortifying.

Oh my God.

What had I just done?

Oh my God!

I knew what I'd done.

I'd ridden in a car with my hand on Raiden Miller's crotch, my mouth in his neck *without a seatbelt*.

Then I'd run after him; he'd thrown me on his bed and I let him fuck me.

Oh.

My.

God.

"Warm afghans, pretty blue eyes, totally dorky and an unbelievably wet, sweet pussy," he murmured against my neck, then lifted his head and looked down at me before he finished on a whisper, "The girl of my dreams."

Okay, that was nice and all. Lovely. Great even.

And the warm, sexy, sated look on his face that I could just about make out in the shadows, even better.

But I'd just let Raiden Miller make out with me on the hood of my car and rode *in* it without a seatbelt because I was busy groping his crotch.

Of course he'd think I was the girl of his dreams.

For tonight.

Tomorrow he'd think I was slutty and easy.

Because I was!

You didn't tell a good girl she had a wet, sweet pussy!

Oh God.

This didn't just happen.

Tell me this didn't happen.

"Don't move," he muttered and brushed his lips against mine. "Be back."

He slid out of me, the area between my legs pulsing magnificently as he did.

Yes, it just happened.

He rolled off me and I blinked at the ceiling, closing my legs, curling them up and twisting my lower half to the side as I felt him disappear.

A light came on from somewhere else, dimly lighting the room, and instantly I became a flurry of activity.

I vaulted from the mattress, and in the dark of wherever the heck I was, I searched for my jeans, panties and flip-flops.

I found my panties, tugged them up and was feeling around with hands and feet for my jeans when an arm hooked around my waist and I found myself back in bed, Raiden on top of me.

"What're you doin'?" he asked.

I shoved at his shoulders, mumbling, "I have to go."

"What?"

"I have to go."

"Hanna——"

"I need to get home. Get some sleep. I have to be up early. Church tomorrow," I babbled, still pushing at his shoulders and squirming under him, freaked, humiliated, scared of what he would think of me now that the heat of the moment had passed.

"Hanna, look at me."

"Really, I need to get going."

"Baby." His arms moved from around me so his hands could frame my face and he held it firm in a way that I stopped struggling and squirming. "What the fuck?"

"I'm not that kind of girl," I announced.

I felt his body, which I hadn't noticed was tense, relax but this had absolutely no effect on me.

I kept talking.

"Never has that happened. Not ever. *Not ever.* I've never done anything like that. I don't even remember a time when I've been *in* a car without a seatbelt much less what…what…" Oh God! "What we did," I finished on a horrified whisper.

"Calm down for me a second," he urged gently, one of his thumbs sweeping my cheek.

That felt nice, but no way could I calm down.

No way.

"I…you…I don't want you to think I'm that kind of girl. I'm not that kind of girl. I don't know what that was. I don't know how that happened. It's never happened before. I don't——"

I stopped speaking abruptly when his thumb shifted to my lips and pressed in.

"Honey, shut up," he ordered, but he did it laughing.

Belatedly, I noticed not only his mouth but his entire body was laughing.

"Raiden——" I tried to say but it came out sounding smushed, mainly because his thumb was still smushing my lips.

"Quiet and listen to me," he stated. "I know you're not that kind of girl."

I blinked through the dark.

"You do?" I asked through smushed lips, and his thumb slid away.

"Yeah, or, I should say, I know you're not that kind of girl for anyone, but me. But what *you* gotta know is that it's all kinds of fuckin' good you're that girl for me."

I wanted to believe this.

I didn't.

I mean, I had girlfriends who had moments where they were that kind of girl and the guys always said that it was good until the next day when they didn't call.

"I really need to go home," I told him, beginning to squirm again.

"No fuckin' way," he told me, and my body stilled.

"Sorry?" I breathed.

"Hanna, honest to Christ, you think out there I get you dorky, head on my shoulder at a movie, holding my hand, riding that preposterous bike, smilin' sweet at me, totally Peggy Sue throwback from the fuckin' fifties, and in my arms, my mouth on yours, you ignite for me. You lose *all* fuckin' control. Give me fuckin' *everything*. And I'm gonna let you crawl outta my bed and go home?" He paused then finished, his voice steely, "No fuckin' *way*."

"I—" I started but Raiden interrupted me.

"It's good you give me that. I *want* that. And I'm fuckin' beside myself knowin' you didn't give some other asshole that before me. It's mine. I'm keepin' it."

Holy Moses.

"Raiden—"

"And I'm gonna take more," he declared.

He was?

That was…he *wanted* more?

"You are?"

"Baby, last night, those kisses, I hoped to Christ that was a preview of things to come and I'm fuckin' thrilled it was. Out there, you can ride that silly-ass bike, but now I know, in my bed, you're gonna let go for me. You're gonna let me play with that body. You're gonna let me work you 'til you're so fuckin' wet you're drenched for me. And when I let you come I'm gonna make it feel like you're coming apart at the seams. And only I'm gonna know you give me that. Only I'm gonna get that. And I'm fuckin' overjoyed that's all for me and only me."

Wow.

That was hot, cool, sexy, sweet and totally freaking scary.

It was so much of all of those, the only response I could come up with was, "My bike isn't silly."

"Babe, it is."

"It's cutesie and girlie," I defended my bike

"It's that too. Absolutely," he agreed.

I tilted my head on the mattress and tried to make out his features in the dim light before I asked, "Are you sure you don't think I'm slutty and easy?"

To that, he hauled us both up the bed and pressed into me. He reached out an arm and I blinked when a light flashed on.

I stopped blinking when my head was again framed by his big hands and I focused on his face which was all I could see.

"Do I look sure?" he asked, and I didn't know how he knew how he looked.

What I did know was that his expression was warm and sweet, but still somehow firm and his beautiful eyes were heated, burning into me.

So I knew he was sure.

Still.

"Just so you know, I've only had three lovers. They were all long-term boyfriends and, if memory serves, the one where we, uh...got to the business fastest, it took three weeks."

"Do not tell me that shit."

Oh boy.

Now he didn't look warm and sweet.

He looked hard and scary.

"I just wanted—"

"Only thing I know, only thing I'll focus on, is now you're mine. I won't share what came before and I'm askin' you now to promise that's the last of you sharin' what came before me. Can you help me out and return that favor?"

"Okay," I agreed cautiously.

"Some men wanna know. I'm not one of those men," he explained.

"Okay."

"Right now, it's just you and me."

"Okay, Raiden."

"And you're not leaving."

My belly flipped.

"Okay," I breathed.

"You should also know there's a good chance you'll fall asleep during church."

I figured I knew what that meant. It brought on a shiver and my arms moved to wrap around him.

"Okay," I whispered.

He rolled so he was on his back and I was on top. One of his arms was clamped around my waist, his other hand in my hair.

"Now, Hanna, kiss me," he ordered, his voice rough and commanding.

"Okay," I repeated then did as I was told.

The roll lasted about two seconds, then he did another one and I was on my back again.

Half an hour later Raiden had me coming apart at the seams.

It was glorious.

10

CHURCH SUNDAY

MY EYES OPENED slowly, and at first I didn't get it.

I didn't get the heavenly softness that covered my body.

I didn't get the bright sunshine that seemed to be coming from everywhere.

I didn't get what sounded like a shower coming from not too far away.

I didn't get the languorous feeling that permeated every inch of my frame.

I didn't get the pleasant ache between my legs.

Then I got it and I shot up to sitting in Raiden's bed, leaning into one hand, the other one clutching the afghan I gave Raiden to my naked chest.

Holy Moses, I slept naked.

Holy Moses! I never slept naked!

But I knew why I did.

I slept naked because the second time Raiden did what he said. He played with me. He worked my body until I was drenched. And when he gave me an orgasm, it felt like I was coming apart at the seams.

He did things to me. Amazing things, wild things, things I knew about and things I didn't. Things that, if I told someone, might sound strange or kinky, but things that, the way Raiden did them to me, were absolutely not.

I let him.

And I loved every second.

And I slept naked because the time after *that*, Raiden did not take an excruciatingly long and exquisite amount of time making love to me.

No.

He took an excruciatingly long and exquisite amount of time *worshipping* me.

There was no other way to put it.

If the first time was fast, wild, out-of-control and phenomenal, the second time was slower, wilder, totally in Raiden's control, but out of mine and it was sensational.

But the last time was like an out of body experience.

It was magnificent.

So much so, waking naked in Raiden Miller's bed the morning after our second date, I didn't feel like a slut or a skank, mortified by either.

I felt happy.

So I smiled.

I looked down at the afghan Raiden obviously wasted no time using and I slid its beauty up my chest, smiling into the cashmere.

Seconds later, I dropped the blanket back to my chest, looked around and my smile died.

I was on a stacked set of queen-sized mattress and box springs that sat on the floor. The sheets were white and appeared clean, bright, even almost new. A comforter with a subtle geometric design in masculine colors of blue and red was on the floor, only the afghan on me.

The bed, as it were, was in the middle of an enormous room made entirely of wood, the walls punctuated profusely by huge, multi-square-paned windows that definitely needed to be cleaned. There was a lamp on the floor by the bed, its ceramic base chipped, a long extension cord running across the rough wood floor, plugged into the wall. Also by the bed was a small pile of condoms, some paperback books and strewn magazines.

Mostly to avoid the pile of condoms and what they said, my eyes wandered.

On the wall across from the foot of the bed was a wardrobe, one door open and dangling drunkenly. Some clothes could be seen hanging haphazardly inside, a variety of athletic shoes and boots spilling out the bottom. More clothes in a tangle on the floor that led to wardrobe.

To one side, a dresser, all the drawers open; tees, thermals and boxer briefs dangling out the drawers.

On the opposite wall, a battered countertop covered in boxes of cereal, crackers, jars of protein powder and piled dishes. A sink that was piled with *dirty* dishes. There was a fridge to one side of the counter that long ago should have been put out of its misery, and a crusty, old range at the other end that might actually be a health hazard.

In front of the scary kitchen, there was an old, chrome sided Formica-topped table with two chairs, their black vinyl seats torn, padding coming out. The top of the table had a laptop and papers, with more papers scattered on the floor.

There was a big, locked trunk against the back wall with a stenciling on the side that read Cpl. Miller, R. In the corner by it, a weight bench and a rack of weights surrounded by a mess of dumbbells on the floor that looked the size only Hercules would work out with.

And last, there was an old, faded plaid easy chair with a rickety standing lamp beside it and an even ricketier spindly table that also was covered to overflowing with paperbacks.

The whole thing screamed Beverly Hillbillies before they struck oil.

The only hints at décor were an alarming number of shotgun racks on the walls, three of them. Two were empty, one had two guns in the slots and boxes of ammo on the shelf under them. I was no gun expert, but they didn't look like shotguns. More like fancy rifles.

And the other piece of decoration was a framed eight by ten photo on the dresser. The space was huge and the picture was far away, but I could see it was a mess of men, some holding guns, all wearing smiles and desert fatigues, probably because a bleak desert landscape could be seen behind them.

Raiden's unit.

The unit that was mostly lost.

Nearly all of the men in that picture were gone.

Holy Moses.

I narrowed my eyes on the picture, like doing this would engage superpower vision I did not have and would make it come into better focus just as I heard the shower turn off.

I twisted to look at a rough plank paneled room that jutted out in the far corner. A room that looked like it had been added in a hurry, the work done by five-year-olds.

The bathroom.

I couldn't believe Raiden lived here, but he obviously did. I recognized some of the cargo pants on the floor from the days I was crazy, creepy stalking him.

Actually, I couldn't believe *anyone* could live here.

He didn't need a housecleaner.

He needed *a house*.

On this thought, hinges screamed in agony. A section of the wood paneling swung open and Raiden strolled out, wet hair slicked back, droplets of water on his broad shoulders, a towel around his hips and the rest of his lusciousness on display.

The second and third time last night, I got to see (and explore) Raiden's body.

It was amazing in clothes.

It was way, *way* better without them.

His eyes came to me. They grew warm and he appeared to be heading to the kitchen-ish area, but switched directions, walking to the bed.

He didn't enter it or put a knee in it. He didn't say hi.

He bent and hooked me around the back of the neck with his hand in a way that I had no choice but to go up, which I did. Once partially up, his other arm closed around me, and when I was crushed to him his head came down and he took my mouth in a good morning kiss that made my toes *and* my fingers curl, the latter of which did it in the hard muscle of his shoulders.

When my hands slid up into his wet hair, he lifted his head, caught my fluttering eyes and said, "Mornin', honey."

"Good morning," I breathed.

He grinned then pulled me out of bed, incidentally pulling the afghan with me as it was squashed between our bodies, and he put me on my feet.

"Get dressed, babe, runnin' late. We gotta get you to your house. You gotta do whatever you do to get cute then we gotta get your grandmother and get to church," he gave his order and after issuing it, he let me go and sauntered toward the end of the bed.

I hurriedly wrapped the afghan around me and watched him go.

Then I froze because now I had his back and I could see marks on his skin. Three of them; red, and in sections the skin was broken.

Scratch marks.

From my nails.

Oh my God.

"Did I do that to your back?" I whispered.

Raiden stopped, turned to me and smiled a smile I felt right at the heat of me.

"Oh yeah," he answered in a voice that ratcheted up the heat so significantly it was a wonder I didn't burst into flames.

He liked that.

A lot.

Wow.

It hit me he said *we* had to get Grams and get to church.

"Uh…" I mumbled before I got lost in watching his lateral muscles shift and undulate as he bent and gathered my jeans, top and underwear from the floor and tossed them on the mattress.

I came out of my stupor when he moved to the wardrobe and the entire thing swayed dangerously as he opened the closed door. I fought the urge to rush across the room and put both hands on the side to brace it before it settled. Raiden reached in and yanked some clothes off hangers. Repeat the swaying and me fighting the urge to rescue his wardrobe before he turned, tossed the clothes on the back of a chair and moved to the dresser.

I found my voice and asked, "Are you going to church with Grams and me?"

"Yep," he replied, digging in a drawer.

I looked down at my clothes on the mattress then reached to grab my panties, finding I was totally okay with that.

I had on panties and bra and was pulling up my jeans when I spoke again.

"Can I ask you question?"

"You can quit askin' if you can ask and just ask," Raiden replied, a smile in his voice, his eyes coming to me. Then he yanked off his towel.

My mouth went dry.

He was perfect everywhere.

Everywhere.

This made me suddenly aware that I was not.

I had great legs, this I'd already noted. I had an ample chest, which sometimes worked for me, sometimes was annoying when blouses gaped at my breasts. I also had a tiny waist, which made buying jeans a pain in the patoot, but looked good in dresses.

I also had a little pouch at my belly that no amount of cycling and snow-boarding got rid of, mainly because I did crunches and pushups about twice a week rather than what I told myself I'd do (four times). I also liked hot fudge sundaes, Grams's biscuits smothered in apple butter and a variety of other things that weren't real good for me, so it was a battle I had no hope of winning.

Raiden had an eight pack (yes, *eight*), noticeably limited body fat and hip muscles so significantly cut you could lose yourself in those valleys for days.

Therefore, I decided no more hot fudge sundaes, definitely five days a week of crunches, pushups *and* I was adding planks. I was also cutting out sandwiches and eating salads for lunch, just in case the rest didn't take.

"Baby, you stare at my dick any longer, Miss Mildred's gonna have to send out a search party."

My body jolted and my eyes shot to his to see the creases at the corners standing out in amusement.

"I was staring at your hip muscles," I corrected.

"Whatever," he muttered, his lips now smiling too, then louder, "just sayin', anything in that vicinity, your eyes on it, it'll get thoughts on its own."

"So noted," I mumbled and shrugged on my top.

"You had a question," Raiden prompted, stepping into some boxer briefs.

I decided to stop watching so I could concentrate on buttoning my blouse, so I tipped my chin down to watch my fingers do just that as I asked, "What is this place?"

"Dad's hunting lodge," he answered and I looked at him again.

He was moving back to the chair and I was shocked at his words.

His sister Rachelle and I were only acquaintances, but friendly ones who had known each other our whole lives. We talked, gossiped, shared news and pleasantries, and if time allowed, sometimes this could go deep, but she'd never mentioned her dad. The same, but obviously less, due to age differences, with Raiden's mom, Mrs. Miller.

What I knew was Mr. Miller took off and was persona non grata in town. He even once tried to come to one of Raiden's football games and some of the men not so cordially invited him to march back to his car, and when he didn't they escorted him there.

He never came again.

I looked back down at my buttons and said carefully, "Your dad?"

"Yep," Raiden replied, and I again looked at him to see he had a pair of suit pants up, zipped but unbuttoned and was shrugging on an attractive, moss green dress shirt.

Surprisingly, he also kept talking.

"When I was sixteen, tracked him down, told him to deed it over to Rachelle and me, seein' as he paid child support when he wanted, which meant never, and Mom was havin' troubles makin' ends meet. It wasn't a surprise, because he's a massive dick, that he wasn't feelin' generous, though his words were that Mom could go fuck herself and I could too. So I drove to his house every night, let myself in and shared my thoughts with my fists. And when he got smart and started to talk his bitches into lettin' him spend the night at their places so he could avoid me, I found ways to track him down and let myself in, shared he was a massive dick who didn't pay child support and when he was at home and had a steady woman, he knocked her around. He suddenly found his choice of beds was dryin' up, so he got smart and deeded it over."

His words slicing through me like a dozen razor blades, I stood absolutely still and stared.

Raiden seemed not to notice my immobility. He went to the wardrobe, slid a belt off a hanger, turned to me and kept speaking as he did up his pants and added the belt.

"Meant we got the monthly money from rentin' out the bottom half where Mr. Lean kept his old tractors and whatever we could get from hunters who don't give a shit where they sleep and cross country skiers on a budget. Didn't help a lot, but did mean we didn't lose our house."

"You nearly lost your house?" I asked quietly, and he smiled at me.

"Seems you didn't pay that much attention to me."

I did.

Still.

"I know you—" I started.

Raiden interrupted me, "Worked nights and weekends. Reason Rachelle is such a great cook is because she did the same at the nursing home, junior nurse's aide. She loved downhome cooking and she pumped old folks for recipes. She's got about eight card files full of 'em."

That explained that.

Now the hard part.

"Your dad knocked your mom around?"

"Yeah, babe, why do you think I set his ass out?" Raiden answered, and I went back to staring.

"*You* set him out?"

"Fuck yeah."

"But weren't you only fourteen?"

"You can fuck someone up, Hanna, you get a good boot in his crotch. He's so busy dealin' with the pain, can't defend himself when you land a fist repeatedly in his face or a boot to his ribs."

I couldn't believe this, and more, I couldn't believe Raiden was so matter-of-fact about it.

My heart hurt and my stomach was clutching, but I forced my mouth to say, "I'll be sure to remember that."

Then I focused my attention on finding my flip-flops, mostly because I didn't know what to do with all the feelings I was having, none of them good, and I had to focus on *something*.

"Hanna," he called as I found my flip-flops and was shifting them with my toes so I could slide my feet in. I looked back at Raiden. "A long time ago and better with him gone. It was worth it. That shit didn't mark me. He was gone, instant happy for all of us, even if things were tight."

I nodded, not feeling mollified even slightly and looked back to my shoes.

"Honey," he called again and my eyes went to him. "Not bullshitting you. Rache, Mom and me, we're close. Him gone, we were happy."

"Okay," I replied.

"You say okay, but your face says something else."

"What does my face say?" I asked, but I knew. I never played poker because I didn't know how and also because I'd suck at it, mostly because I had no clue how to keep my thoughts from showing, nor, until then, had I had any reason to.

"One of two things, can't tell which. Either you're pissed or you're about ready to cry."

I turned my full attention to him. "Both, I guess."

"Right, then, like I said. No need for that emotion because it was and is all good."

"I can sense that, considering the matter-of-fact way you're discussing it, sweetheart," I told him. "But I don't like that you went through that or that things were tight for you guys *or* that you had to get in your dad's face to get him to do something to help take care of his own kids."

"It happened, but it's been done for nearly twenty years."

"I still don't like it."

He grinned. "I'll give you that 'cause it's cute, but you got until we get to your house to get over it."

To that, I returned, "My mom and dad love each other and they loved me and Jeremy. My grandparents loved us until they died. My great-grandmother dotes on me. All of my life, I had love and safety. Life didn't touch me until I decided to start living it, and the worst thing that's ever happened to me was what Bodhi and Heather did, and that's on them, not on me. I never had what you had. I don't know what to do with knowing you had to deal with that. I don't like knowing you had to deal with that. And I just learned about it so it may take longer than the next twenty minutes for me to get over wanting to reenact the boot to crotch maneuver on your dad. Because you're an awesome guy, Raiden Miller. Your mom and sister love you because they have reason. You're a gentleman. You're a kind neighbor. You're even a hero with the medals to prove it. And you deserve a dad who taught you how to be that. Not a life that led you to being that despite having a massive dick for a dad."

I made my stupid speech and shut up.

Only then did I feel the room and fully take in the look on his face.

Both made me take a step back, because the former was pressing on me like a weight I instinctively felt I had to escape, and the latter was reeling me in on a lure so strong it was a wonder I didn't fly across the room and into his arms.

The intensity of both scared the heck out of me.

"You need, right now, to walk down to your car, Hanna," he told me.

That was so weird, I stammered, "I...sorry?"

"I'll be there in a minute."

"But—"

The air in the room got heavier right before he ordered, "Go, Hanna. You don't, we won't. Do you understand me?"

I didn't, not fully.

What I did understand was that I needed to walk down to my car.

So I gave him one long, last look, memorizing the look he was giving me and the way it made me feel: terrified, but at the same time warm and happy.

Then I walked across his crazy pad and unlocked the door, moved through it and descended the steps to get to my car.

Two Hours Later

I WOKE UP when my pillow started shaking.

When I did, I saw I was in church and had my head on the navy blue fabric of Raiden's suit-jacketed shoulder.

A Raiden who was silently laughing.

I bolted straight.

"Sweet Jesus, forgive her," Grams, who was sitting on the other side of me, murmured to the ceiling. "Pastor Wright's sermon is far from inspiring, you hear that, Lord, but still. My precious girl's got better manners."

At this point Raiden's body started shaking so hard the pew started shaking and people started staring.

I turned to him and hissed under my breath, "*Stop laughing*," to which he kept shaking but raised his brows at me.

I gave up on him and turned to Grams.

"We went to the double feature last night, Grams," I explained on a semi-fib in a low voice, doing this out of the corner of my mouth.

"My recollection, it was a triple," Raiden muttered. I turned to him and shouted, *Shut up!* but did it just with my eyes.

Raiden took this in, and of course it made him swallow down an audible grunt of hilarity.

I rolled my eyes to the ceiling and asked for forgiveness for a *variety* of things.

"Mm-hmm," Grams mumbled noncommittally.

"*Shh!*" Mrs. McGuillicutty, sitting down from Raiden, shushed us.

Loudly.

So loudly, Pastor Wright's eyes came to our pew and narrowed, though he didn't miss a word of his sermon.

I looked at my hands that I was folding in my lap and felt about eight years old.

"Shush yourself, Margaret," Grams shot back. A Grams, I'll add, who often acted eight years old, and now was clearly going to be one of those times. "God likes laughter," she finished.

"Grams, let it go," I told my lap.

"Some of us are trying to *listen*," Mrs. McGuillicutty snapped.

"Then listen and keep your nose outta other people's business," Grams returned.

I turned my head and bent into her. "Please, Grams, just let it *go*."

Grams settled back on a wiggle, grumbling, "Shushing *my* granddaughter. Who does she think she is?"

Not one ever to leave the last word, or in all honesty to be nice most of the time, Margaret McGuillicutty didn't let it go either.

"I'm a churchgoing woman who wants to listen to the sermon," she retorted to Grams.

I was too exhausted and riding a high of being with Raiden to do anything about it, but I just *knew* when Grams chose that pew and Mrs. McGuillicutty was in it that we should have found an alternate seating arrangement.

I was right.

Grams leaned across me to say to Mrs. McGuillicutty, "No one's stopping you but *you*."

"And perhaps our choir can have *all* of your attention as they sing their next hymn," Pastor Wright suggested into his microphone, but the comment was clearly directed at us since he was staring straight at us. I knew he loved Grams and me (Mrs. McGuillicutty was up for debate), but he didn't look all that happy.

Raiden lifted an arm and wrapped it around my shoulders. He tucked me tight to his side and dropped his lips to my ear.

"Let 'em battle it out. You're just makin' it worse."

I clamped my mouth shut and my eyes on the choir.

Grams and Mrs. McGuillicutty exchanged a few more barbs before Grams sat back, muttering, "I love this hymn and no McGuillicutty is gonna make me miss it."

Thus letting Margaret have the last word with, "Boudreaux, think they own this town."

Though Grams did get in a, "*Humph!*"

We successfully made it through the final prayer and communal hymn without incident, but hostilities reengaged after Pastor Wright released us.

"Falling asleep and whispering in church like it was a Boudreaux bedroom and kitchen. Shameful," Mrs. McGuillicutty remarked loudly to no one, and all in the vicinity looked away like they wished they could whistle.

This, of course, meant Grams said to her, but directed her remark at me. "Need you to get me a cane, child. Not to walk with it, so I can beat Margaret over the head with it."

Raiden chuckled.

Margaret gasped.

So did I, before I hissed, "Grams, we're in church!"

She waved her hand in front of her face, "God's forgiven me for a lot over ninety-eight years, that's the least of it."

"We gonna get breakfast or we gonna have a smackdown in pew three?" Raiden asked, sounding amused.

Grams didn't miss a beat. "Breakfast. Need my vittles to perform a successful smackdown."

Then she turned and toddled off slowly down the pew.

I leaned around Raiden and said to Mrs. McGuillicutty, "I'm sorry, Mrs. McGuillicutty."

"As you should be," she fired back. "No excuse for rudeness. And falling asleep in church? Appalling."

I gave my apology, therefore did my duty to good manners. She could be ornery. She had to answer to God for that, not me.

Therefore, I was going to let it go and get out of there.

Raiden had other ideas.

He turned his big, tall frame Margaret McGuillicutty's way and looked down at her.

"One, Hanna apologized. The right thing to do is accept, not throw it in her face. Two, Miss Mildred can take care of herself and she's too old to give a damn what you think. Obviously, Hanna cares or she wouldn't have apologized when she had no need to. Now what you gotta know is, if I'm standing next to her or not and I just hear you were rude to her, I'll take it as you bein' rude straight to me and I think most folks in this town know you do not want to be rude to me."

She stared up at him, lips parted while I processed what he said and the fact that any of this was happening at all.

She snapped her mouth shut to hiss at Raiden like he was twelve, not thirty-two, "Well, I don't believe it. I'll be having a word with your mother, Raiden Miller."

"Have at it. She won't give a flying mostly because she thinks you're as foul-tempered and aggravating as everyone else in town," Raiden fired back.

A couple people heard and tittered, proving him right.

I decided we were both done so I grabbed his hand and yanked him down the pew.

Fortunately, he followed me.

We made it to Grams, then we followed in what felt like suspended motion as she made her slow way out of the church, her snail's pace hindered further with the need to call a greeting to everyone she knew, which was just plain everyone.

Raiden made a break for it at the doors, mumbling his excuse of, "I'll go get the Jeep."

Fortunately, this meant when we got to the end of the walk at the front of the church Raiden was there.

Like we had when we came, I climbed into the back and Raiden held Grams steady at the waist while she latched on with a bony hand. He mostly lifted her into her seat, but in a way where it made it seem like she put her foot to the edge of the door herself.

We were on our way when I decided a debrief was in order.

"I don't believe that happened," I remarked.

"Believe it, *chère*. Margaret has always been a sourpuss. Makes it worse, she had her sights set on your granddaddy and never got over losin' him to your grandma."

This was news.

And made the whole situation even more unbelievable.

"Seriously?" I asked. "That had to be fifty years ago, and sorry, Grams, but they've both passed. Holding a grudge when there's no one left to hold it against?"

"Lost love, precious," Grams replied, turning her head to look out the side window. "Stings like a wasp bite that never fades."

This made me pause for reflection, especially the knowing way Grams said it, but Grams wasn't done.

"Probably didn't help, my boy's beautiful granddaughter sittin' next to the town hunk. History, in a way, repeating. Salt in the wound."

My eyes went to the rearview mirror, caught Raiden's and they rolled.

When they rolled back, his were back on the road but they were smiling.

We hit the Pancake House, all pancakes, all the time, (no kidding, they had nothing but pancakes, sausage and bacon on their menu); a weird restaurant that did booming business about fifteen miles out of town up the foothills. It had a fabulous view and the best pancakes I'd ever eaten. So good Grams and I never went anywhere else for Sunday breakfast, and this continued the tradition of Dad and Mom taking us all there every Sunday up until the Sunday before they moved to a different state.

As usual, the pancakes didn't disappoint and breakfast was fun. Grams talked through most of it, which meant Raiden and I laughed through most of it, and Raiden didn't surprise me by being gentlemanly and charming.

We had syrup covered plates and were on our third cup of coffee when Raiden's jacket chimed. He took his arm from the back of my seat, dug into his suit jacket that he'd slung on the back of his chair, pulled out his phone, looked at it and turned to me.

"Gotta make a call." His eyes slid to Grams. "Excuse me." His attention came back to me, his hand came to my jaw and he tilted my face up to touch his mouth to mine.

That felt nice. I liked that he was making a habit of kissing me when he left me, so my lips tipped up against his.

I watched up close as Raiden's eyes smiled. He let me go, straightened from his chair and walked away.

I watched the show.

"Now, *chère*, church with the grandmother and word whizzin' 'round town about holdin' hands, all cozied up at Chilton's, of all places. Good to know early that boy isn't about half measures. But I'm guessing you're sparin' your old biddy of a Grams the details about how you caught the eye of Willow's most eligible bachelor."

I looked at her, grinned a little and replied, "I was running late this morning or I would have called to let you know he was coming with us, but yeah, Grams. Raiden and I are seeing each other."

"Don't kid a kidder," she said softly, and my brows drew together at this unexpected reply.

Unfortunately, she explained.

"Not lost on you I've lived me some years, precious, but they didn't slide by and not touch me. A girl falls asleep at church on Sunday morning because she had too much fun on Saturday night and one look at Raiden Miller says clear exactly what kind of fun he has with a pretty girl."

That was when I felt my eyes get big.

"Grams, I—"

She waved her hand at me. "Don't. Got ourselves enough marks on our soul, disprespectin' God in His house today. Don't add to that, *chère*."

I closed my mouth.

Grams didn't.

"A week ago, he came to my house. I knew why. He's got about as much interest in doing an old woman's yard work as he has in goin' to the ballet. But I looked up at that big, strong man and thought to myself, Raiden Miller? I liked that for my girl. I liked it a lot. You've been alone for a while now and a girl like you, it's a waste, you bein' alone. Always knew in my heart you'd stand by the side of a man like Raiden Miller. Those boys you saw, they were okay, but not one of them was good enough for my Hanna. Now hardly any time at all has passed and he didn't waste a lick of it. He's diggin' deep into that heart of yours, with intent, and child, I'm gonna share, it troubles me."

Again, this was unexpected, but this time not in a confusing way. In an unwelcome one.

"Sorry?" I whispered, stunned.

"Way he looks at you now he's had you, way he is, man like that." She shook her head, her eyes went distant then she focused on me. "Boiling under the surface."

I leaned across the table toward her. "What are you talking about?"

"Had me fooled over sweet tea but now…now I see it."

"Grams—"

"That man is dangerous," she declared.

My heart skipped a painful beat and I stared.

"What?"

"Don't get me wrong, he won't break your heart. He'd die before doin' that. But there's a lotta ways to get a broken heart, precious girl. And he'll do it all the same not even knowin' he's doin' it."

Grams was experienced. Grams was wise. Grams was observant. And Grams was smart.

Therefore, I didn't like this. Not one bit.

Still, I started to explain, "Grams, we've only been out on a couple of dates, but he's really a good guy. A gentleman. And——"

"Dangerous. In every line of his body, hidden deep in his eyes. Missed it then, but he hadn't had you then. I see it now and I see you got bit by his bug. I'm tellin' you, Hanna, you be careful. You go forward cautious. Hard to guard your heart from a man like that who'll do nothing and everything to win it in a way you'll want him to own it forever. But mind this, child. Raiden Miller doesn't find a way to beat back the danger lurking within, he'll go down and he'll take you down right along with him."

She held my eyes, hers bright and keen, and I realized my chest was rising and falling fast. I took a sip of coffee and sat back, trying to force myself to relax.

I was also thinking about the air in his hunting lodge that morning, the look on his face when I said I wanted to give his dad a boot to the groin.

There was something about that that moved me, scared me, spoke to me. I just didn't know what it was saying.

"You find a way to have fun, you enjoy him, *chère*, and I'll enjoy him when I'm with you two. But don't forget what I said," she continued, taking me out of my thoughts.

"Okay, Grams," I told the tablecloth.

"Love you," she told me and my eyes moved to her. "Said what I said and I'll end it with this. If you're the kind of woman who can withstand the blaze of hellfire he's got burning inside, he battles that and wins, you will know nothing for the rest of your life, no taste, no experience, not even the birth of your children that will be sweeter than the love he'll have for you."

Oh my God.

She was totally freaking me out!

"We've only been on two dates," I whispered.

"I see that. And I see he's lost in you so completely it's a wonder he knows his own name."

I was back to semi-panting.

"He's headed this way, precious. Take a deep breath," she ordered, and my eyes went over her head to see added proof to what I'd had repeatedly all my life. That Grams not only had excellent hearing, but eyes in the back of her head.

Raiden was headed our way, but he'd been stopped by Mrs. Bartholomew and her family. He was standing at their table, talking.

I deep breathed before I took another sip of coffee, trying to force back Grams's dire words, fit them someplace in my brain where I could go over them later (preferably with KC). I achieved this feat and had it together when Raiden slid back into his chair beside mine.

He also slid his arm along the back of my seat as he asked, "More coffee or the check?"

"Naptime for biddies, son, so the check. And I'm old, I'm a grandmother, so that means I pay and I don't care how much of a man you are. When you're old and a grandfather you'll know what I mean and you'll be glad you let me do it."

He pulled me into his side and grinned at Grams.

I felt how great we seemed to fit together and frowned at Grams because I loved that feeling and she'd made me terrified of it.

She ignored my frown, lifted her hand and called, "Darla! Child, bring us the check, would you?"

Darla, our waitress, like she did every Sunday when Grams called for the check, scurried to do the matriarch of Willow's bidding.

An Hour and Fifteen Minutes Later

"YOU WANNA TELL me what's on your mind?"

We'd just dropped off Grams. After a glass of sweet tea (well, Raiden and Grams had one, I had diet root beer), Raiden was taking me home.

I turned to look at him and asked, "Sorry?"

"You've been weird since the Pancake House."

"I'm tired," I replied.

Not exactly a lie, just not the whole truth.

"I get you home, you rest. I gotta go out and do something and when I get back I'll bring a pizza. But after pizza, babe, you gotta have energy."

I felt my nether regions quiver as I looked to the windshield.

I forced down that feeling and asked, "Does this something you have to do have to do with your crew and drug dealers?"

"No, it has to do with another job, but that has to do with my crew. Just not drug dealers."

This was an answer, but it still wasn't.

I didn't call him on that.

I just mumbled, "Oh."

"Change of plans tonight," he stated. "Pizza, me sharin' about what I do, then I'll test the recuperative powers of the nap you're about to take."

I turned to him, "Raiden—"

He cut me off, "I tell you, it'll be honest. It'll freak you out, but you'll deal."

Holy Moses.

"What does that mean?" I asked.

"It means I got out, assessed my talents, made decisions about what I wanted to do, I'm doin' it. What I do might come as a shock to you, but then you'll get over it," he declared.

There were more words there, just no explanation.

"Uh, just FYI, this discussion is not conducive to me getting a nap," I shared.

He gave me a quick glance and grinned.

"Right then. I'll tell you I did all the work last night. I'm in the mood to test you to see what you can do, and just a guess, honey, but I 'spect you'll wanna pass."

He would guess correctly.

But that comment also wasn't conducive to me getting a nap.

We were pulling up to the front of my house so I turned fully toward him.

"Raiden, I—"

His belt zipped back and he undid mine. His hand wrapped around the back of my neck and he pulled me to him. My hand came up automatically and crashed into his chest, then I did, scrunching my hand between us.

"What I do isn't bad," he said quietly. "It isn't conventional but it isn't bad."

"Okay, so now I'm not totally freaking out, I'm only kinda freaking out," I replied.

"Babe, a day ago, you found out two of your friends played you. You freaked out, felt the pain, sucked it up, hung up on that fucker when he tried to phone and moved on. You take care of your grandmother, not like it's a burden like everybody else would treat it, but a boon. That translates to her so she doesn't feel the burden of being a burden and she can just enjoy the life God's seen fit to grant her. What I do is what I do. It's part of who I am. It came from what life threw at me and you're gonna suck it up and deal with that too."

This was a cool speech, but it was also a scary one.

So I asked a pertinent question.

"What's happening here?"

"I'm about to kiss you good-bye, you're about to take a nap, and in a few hours I'll be back with pizza."

"I mean with you and me."

His eyes held mine, his hand slid up into hair and his other hand lifted to wrap around the side of my neck as he replied gently, "You know the answer to that."

I had a feeling I did, and it exhilarated and terrified me.

"Raiden, maybe we should——"

"If you're gonna say slow things down, baby, enjoy this because this is as slow as it's gonna get."

I felt my eyes get wide.

"Yeah," he confirmed to my unspoken cry of shock. "If you can take it tonight, I'll explain that too."

"Now there's no way I'm getting a nap," I mumbled.

"You wake up happy?" Raiden asked and I blinked at him.

Then I whispered, "Yeah."

"I did too. When was the last time for you?"

"The last time, what?"

"The last time you woke up happy."

Oh God.

Before him, I wasn't unhappy. I also wasn't exactly happy.

What I knew was this: waking up in Raiden's bed, I *definitely* was happy.

"I don't remember," I admitted.

"Me either," he replied.

Oh *God*.

I liked that and hated it. I understood it just as much as I didn't. I wanted to know why he wasn't happy just as much as I was scared to find out.

"Raiden——"

"We're holding on to that," he declared, and like it had a mind of its own my hand slid up his chest to curl around the side of his neck like it was answering his statement for me and doing it by agreeing.

He knew it, felt it and understood it.

Therefore, he stated in his rough, commanding voice, "Yeah."

I dropped my head to his shoulder.

He was right.

Yeah.

I knew what was happening here.

His hand slid out of my hair so he could wrap his arm around me. "What do you like on your pizza?"

"Everything but onions, peppers, sausage, pineapple, ham, anchovies and olives."

His voice was smiling when he remarked, "So you're sayin' you like pepperoni and mushroom only."

I lifted my head and looked at him. "I like all that stuff, just not on pizza. All that stuff makes it complicated. I'm into simple pleasures."

His amazing eyes warmed and his amazing lips murmured, "I'll remember that."

I could get lost in those eyes. I *wanted* to get lost in those eyes.

But I needed to stay on target.

"Can you tell me something?" I asked suddenly.

His eyes got warmer and his smile hit his lips when he replied, "I can tell you that you asking me if I can tell me something is the same as you askin' me if you can ask me somethin'. In other words, you don't have to ask."

"Noted," I muttered.

"So ask, I'll tell," he prompted.

"Whatever you're going off to do, are you safe?"

His smile faded and I stared in horrified fascination as it did.

Holy Moses!

I'd been guessing!

"It isn't safe?" This came out as a squeak.

"We'll talk about it later."

"Holy Moses!" I cried, no longer semi-freaked. I was gone.

"Hanna, we'll talk about it later."

"Will you be *back* later?" I asked, borderline hysterically.

His smile came back. "Yeah."

"Just pointing out, Raiden, you're about to drop me off, telling me to take a nap but you've got some things to share with me later that you told me straight up I have to *deal with*. Then you intimate *strongly* that whatever it is you do is unsafe, and you're off to do whatever it is you do *right now*. So I'm not in the mood to smile nor am I in the mood to watch you do it, no matter how hot you are when you do."

He didn't quit smiling.

Instead, he asked, "You wanna talk more about us going slower now?"

Was he serious?

I tore out of his arms, twisted to the door and threw it open, announcing, "Time for my nap!"

I found an arm hooked around my waist and was twisted back into the Jeep and Raiden's arms, this time both of which he locked around me.

Then is eyes locked on mine.

"I'll be back safe and you'll be cool with what I do, Hanna," he declared firmly.

"Right. I believe you. But can I make the request now that I have at least a date number five before you rock my world again?"

Another grin then, "I think I can accomplish that."

"I'd be obliged."

"You wanna quit bein' cute so I can let you go, you can get your nap and I can get this shit done?"

"I'll remind you not a minute ago I tried to exit this vehicle, but you hauled me back."

"I'll take that as a no."

I glared.

Raiden kept smiling.

Then he muttered strangely, "My reward."

I lost my glare and asked, "Sorry?"

He lifted up, kissed my forehead and whispered there, "Nothin', baby." He pulled away, ordering, "Go. Rest."

I needed to go. I hoped I could rest, but I studied him a moment before I leaned in to touch my mouth to his.

His arms came around me, his mouth opened over mine and my touch became a hot, heavy *kiss*.

Raiden broke it and ordered again, "Go."

"Okay," I mumbled. He let me go and I went.

I stood at the door in numero uno of my Sunday's finest dresses (I *did* go to church with Raiden Ulysses Miller) and waved.

He didn't wave back, but I did see him smile.

I closed the door and wandered up the stairs, listening to his Jeep drive away.

I took off my heels by the side of the bed. I climbed in, pulled an afghan over me (mine, not cashmere but still lush) and stared at my pillow, thinking this was how it felt.

This was how it felt when something huge was happening.

It felt fantastic.

And I was scared out of my wits.

11

CRIMINAL

That Evening

I SAT TUCKED into the corner of my frou-frou, fluffy, girlie, cutesie couch in my countrified, quirky living room and watched Raiden, who'd just gone to the kitchen to get his second beer, fold his long body at the other end.

The pizza was annihilated, that always awkward sliver of a slice the only piece left. Raiden had got it from the place in town so it was the best and I was hungry so I tucked in, forgetting (momentarily, like always) about the little stomach pouch I needed to get gone.

It was a minor miracle, considering all that was on my mind, but I'd managed a two hour nap.

Then the phone started ringing.

Apparently, the town of Willow had decided they'd given me enough time to cope, that time was up, so all and sundry called to check if I was okay after the Bodhi and Heather debacle. This invariably segued into digging for gold, thus most of them asked if it was true—since I was seen at Chilton's, Rachelle's, the Deluxe and at church with him—if I was seeing Raiden Ulysses Miller

It was not lost on me that things were moving fast with Raiden, but regardless I knew very little about him. However, I sensed he was the kind of man who would not be fond of people in his business. So although I confirmed what me being seen all over town with Raiden stated, since it was the truth, I didn't get into any details. After that, I explained the last few days had been trying, I was exhausted and I needed some time to process it all.

Luckily, the folks of Willow were kind, so they left it at that. Unfortunately, there were a lot of residents of Willow I knew since I'd lived my whole life there, so that message didn't get relayed quickly enough before others picked up the phone and called.

Therefore I had the phone to my ear when I opened the door to Raiden holding a pizza box in one hand and a six pack of Fat Tire in the other.

He grinned at me.

I rolled my eyes, let him in and did my best to get rid of my caller as Raiden dropped the box on the coffee table in the living room. He sauntered to the kitchen like he'd lived in my house since birth, came out with two plates, napkins and two opened beers. He'd already dug into a slice by the time I beeped the off button on my phone and joined him.

All this activity meant I didn't have time to freak out about the upcoming talk with Raiden, which was good.

What was bad was that he drank and ate. He asked about the call, the rest of the calls (once he'd learned of them) and my nap. But he did not do what I'd hoped.

And that was launch right in to the conversation we needed to have that included me freaking, then dealing with learning about whatever he did for a living.

So I gave it until there was only that awkward sliver of pizza left and Raiden got up to get another beer, asking me if I wanted one. I was sipping, keeping my wits about me. Raiden was taking long, manly pulls, therefore I had half a beer left and I declined.

He got his beer and was putting it on the coffee table, not going for the last slice, which I decided indicated he was done eating, so I also decided it was time.

As he was settling back in the couch, I prompted cautiously, "Raiden, you were going to tell me some things."

He wasn't fully back, and at my words he stopped, his head turned to me and he studied me for long moments that made me fight to keep myself from squirming on the couch with worry and impatience.

He sat back and spread his arms out. One he draped on the armrest, the other on the back, claiming my frou-frou, girlie sofa so thoroughly with his sexy, masculine vibe that for a second my mind blanked.

Then his deep voice announced, "I'm a bounty hunter."

My mind came back into the room.

Was that it?

A bounty hunter?

Sweet relief swept through me.

Sure. Raiden had been right. Being a bounty hunter was unconventional.

It was also *totally cool*.

Therefore I grinned huge and cried, "That's totally cool!"

He took in my grin, his face blank, and shook his head.

"No, Hanna, not the badge carrying, having arrest warrants, extension of law enforcement kind of bounty hunting. Cash under the table, getting a fuckuva lot more money kind of bounty hunting."

I didn't know what to do with that since I had no idea what he was talking about.

"I don't get it," I told him.

"I hunt fugitives and they definitely act outside the law," he explained. "But, when I find them, I don't deliver them to the police so they can do jacked shit, get caught, get bonded out, do more jacked shit, go on the run, get caught, then some bondsmen bonds them out again so they can do more jacked shit. I deliver them to people who are willing to pay a lot of money to have them delivered."

This didn't sound good, but I still didn't get it.

"I'm sorry, sweetheart," I said softly. "I'm still not following."

He didn't move and his eyes never left my face as he kept talking.

"Then I'll explain. Right now, I got several jobs goin', the primary one bein' Knight's. He's a buddy of mine. He's got an enemy who keeps gettin' bested but won't let his grudge go. Knight had some shit happen to his business because of this guy and he asked me to do him a favor. A favor he's payin' me to do. And that favor is find the man who infiltrated his business, injecting dope into it. This guy is doin' a favor for the *other* guy who's tryin' to fuck with Knight. But when I find him, I won't turn him and any evidence I have as pertains to his criminal activities into the police. I'll deliver him to Knight and walk away. When I do that, what Knight does with this guy and the shit I give him is not my business. I just walk away. I *always* walk away."

This didn't sound good, either. In fact, it sounded worse, and the stuff before it already sounded bad.

I wasn't sure I wanted to know and was leaning towards not wanting to know, but still, I asked, "So this Knight person asks you to find someone. You find him and give him to Knight, he pays you in cash then your part is done?"

"Yep," he answered.

"And you don't just do this for Knight. It's your job and you do it for other people?"

"Yep."

"Is that legal?" I queried.

His body moved minutely. I almost didn't catch it, but I did and then he sat there looking at me like he had been. No change, except I felt it.

He was tense.

"Strictly speaking," he began, paused, and finished, "no."

Oh God.

"I…you…is it…?" I stammered, pulled myself together and went on, "Are you telling me you're engaged in criminal activities?"

The tension started pouring off him in waves, making me tense. Big time tense.

In fact, wired.

"Strictly speaking," he began, paused, and finished, "yes."

Oh God!

I'd put my plate on the coffee table, which was fortunate. It freed me to lift my feet to the seat of the couch and curve my arms protectively around my shins, hugging my legs to my chest.

Raiden's eyes dropped to my posture. He closed them slowly, then opened them and looked at me.

"Told you yesterday, years ago, I tracked down my dad. To this day, I don't know how it came to me how to do it. We hadn't heard from him in two years. He lived two hours away. I had no resources, no experience, no money, not that first fuckin' thing to go on, and I was a minor. But it took me a week to find him. It just came natural, askin' questions to the right people, bein' smart about it, turnin' over rocks. Same went for when I drove my ass up there and found his house empty. Didn't know that town, didn't know his MO. Still tracked his ass down at his bitches' houses. Same went for me breakin' in. Bought a lock at the hardware store, examined it, fucked with it for hours until I figured out how to pick it. All this came natural. Some people are good with numbers. Others good with their hands. I'm good with this shit."

None of this made me feel any better.

Raiden wasn't done sharing.

"I went into the Marines and I did it as a career choice. What I mean by that is I never intended to get out. Had no dad who could help guide the way, never had any dreams of wantin' to be a cop or a fireman or an astronaut. But I examined my life to that point and knew where I was comfortable. I figured I needed discipline and someone to guide me, tell me what to do. I was good on a team, playin' sports, gettin' coached. I thought that was a natural progression. Once I got a directive, if I was trained how to do it, I went all out. And I was right. At first, the Corps worked for me."

His face changed, went hard and his eyes started burning.

"Then it didn't," he stated.

I understood why and understanding it killed me, but I stayed silent.

Raiden continued talking.

"I got out and remembered trackin' Dad. Figured I'd be good at bounty hunting, better at it after what I learned in the Corps. So I looked into that. Didn't like the way it played out. It was part of a system that was totally fucked. Lots of rules. Lots of paperwork. But absolutely no reason to any of it. It was a dysfunctional cycle. To be successful, I had to write bonds, put my own fuckin' money on the line and live a life filled with lying scum, most of them intent on fuckin' me over. A buddy from the Corps came to town. We went out for beer, I shared this shit with him, he told me about a man he knew named Deacon."

When he stopped and didn't carry on, I asked, "Deacon?"

"Bounty hunter, like I am now. But a cold motherfucker. A six foot two, two hundred twenty pound wall of sheer ice. He got into it like I got into it. His wife went missin', the cops couldn't find her, so he descended into a world that was not his to find her. What he found was that he fit in that world. It was on the periphery, but he had talents in it, he had a place, so he stayed."

"Did he find his wife?"

His gaze, already locked on mine, bonded with it.

"Yeah."

Whatever this Deacon person found was not good and I didn't want to know. Luckily, Raiden didn't tell me.

Unluckily, he continued to tell me other things.

"My buddy hooked me up with Deacon. He's a loner, but he's also the best in the business. Lots of work, not enough of him to go around. The thing was he didn't have anyone he respected enough to punt business to. He must have liked the feel of me 'cause he took me on a couple jobs before he let me loose and started referring work to me. I did the jobs, established a reputation, got more work. So much I had to recruit and train a crew. I did. All the men left from my unit in the Corps who got out like me and found, also like me, they didn't fit back into the world they left when they entered the Corps. But they fit into this other world."

Suddenly, it came clear to me.

And it broke my heart.

"Raiden, this sounds like—"

"Save it," he bit off, interrupting me. "They don't know all this I'm tellin' you, but they know me and I figure they can guess. Not the specifics, but enough to tweak them, so I got that shit from Mom. Got it from Rache. Didn't listen to it from them either. I live it, Hanna. I get it and I know my place, where I'm comfortable, where I fit and this is it."

"I'm not sure you're right," I told him carefully.

"You watch a friend you thought would be a friend for life—who'd stand up at your wedding, who you'd name your kid after, who you'd watch go gray while listenin' to him bitch for the next forty years about his wife spending too much money—get blown to fuckin' *bits* by a landmine, babe, you'll be in a place to say. Since that shit will thankfully never happen to you, you aren't."

My heart broke more, but after that I stayed silent.

"You know all that, I'll give you the rest," he declared. "All of this is sorted. Knight's a buddy because Knight's connected to Deacon, Deacon connected me with Knight and Knight did me a favor. I get paid cash. None of that is on any books, but Knight's got a business and he cleans my money. I use a bogus partnership with him, which means I use his accounts to pay myself, my boys, make investments and pay taxes. It's all above board and legal as far as the government knows. We do legitimate jobs that have no results in a way no one will ever cotton on that the jobs we do are not legitimate. IRS takes their cut, turns the other way. I got an address. I vote. I got a license. Plates on my car. An honorable discharge from the Corps. As far as anyone's concerned I'm a respectable citizen, a veteran and a small business owner and the shit me and my crew do is buried so deep under that respectability, it'll never be dug out."

"Paul Moyer said you were off the grid," I blurted, and his eyes got scary sharp before he appeared to relax.

"Paul Moyer talks smack because he wants to sound cool. For all intents and purposes, I operate off the grid, but I'm not off the grid. You meet Deacon, you'll understand off the grid. That is not me. I come home for a few days at Christmas, but don't reestablish life in Willow after gettin' out, he knows what went down with my unit, Moyer thinks he knows his shit and runs his mouth. He doesn't know his shit. He doesn't know anything."

"You said this was unsafe," I reminded him.

"Men who want men hunted and are willin' to pay tens of thousands of dollars to have them delivered, and the men who are runnin' from them tend not to be people you wanna ask to dinner," Raiden remarked.

This was very, *very* true.

God.

"This scares me," I admitted.

"Yeah, but you'll get used to it."

He seemed very sure.

I was not.

"I don't think I like this," I told him, my voice small. "Any of it."

Raiden didn't move.

But he did speak.

"Then you need to understand why I do it."

This meant there was more, and I really did not want more.

He gave it to me.

"Everything, every living thing on this earth, from plants to animals to humans, has a natural order. It's absolutely crucial to keep that order, Hanna. I've been in the thick of chaos and it is not a fun place to be."

Raiden went quiet and I nodded for him to go on, my heart clenching and the pizza in my belly sitting there in a nauseating lump.

He went on.

"The men who hire me keep order in their worlds. Each one of them rules their own empire. If something breaks free of their rule, chaos can result. In the worlds those men rule, if they keep control, it is very rare there's collateral damage. But someone steals from them, someone conspires to overthrow them, hell can break loose. And when those fires burn, baby, they take out anyone in their path."

Weirdly, this made sense so I said, "Okay."

"When chaos can result, they call me in. I rein it in but I don't extinguish the threat. I'm not a moron. I know when I deliver a man who fucked one of these guys over they don't sit him down in group counseling and work out their issues. But I don't give a fuck. I control chaos. No wife or mother or kid or girlfriend or just a person on the street who was in the wrong place at the wrong time gets pulled in to make a point, carry out a threat or used as shield, then I did my job and got paid huge to do it."

This made sense too, and was kind of honorable in a twisted, criminal underworld kind of way.

I did not tell Raiden this. I just stared at him.

So he continued.

"That's my work, and the way you're lookin' at me I see it hasn't penetrated yet that in the natural order of things it's good work. I got a code. I don't hunt women no matter what shit they pull—and they can pull some serious shit—but that is not my gig and never will be. And if the man I'm huntin' is twenty or younger, I don't take the job. At that age, they can pull their shit outta that life, turn themselves around. I don't ask questions. I don't counsel my prey. I tag and deliver. The kid might be pullin' shit, but I won't know that and I won't live with it on my conscious that he's off tryin' to find a better life and I was responsible for dragging him back in."

Raiden went quiet.

"Is that it?" I asked, thinking that was at least something but not much of a code.

"Nope," he answered. "I don't do side jobs, deliverin' shit if they know I'm headin' somewhere, which would usually be dope or firearms, but it could be anything. I do not touch any of their business because no matter what it is it's tainted, and that is not part of my life. I am not muscle. I gotta get physical on the capture, I do that. But I don't inflict injury unless it's unavoidable. I am contract only and not on any payroll. It is known wide I'm not looking for employment. Now they don't even offer no matter how good I do what I do and they want me on their crew. As for what my crew and I do, we do one thing. The job and only the job. There is not a menu of services available. We don't accept add-ons no matter the amount they're willing to pay. And unless I trust a man—and there are few I trust outside my crew, Deacon and Knight—I don't grant favors and I don't ask for them."

Raiden again stopped speaking.

I said nothing.

So he asked, "You got any questions?"

I shook my head but told him, "I think I need to process this."

He studied me a moment before his eyes warmed, his voice dropped and he ordered, "Then come here and process it closer."

My throat clogged. I shook my head, but swallowed and forced out, "I think this is the kind of processing you need to process alone."

A look that was hard to witness moved over his face.

He understood me.

That killed too.

"Hanna, come here," he whispered.

"I can't."

"Why not?"

Why not?

"Raiden, you just told me you're a criminal and I'm not sure I'm down with that or if I'll *ever* be."

And I wasn't.

And that's why this was killing me.

"I'm not a criminal."

"You participate in criminal activities," I pointed out. "With understanding *and* intent."

"I do shit that's considered illegal," he amended.

"It isn't considered illegal, Raiden. It just *is,*" I told him.

"And who do I hurt?" he shot back, and my mouth clamped shut because that was actually a good question. "Who do I hurt, Hanna?" he pushed.

I said nothing.

What I did was push back into the couch when Raiden leaned toward me, putting his elbows to his thighs and kept talking.

"I don't push dope. I don't run guns. I don't pimp women. I don't steal. I don't con. I don't blackmail. I don't squeeze people for protection money. I do not act as an enforcer. My business never touches the lives of honest citizens. The people I deal with made their choices, the wrong ones, and I'm a consequence of those choices. I didn't force their choices. I do not do one fuckin' thing that contributes to their business or the shit they do. They fuck up and wander into the real world where there's a possibility that they can make decisions that will put good people doin' their best to live decent lives in jeopardy, I reel them back in so that shit does not happen. I'm not tryin' to convince you that that shit always bleeds. Sometimes it's contained, but there's always the possibility that someone could get tweaked, panicked, do something entirely fucked up where someone innocent pays, and what I do stops that before it could even start."

He was scaring me. All of this was, but still, I found the courage to note, "Raiden, it's clear you're determined to do what you do and you have your reasons, but, honestly some of it sounds like rationalizations."

"Yeah?" he asked. "You stopped Bodhi and Heather from fuckin' you up the ass. You let that play out, I would have stopped those shipments from goin' out with your afghans *and* I would have eventually traced all that shit back to the man who's instigating it. Now he's gonna find another Bodhi and Heather who will likely find another Hanna Boudreaux they can fuck up the ass and she might not be as lucky as you."

Oh my God.

That totally made sense.

"People do a lot of shit," Raiden told me. "You're so insulated by family, friends and Willow, thank Christ, you'll never know all the seriously jacked up shit people can get up to. And I didn't tell you that about Bodhi and Heather to make you think I'm on a crusade to shut down drug dealers or any kinds of other scum. The men I work for, I don't make judgments and I don't get involved. But when shit bleeds and I staunch the flow, that jacks up job satisfaction and it does it huge. You want it straight up, odds are Bodhi and Heather were good people who got caught up in something they couldn't control. They were squeezed. They were forced to make a choice. I don't know what happened and I don't give a fuck, but I've seen a lot of people, and those two do not have black souls. But they jacked up somewhere along the way, felt the consequences and that's fair. What isn't fair is they roped you into that shit and I don't get to feel good about disentangling people like you often. It happens enough that I like what I do enough to keep doin' it until I have the money to quit doin' it, kick back and have a decent life where I answer to no one and I can just breathe."

He stopped speaking and I said nothing.

We held each other's eyes.

This went on a good, long while as my mind turned over what he said, *everything* he said, and a lot of things he didn't say.

I had to admit, all of it made sense. It was his sense because Raiden had untwisted some scary, twisted stuff and forced it to make sense, but he did it in a way that it even made sense to me.

It was what he didn't say that penetrated, dug deep and settled with the intention of staying awhile.

Maybe forever.

As I thought this he watched my face, and I knew he knew when he sat back and ordered quietly, "Now, Hanna, come here."

I didn't decide to do it. I couldn't actually believe I was doing it even as I did it.

I let my legs go, curled them under me, put my hands to the empty seat between us and crawled his way.

The instant I got close he leaned toward me and his arms sliced around me so tight my breath constricted. He hauled me to him, his hand at the back of my head forcing my face in his neck and I felt him bury his in mine.

"Jesus, fuck," he whispered, relief dripping heavy in those two words.

I closed my eyes, and again I didn't decide to do it, but still my arms shoved into the cushions of the couch so they could round him.

He shoved his face further in my neck and squeezed tight.

I let this continue because he needed it, and maybe I needed it. Eventually I couldn't let it continue because I didn't need to pass out.

"Raiden, I'm finding it hard to breathe," I rasped.

His arm loosened.

"Are you with me?" he asked my neck.

Oh boy.

Oh God.

Heck.

"Yes," my mouth decided for me.

His hand in my hair fisted and he repeated, "Jesus, fuck."

Grams was right. She always was.

Raiden was dangerous.

And I knew I shouldn't. She warned me to be careful.

But for some reason I didn't understand I couldn't stop myself from being that woman who tried to withstand hellfire.

No.

I knew the reason.

It was because I wanted to know nothing for the rest of my life sweeter than the love Raiden could have for me.

It was also more.

I wanted him to know nothing for the rest of his sweeter than what I could give him.

"I think I'm in trouble," I told his neck.

"That feeling will fade," he told mine.

"I think I'm scared," I kept going.

"That'll fade too."

"Just saying, you might be in a little bit of trouble, too."

His head came up, his fist loosened in my hair so mine could go back and he caught my eyes.

His were still amazing.

The relief in them was not hidden.

He'd been worried.

Raiden Miller was *so totally* into me.

God.

Grams was *so totally* right.

How did this happen?

"How am I in trouble?" he asked.

I didn't tell him what he knew, but obviously, from what he said, refused to do anything about.

That he was damaged and he needed fixing.

I also didn't tell him I was going to do it.

I wasn't going to do it because he was Raiden Ulysses Miller, a beautiful boy that turned into a gorgeous man I'd been crushing on for forever.

No, I was going to do it because he was Raiden, a gentleman, a hero. A man who, as a boy, went through terrible things and came out amazing because that was just who he was and he deserved someone who cared enough to put the effort in to fix him.

I didn't want to change him. What he did was who he was and however that progressed I knew he was the kind of man that I would have to leave that alone.

That would be up to him.

But I was going to right the damage because I cared enough to put the effort in.

Instead, I told him, "I'm totally Peggy Sue, Raiden, and you do what you do and obviously you intend to keep doing it, but you should know I'm going to ignore that and keep right on being Peggy Sue."

"Thank fuck," he replied so immediately I blinked.

"Sorry?"

"You gotta know my work because you gotta know me," he explained. "Now you know it. But from now on, it doesn't touch you. So you keep bein' you because that's you but also because that's exactly what drew me to you, baby." He grinned. "That and your long-ass legs and that sweet ass, and, bein' honest, your great tits and fantastic fuckin' hair." I rolled my eyes, his grin got bigger and he kept talking. "But, back on track, bottom line, I wouldn't want it any other way."

I liked that. All of it, including the stuff about my legs, booty and the rest.

So I smiled.

Then I relaxed.

Raiden felt it.

And I felt him relax.

Then he wasted no further time and kissed me.

It was nice, but too short.

I would know why when he broke it, looked me in the eyes and stated, "Now that's done, time for a tour of your house. A tour that's gonna end in your bedroom."

His words made me shiver.

I was about to have sex with an amazingly gorgeous, criminal underworld bounty hunter with questionable ethics that at least made sense to him, even if they didn't entirely make sense to me. He was dangerous. He was damaged. He was into me. I instinctively knew this was not the end of my world shifting because Raiden Ulysses Miller entered it.

And still…

I could not wait.

12

TRUST IT ALL TO ME

THE TOUR OF my house didn't last long, and as Raiden said, it ended in the bedroom.

It lasted long enough that by the time we got there my breasts had swelled and my legs were trembling so much I didn't know how I stayed standing.

That didn't mean I didn't watch closely as he entered my room. I was unbelievably gratified when he took in my intricately scrolled white iron bed; the frills, the flowers, the pastel pinks, blues and greens, and I saw his face get soft. His lips quirked and I knew he liked it.

I definitely knew I liked Raiden in my room and this *did* have to do with the fact that I spent a fair amount of time imagining him right there.

And there he was.

Right there.

I enjoyed this feeling for a second before he took my hand and led me to the bed, then I was back to concentrating on my breasts swelling and my legs trembling so badly I found it hard to stay upright.

Once we got to the bed, though, he did something strange.

He sat on the side, opened his legs and pulled me between them, but then he let my hand go and both of his spanned my hips in a firm way that said without words I was to stay right there.

I stayed right there.

He tipped his head back to look at me.

"Downstairs, you made a decision," he stated quietly, and my breath started to quicken.

He was very right. I did.

I nodded.

"I know it freaked you, baby, but I hope you come to understand what I gave you downstairs was a gift that, in giving, means a fuckuva lot to me."

I could see that already so I nodded again.

He took in my nod, nodded back once and the pads of his fingers dug into my hips.

"I trusted you with that, Hanna. No one but the people I work with knows that shit about me. Not my mom, my sister, not anybody."

"I won't say anything," I assured hm.

"I gotta trust that, honey."

This was big. I understood why, so to make my point my hands covered his at my hips and I whispered, "You can."

Raiden studied me.

Then he said, "Okay."

I let out a deep breath.

His hands slid up to my waist and his eyes held mine. "Now, you've had a lot happen. You're learnin' some serious shit and this is goin' fast for you, but even so I'm gonna ask you to take more."

Oh boy.

"Okay," I replied but it was hesitant.

"Last night, you got off on what we did. I get who you are, where you come from, but you let yourself go with me and I loved that, every second. I'm gonna trust you with what I gave you downstairs and take it from you that since I'm sittin' on your bed, you took that from me and still trust me. But I need you to trust it all to me."

I was again confused. "Trust all what to you?"

"This." His hands slid up to my ribs and tightened. "You. *All of you.* I want you to trust it all to me."

I was right.

Oh boy.

"Raiden——"

"I like to play."

I shut my mouth.

"You got a hint of that last night," he went on.

A hint?

Oh God.

"Yeah?" he prompted.

Oh yeah, I got it, but I didn't know it was a hint.

Still, I nodded.

"And you got off on it," he noted.

I *so* did.

I nodded again.

"I wanna give you more."

Oh my God.

My legs again got weak, and my hands that had dropped from his when his moved lifted to hold on to his shoulders.

"Which means you're gonna take more," he continued.

Oh my *God*.

"And you're gonna give more to me," he kept going.

I started breathing heavily.

"But anything I do, anything I ask you to do, it doesn't work for you, it doesn't turn you on, no matter how deep we are in it, Hanna, you say the word 'solitaire' and we switch it up, find somethin' we both enjoy that gets us both off."

I knew what he was saying. I'd heard about it.

He was talking about a safe word.

Which meant when he said he liked to play, he meant he liked *to play*.

Even as my breath came faster and my stomach clutched I still felt my nipples tingle and heat start to pound between my legs.

"You with me?" he asked.

I never expected this. I never even thought about it. It didn't occur to me I'd have to make this decision, much less make it with Raiden Miller.

Still, I didn't hesitate before I breathed, "Yes."

His fingers at my ribs dug in again and his voice got rough and commanding when he said, "Hear me, Hanna, you don't like what we're doin', you stop it. I got what I got from you last night, honey, and I did not lie. It was fuckin' phenomenal, so I push you to an edge you don't wanna go over, you put a stop to things. I know what's standin' in front of me and I want it just like it is, however that comes. We explore, I'll be happy. But if I get nothin' beyond what you gave me last night, this will make me far from unhappy. Right?"

I nodded but it was tentative.

Raiden didn't miss it. "Baby—"

"I'm Peggy Sue," I whispered and his lips turned up.

"No down-to-her-bones-Peggy Sue gets her freak on like you did last night, honey."

I had to admit, this was true.

"Do you trust me?" he asked, and my fingers tensed into the muscles at his shoulders.

"Yes."

"Then trust it all to me."

I swallowed before I licked my lips, rubbed them together and stared at him.

A handsome man.

A dangerous man.

A damaged man I intended to fix.

On those thoughts, determination stole up my spine and I again nodded.

His fingers dug deep as his eyes started burning and he growled, "Fuck."

Raiden was pleased.

Oh *God*.

His hand slid back down to my hips and his voice was deeper when he said, "Right. Now, Hanna, take off your clothes."

Oh.

God.

Suddenly that determination in my spine didn't feel so determined.

I sucked it up, started to take a step back but his fingers flexed and I stopped.

"Right there, honey," he instructed, and I was a bit confused.

I was standing between his spread legs. There wasn't a lot of room to move.

Still, I went for it. I put my hands in the hem of my t-shirt, whipped it off and threw it to the floor.

"Slow," Raiden ordered and I bit my lip.

Okay, I could do that.

Or maybe I could.

Even as my fingers went to the button on my shorts his hands didn't move from my hips, so when I slid down the zipper and, holding his heated eyes, very slowly glided them over my hips, I pulled them out from under his hands, but they stayed right where they were.

My shorts fell to my feet. I shifted from one foot to the other, getting them off and kicking them behind me.

His eyes never leaving mine, Raiden demanded, "Your bra now, baby."

Okay. Oh boy.

Um…

My skin tingling, nerves jangling even as the heat gathered between my legs at the look in his eyes, I put my hands behind my back and very slowly unhooked the first hook then the second. I dropped my hands, rolled my shoulders forward and the bra fell away.

His eyes dropped to my chest. His fingers dug in and I began to pant softly, the heat now swelling between my legs as I caught a strap of my bra in one hand and tossed it aside.

Raiden's gaze came back up to mine and he growled, "Panties."

I swear I felt the rumble of his growl at the heat of me as I did my best to maneuver around his hands that still didn't move and very slowly tugged my panties over my hips until they fell down my legs. I repeated what I did with my shorts, kicking them behind me.

Then I was naked in front of him, sitting fully clothed on my bed, and I felt weird. I felt wonderful. I was a little scared. I was a lot excited. And I was wondering, with not a small amount of eagerness, about what would happen next.

He didn't make me wait as his hands finally moved on me, whisper soft, but he didn't watch them. He watched my face.

It felt good, it felt nice and the more he did it, it felt better.

"Can you get your legs open for me?" he asked gently, and I actually felt the wave of wet that saturated between my legs as I did as he asked. I didn't have a lot of room but I gave him what I could.

"That's it," he whispered, one hand swooping over my belly and in. I braced for his fingers to touch me *there*, or better yet, to invade but they swept feather-light along the inside juncture of hip and thigh and that was when it began.

Minutes that seemed like hours of just that.

Raiden watching my face, his hands moving on me, coming close to the good stuff, gliding along the side of my breast but then not touching my nipple, knuckles grazing the underside of my breast but not hitting the target, finger-tips sliding up the inside of my thigh only to go away right when I thought they'd find me.

It was brilliant. It was torture. The longer it went on, the more it thrilled and frustrated me.

I whimpered and lifted my hands to clutch his shoulders, but before they made it to their destination, Raiden ordered, "Clasp them behind your back."

"What?" I panted.

His hands spanned my ribs again, holding firm and his eyes locked with mine. "Do it, baby."

Oh God, this was hot.

This was scary.

This was crazy.

I clasped my hands behind my back.

One of his hands slid in, down; his fingers went through the hair between my legs and whispered over my clit then it was gone.

A reward.

An infinitesimal reward.

God.

Torture.

Brilliant.

"Good, Hanna, now keep your hands clasped. No matter what you feel, what I do, what you want. Will you do that for me?"

"Yes," I gasped.

"Good, baby, now arch your back for me."

Oh God. God. God. *God.*

I arched my back for him and he immediately leaned in and added his lips and tongue to the torture his fingers were perpetrating. They moved, they touched, glided, grazed and they did this an eternity before just the tip of his tongue glided over my nipple.

I was so primed, heat bolted through me and I whimpered, "Raiden."

"Keep arched for me, honey," he murmured to the skin between breasts.

He kept a hand giving nothing but constantly toying between my legs, the other one held me at the hip, and then suddenly his mouth closed over my nipple and he pulled deep.

I was so ready, I *needed* that so much, my entire body bucked. I cried out, my hands came unclasped and I almost drove them into his hair to hold him to me before I remembered, pulled it together and clasped them behind me again.

He stopped suckling.

No!

"Raiden." It was a plea.

"Stay still, Hanna."

"Sweetheart——"

Another glide of just the tip of his tongue over my nipple; my clit pulsed, my body jerked and I moaned.

"Trust me," he whispered.

Oh God, oh God.

God.

More toying, more nothing, all of it full of promise; more torment, then both of Raiden's hands slid back to my ribs, his mouth moved from me and I tipped my head down to see his tipped back.

"Climb on, baby."

Finally.

I didn't hesitate. I put a knee to the bed on one side of his hips, one on the other side and settled in.

"Hold on to my shoulders," he ordered and I put my hands on his shoulders.

His hand went between my legs, and no fooling around, he drove two fingers inside.

Oh yes.

Yes.

Finally!

I gasped, my head fell forward and hit his shoulder and his turned so his growl went directly into my ear.

"Ride those."

I rode them. Oh God, did I ride them. My head turned, my face pressed into his neck, my hands grasping his shoulders, I rode his fingers and I did it desperately because I needed it. I needed it to hold me together. I needed it because I was coming apart at the seams.

"Stop," Raiden demanded.

"Oh, honey, please, no," I gasped.

"Stop, Hanna."

I stopped on a mew of reckless despair, but I got more instantly.

"Free me," he ordered.

I lifted up, looked in his eyes and he was shifting. His hand to the back of his jeans, he pulled out his wallet.

Oh yes.

Thank God, yes.

He unearthed a condom, tossed the wallet on the floor as I held his eyes and clumsily worked his jeans.

I finally got them as I needed them and pulled him free.

His cock was big, long, thick and rock-hard, and I wanted it inside me.

"Take the packet, Hanna, and roll it on me." He barely finished his order when I snatched the packet out of his hand, but he said, "Slow, baby."

Darn.

I looked at him and forced myself to go slowly. This kind of worked, mostly because my hands were shaking so badly and they got to shaking worse when his hands moved to my breasts, his thumbs started circling my nipples and I lost concentration as that throbbed from nipples to clit.

I finally did it and I was about to wrap my hand around his cock when his words stopped me.

"I'm gonna guide you on me then you're gonna take over, and when you do, you're gonna fuck me slow."

I held his eyes and my voice trembled when I told him, "I don't know if I can do slow, Raid."

When I said his name, his eyes flashed, but his lips said, "Slow, Hanna."

"I—"

"Trust me."

I swallowed and nodded.

"Hold on to my shoulders again, honey."

I did as I was told.

Raiden did as he promised, moving me, positioning me, and with a hand around his cock, his other arm around my hips, he guided himself in as he pulled me down, filling me.

My head fell back at the sheer beauty.

His hands spanned my hips.

"Look at me." I forced my head forward. His eyes caught mine, the pads of his fingers dug in and he ordered, "Lips to mine, baby, the whole time you fuck me slow."

Yes.

I could do that.

So I did it.

Lips to his, my eyes open, his eyes opened, I moved on him.

Instantly, I needed more.

"When can I go faster?" I asked.

"Slow," he answered.

"Yeah, but when can I go faster?"

"I'll tell you, honey, now slow."

I went slow.

I couldn't do slow.

It was undoing me.

My hands slid up to the sides of his neck and I begged, "Raiden."

One of his hands slid up to my breast, covered it and his thumb rubbed hard against my nipple.

I moved faster and gasped, "Raiden!"

"Slow down, Hanna."

"Oh God," I whimpered as I forced myself to do what he said.

His thumb kept at my nipple, and it built, and built, and built until I felt like my skin was going to split open.

"Raiden, honey, *please*."

His other hand moved up my back, his fingers went into my hair, fisted and he growled against my lips, "Okay, Hanna, fuck me hard now, baby."

Instantly, I complied.

Just as instantly, Raiden's finger met his thumb, he tugged hard at my nipple and that seared through me.

I moaned against his lips and rode him harder.

"Fuck, but my girl is fucking magnificent," he rumbled. "Harder, baby, fuck me."

I fucked him harder, gasping, whimpering, moaning. One of my hands slid into his hair and just like his at mine, it fisted. Hard.

"That's it, baby, ride me," he grunted as I moved. "Fuck. Magnificent. You gonna give it to me?"

"Yes," I whispered, and his hand left my breast, traveled down and shot between my legs.

"Then give it to me," he ordered.

His thumb tweaked my clit and that was all I needed.

I drove down and grinded in. My head flew back, my back arched and I cried out as I flew apart.

"Un-fucking-believable." I heard Raiden rasp.

Then I was on my back, Raiden's hips slamming into mine and I took him, still coming, my limbs clutching him to me, my hand still fisted in his hair. I lifted my hips to give him more even when it left me and I shoved my face in his neck.

"Fuck me harder, sweetheart," I gasped into his neck. His hand still in my hair tugged back, but his face stayed in my neck and his cock drove hard and deep.

I felt his teeth sink into my flesh as his fingers fisted tighter in my hair. I whimpered as pain that came as pleasure hit and an aftermath shiver of pure bliss whispered through me.

Raiden planted himself to the root. I felt him come, and when he did he groaned so deep into my neck it traveled through my throat and felt like it shook the bed.

I held on and gloried when my body jolted as his hips jerked through his own aftermath of thrusts, pounding into me, once, twice, again and again, then finally his orgasm began to wane and the thrusts gentled, became glides and he stopped deep.

He didn't stroke me, he didn't work my neck with his mouth. He didn't say anything and I didn't either. I just held on and laid there, feeling him connected to me, in my bed. All we'd just done, what he'd demanded from me, what that meant he gave to me and the fact that I'd trusted it all to him. And Raiden had made it worth it.

Completely.

That was hot.

It was amazing.

And it was beautiful.

He made it more beautiful when his lips slid to the skin under my ear and he muttered, "Be back," then his lips slid over my jaw as he slowly, so slowly, slid out.

He barely moved his body from over mine before he dragged my afghan over me to cover my nudity, and rolled off the bed. I curled up on my side and watched as he walked into my bathroom.

I lay there, sated, feeling so fine I didn't know anyone could feel that fine and thinking that I just took off my clothes, and naked as the day I was born fucked a beautiful fully clothed man and came so hard I might not need another orgasm for a decade.

This made me grin, which was what Raiden caught me doing when he walked out of the bathroom.

When he caught it, his amazing eyes warmed, his entire face softened and Raiden Miller in my bedroom grinned back.

Then he gave me more beautiful.

He stopped at the side of the bed and he did something remarkable, something I'd remember for the rest of my life.

It wasn't the same, but it still was. While I watched, taking his time, Raiden took off his clothes. Giving me what I gave him, making what already was a happy memory for me, trusting that he would take care of me, do right by me, give me beauty, a happier memory when he gave it right back to me.

Then he put a knee to the bed, lifted the afghan, slid under it with me and pulled me into his arms.

On our sides, front to front, my arms around him, my head tucked under his chin, my forehead to his throat, cheek to his collarbone, I heard and felt his rumbled, "You good?"

"Um…they haven't measured this level of good, thus it has as yet gone undefined, so the answer is yes, but the word is wrong."

His arms tightened and his body started shaking.

Idiotically, I kept talking. "I'll be contacting Webster tomorrow. My suggestion will be absofuckingmazing."

Raiden's body started shaking harder.

That was all the idiocy I had left in me. My orgasm drove the rest of it out, so I had nothing left to give except silently cuddling closer to Raiden.

He got control of his hilarity, his body quit shaking and his neck moved before I felt his lips on top of my hair where he murmured, "My girl came hard."

I *so* did.

"Yeah," I whispered.

"I think you're gonna have fun with the way I like to play," he noted.

He was not wrong.

I didn't answer. Just cuddled closer.

"Yeah, she's gonna have fun," he muttered into my hair, and I heard the smile in his voice. But there was no smile, his voice was gruff when he finished with, "My reward."

That was twice he said that, but I let it go, mostly because I had a feeling he would tell me what that meant when it was his time.

He fell silent. I remained that way.

We held each other and Raiden only moved once, to lift a hand and brush the tips of his fingers tenderly along my neck at the place where his teeth sank in before his arm moved back around me to pull me closer.

There was something about that gesture, that touch. Something significant. Something I wasn't sure I got, but something I liked. I didn't question it, didn't say a word; not willing to break the mood, not about to question that gesture of tenderness Raiden gave me, happy just to accept it silently.

After a while, I tilted my head back and his chin dipped down so I could catch his eyes.

Those eyes.

In my bed.

Looking at me.

I let that settle as I asked an important question.

"You want a hot fudge sundae?"

"Yeah," he answered, lips twitching.

"I make homemade hot fudge," I shared.

"Then fuck yeah," he replied, now smiling.

I reached up, touched my mouth to his and said, "Let's go."

He lifted up, taking me and the afghan with us so I was still covered, which was again sweet.

He pulled on his jeans commando.

I rooted under my pillowcase and pulled on my pajama shorts (commando) and my tank top (also commando).

We went downstairs and I started a pot of hot fudge sauce that eventually burned beyond being edible.

This was because as I was preparing to assemble the sundaes, I got out a spray can of whipping cream

And Raiden saw it.

So the hot fudge ended up burned.

But I ended up naked on my back on my kitchen table getting another orgasm that had everything to do with Raiden, his hands, his mouth, his tongue and a can of whipping cream.

It was better than any sundae I'd ever had.

Much better.

13

THAT KIND OF LOVE

The Next Morning

I WAS IN the kitchen standing at the counter in my pajamas, arranging the cinnamon apple slices on top of the coffeecake batter, when I sensed movement to my side.

I turned my head.

Raiden was there.

This wasn't a surprise. I'd heard the water going in the bathroom upstairs.

But it *was* a delight, seeing as he was wearing nothing but jeans, his hair a sexy mess, his eyes drowsy but warm and on me as he sauntered my way.

I smiled. "Morning, sweetheart."

His "morning" was better.

He said no words but fitted the front his big body to the back of mine and wrapped his arms around me. Then he bent his head and kissed my shoulder.

Yes, a whole lot better than mine.

His stubbled chin came to rest on my shoulder and I knew he was watching my hands arrange apple slices.

This was proved when he rumbled, "That looks good," his voice deeper because it was like his eyes, still a hint sleepy.

"Apple cinnamon streusel coffeecake," I told him.

"Jesus," he murmured, sounding slightly stunned, as he would considering the countertop was a mess of bowls, ingredients and coffeecake preparation residue.

Suddenly, I felt tense, nervous and hurried to explain, "It's not an, um... everyday thing but I kind of felt in the mood for something..."

Oh God! I should never have pulled out the big gun coffeecake that took forever to bake and assembly was seriously fiddly.

What was I thinking?

"Special," I finished lamely, thinking that said too much too soon.

Raiden wasted no time communicating he didn't think it said too much, too soon.

One of his arms around my middle let me go only to lift and wrap around my chest. He pulled me deep into his body, and this time he kissed the skin below my ear.

"Haven't tasted it yet, but already know it's perfect," he whispered there, and I relaxed into his hard frame.

He gave me a squeeze before his arms loosened, and I informed him, "Coffee's made. Cups are in the cupboard over the coffeepot."

Raiden let me go, but did it sliding his hand across the skin of my chest, the other one across the material of my tank at my midriff before his body disappeared.

He got a mug and was filling it when he asked, "You need a warm up?"

I was smoothing the top layer of batter over the apples when I answered, "Yeah."

He brought the pot to my mug and topped it up, asking, "See milk, babe. You need more?"

"Yeah, sweetheart. I use the creamer in the door of the fridge."

He went, grabbed the French vanilla-flavored Coffee-mate and splashed some in my cup.

I spread the streusel on top of the batter thinking this was fabulous. Me cooking. Raiden topping up my coffee. Couple stuff that felt natural and right, even though we'd only had two dates.

Maybe Raiden's brand of slow was good.

He leaned a hip against the counter as I slid the cake in the oven and went to wash my hands at the sink.

"Your day?" he asked as I dried my hands.

I moved to stand in front of him, grab my mug and leaned against the counter, too.

I took a sip and told him, "Grams to mah jongg then me to my place in town, if the cops will let me get in. I need to see what Heather got up to, if I'm caught up, orders filled, get back on top of that."

"You need me to talk to Joe to make sure you have access, I'll give him a call," Raiden offered and I smiled.

"I think I'm good, but I'll let you know."

"All right, honey."

I repeated his question, "Your day?"

He took a sip and dropped the mug to the counter. "Hardware store, back here, installing new locks for you. Then I gotta go into Denver and see to some shit."

Two sentences, a huge amount to go over.

"New locks for me?" I asked.

"Your lock sucks," he answered.

"But—"

"And, Hanna, it's good we're on this because you answered the door to me last night and I didn't hear the lock go."

My brows drew together in bewilderment.

"But...I was home," I told him something he knew.

"You were a woman at home alone. You should lock your doors."

"Raiden—"

"No," he cut me off. "I'm tryin' to ignore the thought of you takin' a nap without your doors locked. Bad enough they're not locked when you're awake."

"I live in the boonies," I reminded him. "No one comes out here. No one even knows there's a here to come to. But the ones who do, I can hear them coming."

"Don't give a fuck. Just a guess, you don't have a gun. Your lock is total shit and wouldn't keep anyone out who knows rudimentary lock picking or has the power to land a solid kick to your door. You gotta have a new lock. I'll check this one," he jerked his head to my back door, "and you might get two. But when you're home, you lock both."

"This is the house I grew up in, Raiden. I've lived here all my life. I know that it's—"

I shut up when his hand curled around the side of my neck and slid right up into my hair, pulling up so I went on my toes even as he bent into me, and I saw his face was not sleepy-ish handsome anymore. His eyes were hard and sharp and his jaw was tight.

"Lock. Your. Doors," he commanded.

"Okay," I whispered instantly, and he let me go.

I rolled back to my feet and hid my discomfiture at his extreme authoritarianism and easy ability to underline that by getting physical.

"Hanna," he called.

"Mm-hmm," I mumbled into my mug.

"Honey, give me your eyes."

I lifted my eyes to him.

"I know the threat that lurks out there. What I want is to know that threat won't threaten you. If shit can happen, it will. Odds are, no threat is gonna wander down that lane and stop at your house. But if it does, I want you to have five minutes to call 911 and get yourself safe so you don't learn exactly what a threat is. I get thinkin' about it for the second it takes every time you flip a lock is unpleasant. Livin' a lifetime with the consequences of not doin' it would be far fuckin' worse."

This made sense.

It was even sweet he was worried about me and wanted to protect me.

However.

"You could have explained that instead of grabbing me and going all drill sergeant," I told him.

"Did I get your attention?" he asked.

"Yes," I answered and hesitantly added, "in a way I didn't like very much."

"Then next time, don't backtalk," he returned.

I blinked.

He took a sip of his coffee before he asked, "How long's that cake take?"

I opened my mouth, closed it, and opened it again to reply, "About an hour."

Raiden looked at the clock on my microwave then pulled my mug out of my hand, put it on the counter, tagged my hand and dragged me toward the doorway, muttering, "Then I gotta eat you now before the cake."

My nipples started tingling and I missed a step but Raiden didn't notice.

He pulled me behind him up the stairs and to my bedroom, and before I could get my thoughts together, I was on my back in my bed. My panties and pajama shorts were gone, Raiden's mouth was between my legs and I had no thoughts at all except how unbelievably good he was with his mouth.

He had me before cake.

And I had an orgasm before cake.

Early Evening, the Same Day

MY CELL RANG and I grabbed it. The display said Raiden Calling, and I was undecided about answering it.

I knew why this was.

I didn't like how things turned so drastically in my kitchen that morning. I also didn't like that Raiden didn't give me the chance to address it or that I'd allowed him to take my mind off it. Not to mention the fact that after, there wasn't enough time to go back to it, but more, I didn't have the guts to do it.

But the bottom line was what Raiden did was uncool. I didn't like to think of him as uncool. I really didn't like to think of myself as a woman who would put up with uncool because she was hanging onto the man of her dreams. A man who gave her a scary indication that she shouldn't live with (on top of other scary indications she was telling herself she could) that he wasn't cool.

And I figured I needed time to sort through all this.

Nevertheless, being an idiot (though, this *was* Raiden Miller), I took the call and put my phone to my ear.

"Hey," I greeted.

"Hey, baby," he greeted back, and my insides melted.

There it was again. He did something dreamy and that something dreamy was simply calling me "baby," and I forgot he could be not-so-dreamy.

"Where are you?" he went on.

"At home," I answered.

"Things cool in town?" he asked.

"Surprisingly, or maybe not so much, seeing as she had two jobs to do and she was getting paid for both; Heather was totally on top of things. It's going to stink, having to put together my shipments again, but I'm not behind."

"Excellent," he muttered then continued, "I'm just headin' outta Denver. Be home in about forty. I'll pick you up. We'll go to Rache's for dinner."

"Uh…I already put a chicken in the oven."

"Right, then be there in forty."

I didn't exactly ask him to dinner but it seemed he didn't exactly care.

"Raid—" I began, but he interrupted me.

"See you soon."

Then he was gone.

I stared at my phone.

Okay, I'd talk to him at dinner, and I promised myself I *would* talk to him at dinner.

I dealt with things in the kitchen. After I did that, I opened a bottle of white wine, poured myself a glass, got my wool and headed out to the front porch.

I was swaying sideways on my swing, one leg bent, my foot in the seat. The outside of my leg was resting against the back of the swing. The other leg was down, tips of my toes swaying me. The makings of an afghan were in my lap and Carole King was coming soft through the windows of my living room when the Jeep pulled up.

I watched it, steeling myself to do what I promised, and I kept steeling myself as Raiden unfolded his body encased in tan cargo pants, tight hunter green tee and boots out of the Jeep. I continued steeling myself as he slowly walked up the steps, eyes on me and stopped at the post by the stairs.

"Hey," I greeted.

"Hey," he said back in a way that that one word glided across the space and wrapped warm and snug around me like one of my afghans.

I quit steeling.

But I did make to move, saying, "You want a—?"

"Don't move."

I settled because there was a command to his voice, but it was different. It was like the way he said "hey" except more. A lot more. I stayed where I was, eyes glued to him, feeling funny in a way so good, it was absofuckingmazing good.

When he just stood there, his eyes moving over me, I asked softly, "Sweetheart, are you okay?"

His eyes came to mine. His body slanted to the side so his shoulder was resting against the post and he replied, "You, just like that, any man would fight and die for the privilege of comin' home to that every day."

My breath left me in a soft, audible "*oof*," like Spot had jumped up on my chest.

Raiden wasn't done.

"Better, she accepts you just as you are, then makes a special coffeecake with apples and doesn't skimp on the streusel, which is the best part. All that to celebrate you givin' her your trust and her givin' hers right back to you."

Tears crawled up my throat and started clawing the backs of my eyes, so my voice was husky when I whispered, "Raiden."

"And you know, she learned at the hand of Miss Mildred, the chicken in the oven is gonna rock your world."

It totally was. Grams taught me everything she knew, but my mom was also no slouch in the kitchen.

"Please stop talking," I begged.

He didn't.

"Fight and die for that privilege, Hanna."

I swallowed back tears and warned, "If you don't shut up, you're going to make me cry."

Raiden shut up, but didn't move. He just stood there staring at me.

So I asked what I was going to ask before, "Honey, do you want a beer?"

"I'll get it."

"Okay."

He pushed away from the post and walked into the house.

I did not find the courage to talk to him about my concerns about our morning conversation.

No, the truth was that sharing my concerns didn't once enter my mind.

That Night

RAIDEN WAS BACK on his calves, his hips powering up. I was straddling him, back to his front, his arms around me, his hands moving everywhere.

I was unraveling.

His hand slid down then glided across my belly, and not even thinking about it, my hand covered his and slid it up.

Taking mine with it, his slid back down to my belly.

I slid it up.

His hand stilled then glided to my side, down and in. My hand still over his, I felt his middle finger press in, circle. His hips surged up, he filled me, my head flew back, a moan drifted up my throat and I shot to pieces.

Twenty Minutes Later

NAKED IN RAIDEN'S arms, I cuddled closer, my eyes drooping, sleep close.

"What was that?" his voice rumbled into me.

"Sorry?" I murmured.

"With your belly, baby."

I blinked into the dark, suddenly not sleepy in the slightest. "Uh…sorry?"

"Want all-access, Hanna. You got some issues with me touchin' your stomach?"

Oh God.

"Um…" I mumbled and said no more.

Raiden's body tensed then pressed into mine so I was on my back and his shadow was looming over me.

"Fuck," he grunted.

"What?"

"Do not wanna ask this shit, but did some fuckwad do somethin' fucked with your stomach?"

I was baffled by this question so I repeated, "What?"

"Babe, you don't want it, we won't do it, but like I said, I want all-access and that might include me comin' on you. Is that gonna be an issue for you?"

I didn't answer. My mind was filled with Raiden coming on me, and how if he did that I'd get to watch, and how I kind of wanted to do that immediately.

"Hanna," he called.

"What?" I answered distractedly.

His hand came up and cupped my jaw. "Honey, talk to me," he urged gently.

God, he was being sweet and he totally had the wrong end of the stick.

So I found myself blurting, "I have a pouch."

I watched the shadow of his head twitch and he asked, "You have a what?"

This was not fun in any way.

But I couldn't have him thinking some "fuckwad" did something "fucked" to my stomach.

"I, um...well, am not exactly *toned* there like you're, well...*toned*...or more like *cut*, well...*everywhere*."

"So?"

I blinked into the dark.

"So?" I repeated.

"Yeah, so?" he asked.

I didn't know what to do with that question so I remained silent.

Raiden didn't.

He asked strangely, "Are you shitting me?"

I didn't know what do to do with that question either. What I did know was I wasn't shitting him, though I also didn't know what he thought I was shitting him about.

"Well, no," I answered, and suddenly his shadow was gone and the bed swayed because his big body landed on its back beside mine.

"Jesus, women are so fuckin' whacked," he informed the ceiling.

I pulled the covers up to my chest, lifted up on an elbow and twisted his way. "Sorry?"

I felt his eyes on me in the dark. "Babe, guys like pussy," he declared.

"Okay," I said slowly.

"A woman's gotta smell good and she needs to take care of herself. By that I mean, she's gotta wash her hair, shave her legs and work it, whatever it is she's workin'. Her clothes, the way she does up her face, the way she moves, it doesn't fuckin' matter. She does that and has a sweet pussy, a guy does not give a fuck and gets off on whatever wraps that package."

I wasn't sure that made me feel better and I communicated this by saying a disbelieving, "All right."

Raiden got up on his elbow to face me, his arm moving to wrap around my waist and haul my lower body against his.

"That's not entirely true," he carried on. "Some guys like big tits, some guys don't give a shit about tits and like a round ass. Some want long legs. Some want short women they can protect or feel like they can dominate. But brass tacks, it's about the pussy."

I *was* sure this didn't make me feel better, therefore I asked, "So essentially, if it's female, a man will sleep with it?"

"No, essentially a man won't fuck anything he doesn't want and women have got to get it in their heads that if he's givin' her his dick, he likes what he's burying his dick inside."

Well, that was certainly clear, if crude, and something that again left me with no response.

"Hanna, baby," his voice had gentled and his arm pulled me closer, "what I'm sayin' is, we like what we like, we're drawn to what we're drawn to and I wouldn't be fuckin' you if I didn't want what you're givin' me. *All* of what you're givin' me. You're pretty. You smell good. You're legs are fuckin' amazing. You've got great tits. You're toned and in shape but soft in great fuckin' places and I like it like that. Add you bein' cute, dorky, sweet and fuckin' hilarious, it's perfect. *All* of it."

Okay, *that* made me feel better.

I thought, for the first time in a long time, about the woman I saw him with, petite and skinny-minnie.

"So, you, uh…like tall and curvy, not short and skinny?" I asked.

"No, I like tits and hair, however those come, but what they gotta come with, what turns me on most, are smells and personality. You might think that's bullshit, but it's true. You got all that, but add your legs and I don't have to court a backache in order to take your mouth, major bonus."

That absolutely made me feel better so I smiled.

Raiden must have seen it in the dark because he leaned into me, taking me to my back and again loomed over me.

"So, you gonna stop that shit with your stomach?" he asked.

"Yeah," I answered.

"All-access?" he pushed.

"Yes, sweetheart," I promised.

"How about you give that to me now," he suggested and a pulse pounded between my legs.

"Okay," I breathed.

"Spread for me, Hanna."

I opened my legs at the same time I had a minor preliminary orgasm.

Raiden put a hand flat between my breasts, slid it down, glided it over my belly then it dipped between my legs.

My hips lifted and I bit my lip.

He shifted and ordered gruffly, "Wrap your hand around my cock, honey. Jack me off while I play with your pussy."

Readily, I did what I was told.

I came first.

Five minutes later, Raiden anointed my belly.

And I got to watch.

After cleaning him off me, I fell asleep with Raiden spooning me, big hand splayed at my stomach.

And I fell asleep thinking this was good news for my sundae addiction, I liked my little pouch and I was going to keep it.

*

That Friday Afternoon

GRAMS WAS SITTING on her back porch, feet up, eyes closed. I'd dragged her chair to the end of the porch so she was bathed in sun.

Raiden was at the far end of the backyard with the push mower, its engine droning.

I had a mess of afghans all over Grams' porch furniture and my basket of ribbons with me. I was folding, tying and tagging them.

Spot was lying on the floor inside the back door, his enigmatic kitty face studying my movements. I didn't know if he wanted me to let him out so I would cease my work and give him cuddles or so he could do his best to draw my blood.

Grams's house was in the residential area of town, two blocks down from the end of the businesses, one block in. As we were somewhat removed from the big city, not a suburb but not far away, thus we had wildlife, but the scary stuff didn't stray into town, making clawless Spot a ready-meal should we let him out. Still, we didn't let him out, just in case.

Therefore, being confined indoors was one of many things that didn't make Spot happy, and I suspected he was studying me and plotting ways to draw my blood.

"See my precious girl's decided to play with fire," Grams told the backs of her eyelids.

I pulled a bow tight on an afghan and looked at her.

Then I looked at Raiden in jeans, a now sweaty tee and running shoes, mowing my grandmother's lawn.

I looked back at Grams.

"Yeah," I answered softly.

"Mm-hmm," she mumbled ambiguously.

"It's not mine to share, what he's shared with me, Grams, but you were right. He's dangerous," I told her.

"Know that, *chère*," she replied.

"He's also worth the risk," I finished.

Her eyes opened and came to me.

"Talk in town and lots of it. Shocked you and that boy haven't received your invitations to be grand marshals, sittin' on a float in the parade the town intends to plan to celebrate your togetherness, what with them bein' beside themselves with joy their local hero's courtin' the town's sweetest girl."

I knew she was worried. I didn't want her to think I was going in with anything but my eyes wide open, but I couldn't stop the goofy smile that I knew hit my lips.

Grams wasn't done

"Those in the know about that fire within, that would be his momma and his baby sister, they got all kinds of faith in you. Especially with Rachelle practically havin' the menu planned for your wedding and Ruthie Miller grumbling about the bike shop bein' closed, seein' as she wanted to buy her boy a bike so he could ride alongside his girl."

The news of Mrs. Miller and Rachelle approving was so welcome I had to bite my lip so I didn't break my face smiling huge.

I felt Grams eyes sharpen on me and my smile faded.

"Don't get ideas. That boy's behind won't mount a bike, precious. He might blow one up in a military exercise, but he's not gonna ride alongside you while you mosey into town and pick up salad fixin's for dinner."

This was true. And it was funny.

I beat back the laughter and agreed, "I know, Grams."

Her voice got sharp when she warned, "Do not take this lightly, child. You knew the danger, you still made a decision, took on this job and now you got people countin' on you. His momma, his sister, me, the town and, most importantly, *him*."

My amusement fled. I held her eyes and nodded.

"Proud of you," she said and she sounded it.

My heart warmed, but the smile I gave her was shaky. "Thanks, Grams."

"I'm proud, but that don't mean I'm not worried. Fire's gonna get hot, *chère*. You made your choice. You do what you gotta do to take the heat."

I nodded.

"Hope I live to see it," she continued and my heart lurched.

"Grams—"

"Want one thing before I die: to know you'll go on after me and do it safe and happy. That boy's got the capacity to give you both, he doesn't destroy you in the process. I hope I live to see him battle that blaze so he gives my girl safe and happy."

"You're going to make me cry," I warned.

"Boudreaux do not cry, *chère*. You know that. Place to cry, on the back porch in the sun is not it."

I pulled in a deep breath through my nose and again nodded.

"There'll be good times, Hanna. Fill yourself up with them, hold on to them tight, 'cause when the bad times come, you'll need them," she advised.

"Now you're scaring the pants off me," I told her.

"Boudreaux don't show fear. There's a place to feel fear and on the back porch in the sun is not it."

I avoided her eyes by setting the afghan I'd finished aside and getting another one.

"Listen to your grams, precious," she ordered.

"I'm listening," I told her, shaking out a blanket in preparation for folding it.

"You keep your chin up, you control tears and fear, you'll be all right," she told me.

"Okay," I replied.

"Proud of you, *chère*," she whispered.

I looked at her and smiled. "Love you, Grams."

"I know, child. What do you think's keepin' me on this earth? Not easy to let go that kind of love. That kind of love's got the power to hold you tethered to a world you should have left a long time ago."

Oh my God.

Tears stung the backs of my eyes. I dropped the afghan and moved to her. Then I pulled her little, bony body in my arms and hugged her as tight as I dared.

She hugged me back.

Then she pushed me away, demanding, "Need a refill of tea. And get your boy one. He's losin' water."

I pulled myself together, did as I was told and discovered I was right. Spot was lying in wait, not for cuddles but for blood. I discovered this when he hissed and launched an attack on my ankles the minute I stepped inside.

I stopped and looked down at him. "You don't fool me, buddy. I know you love me."

He reared back, hissed again, batted my toes then jerked away. He ran-waddled down the hall and disappeared.

I went to the kitchen, thinking that my days were filled with work and my evenings were filled with Raiden. I needed to figure out how to spend some time with KC so I could share things I needed to share without sharing things I couldn't, and load up on more resources to fight fire so I'd be prepared when the time came.

Because no matter how good it was, and it was good, always underlying it was the understanding the time would come. I knew because I felt it and my wise grandmother told me.

And I had to be ready.

14

SCORCHED

Sunday Evening

I PARKED MY Z next to Raiden's Jeep, got out and jogged on my toes to the side steps of his place.

He'd taken off early yesterday morning on unexpected business, which stunk, but he phoned an hour ago saying he'd be home soon and telling me to meet him at his place.

So I'd had my first almost two days without Raiden in a week.

I should have taken this time to phone KC, get her up to speed and load up my resources. More to the point, I should have taken this time to phone my pregnant friend and make sure all was good in her world too. She had a toddler, a husband who worked long hours, a huge house and volunteered at three charities.

Both of us being busy, it wasn't unusual for days to pass where we didn't check in, even weeks sometimes. But since she had a lot going on in her life and I did too, this was not one of those times I should allow things to slide.

I just didn't do it. I didn't know why.

Maybe I was holding this time precious.

Maybe I was just an idiot.

I determined I'd call her the next day as I jogged up the steps and stopped outside Raiden's door.

I knocked, calling, "It's me!" I turned the knob and stepped in.

Raiden was at the kitchen-ish area wearing cargos, boots and a skintight tee.

My belly fluttered. I smiled and greeted, "Hey," as I turned and closed the door.

I turned back, saw he'd turned fully toward me and I was about to take a step toward him before he said, "Stop."

I went still and my head tipped to the side.

"Is everything okay?" I asked.

"Don't move until I tell you to and then do exactly what I tell you to do."

Oh my God.

He was in the mood to play.

Instantly, I felt myself get wet between my legs as my heart started hammering and every inch of my skin began to tingle.

He leaned back against the counter, crossing his arms on his chest, his eyes moving over me. I added my nipples getting hard to the rest, marveling at the same time, glorying in the fact I had all that from him with a few words and a look from across a room.

As the seconds slid by, my breath began to get heavy.

Suddenly, he asked, "Trust me?"

"Yes," I answered immediately.

"Then on all fours, baby, crawl to me and do it slowly."

Oh God.

I didn't know if I could do that. I didn't know why, but I didn't know if I could do it.

I held his eyes.

"Raiden," I whispered.

"Do you trust me?" he semi-repeated.

I swallowed before I nodded.

"All fours, Hanna. Slow."

I closed my eyes telling myself this was Raiden. He wouldn't humiliate me. He wouldn't debase me. I could trust that he would lead this to something good.

I opened my eyes again, kept them on him and slowly dropped to my knees. Keeping my head back, I fell forward to my hands.

Then, as he asked, slowly, I crawled toward him.

My stomach lurched when I was almost there and he uncrossed his arms and moved toward the bed. Confused, guessing, uncertain I liked this, the word "solitaire" on the tip of my tongue, I followed him.

He stopped at the foot of the bed.

I stopped two feet away from him, neck arched way back, eyes on his.

"Closer, Hanna, then up on your knees," he ordered.

Fighting my nerves, I moved closer then got on my knees. I still held his gaze but my face was in line with his groin.

Okay, this could be better.

Maybe.

His hands went to his belt but his gaze stayed locked to mine as he pulled himself free.

"Hands on my hips, give me your mouth, honey," he demanded.

Okay, this was better.

I did as I was told. I opened my mouth in preparation for taking him, but I didn't give it to him. He took it, sliding inside.

Yes, this was better. So much so, I moaned against his cock.

"Fuck, my girl likes my cock," he growled, sliding in and out of my mouth. "Hand in your shorts, Hanna. Touch yourself while you suck me off."

Okay. Yes. Totally.

This was better.

I left one hand at his hip. The other one I used to open my shorts and I slid my hand inside. The minute my fingers touched the slick skin, I whimpered.

I sucked, I licked, I touched myself, my hips rolling and pressing into my fingers and I moaned against him. It was good, way good, tremendous and I worked him harder, urging him to take my mouth with my hand it his hip.

"Gentle," Raiden said, his voice hoarse. "I fuck your face, I do it gentle." My mouth sucking hard, my eyes lifted to his, he groaned, "Fuck," and started thrusting into my mouth.

Yes.

I was working him. He was taking my mouth. My fingers were moving as desperately as my hips when he pulled out of my mouth and hauled me to my feet.

"Clothes off, now. Everything. Then get ready for me. Hands and knees on the bed."

Okay. Now this was *way* better.

Rushing, I carried out his commands.

No sooner was I in place when his cock slammed into me.

My head flew back and I came.

I wasn't close to finishing when he pulled out, turned and lifted me and impaled me on his cock. Then I was back to the bed, taking him until he thrust to the root, grinding, and he came for me, his face in my neck, his teeth sinking sharp into my skin.

That would leave a mark, but then again Raiden often left a mark.

He liked it and, it must be said, I did too.

Raiden barely finished before he rolled so I was on top, he tucked my face in his neck and his voice was rough when he murmured, "Missed you, honey."

I loved it that he did.

I closed my eyes and pressed closer.

He was gone only two days, but I missed him, too.

Before I could share this, his arms around me got tight and he went on, "But don't do that shit again."

I blinked into his skin.

"Sorry?"

"You didn't like it."

I lifted my head and looked down at him. "I didn't like what?"

"Crawling for me. I know it now, won't ask you to do it again, but you didn't like it and you did it. Don't do that again."

"But I…" I stopped and started again. "You told me to trust you. I trusted you. And it worked out in the end."

"Did you like it?" he asked.

"I was…uncertain," I admitted.

"You're uncertain, we do something else and talk about it later. After we talk about it, maybe you'll want to try it, maybe you won't, but it's your choice, Hanna. You're on your hands and knees on the floor. Not me."

I studied him. I couldn't tell for sure, but it seemed he was upset.

I had to know so I asked quietly, "Are you angry at me?"

His eyes narrowed and his arms around me tensed. "Fuck no."

"Then——"

"Babe, you gave that to me, beautiful. But playing is supposed to be fun *for both of us.* You play like we play, communication is crucial."

That was great and all, but I was confused. "If you knew I didn't like it, why did you keep doing it?"

"I've done stuff to you; you hesitate but then let go and get off on it. I couldn't tell until you were closer and I moved. I had more planned, saw you were not with me on that, gave you my cock."

"Oh," I whispered.

"So promise me. I know you wanna please me and I like that a lot, honey, but don't do that shit again."

I looked into his unusual, amazing green eyes. I felt his hard body under mine, his cock still inside me, his arms tight around me and I knew it wasn't Raiden who was going fast.

I was picking up speed, doing it as I fell, falling faster and faster.

For him.

Obviously, I didn't share this.

Instead, I said, "I promise."

"Good," he muttered. He lifted up, touched his mouth to mine, fell back and ordered, "Now slide off me, baby. I'll be back."

I slid off his cock and rolled off his body. Raiden leaned in to kiss my jaw and his lips trailed down so the tip of his tongue could glide over where I knew his mark would be before he reached out and pulled the afghan over me. Then, naked, he got off the mattress and moved toward the bathroom.

I gathered the afghan close around my body and stared at his pillowcase.

I'd crawled across a room for Raiden Miller.

And it was him, not me, who stopped it because I didn't like it.

Which made me look back and like it.

Because he just demonstrated (again) he was going to take care of me.

I needed to pull it together and start the process of taking care of him.

I just didn't know how. What I did know was that what I just did was not the how.

So I had to figure out the how.

The Next Morning

THE MINUTE THE hinges on the door screamed after Raiden went into the bathroom to deal with the used condom, I tossed the covers back, grabbed his tee from the side of the bed and pulled it on as I dashed silently across the room to the picture frame.

I needed to understand.

But I couldn't ask him.

Not yet.

I had to learn as much as I could without him.

Snatching up the frame, my heart racing, my eyes moved over the faces of the men in the picture.

I couldn't take them in, not yet.

I was looking for Raiden.

I found him, back row, one in, his arms slung around both men at his sides. The one at the end had a scary-huge gun, butt to his hip, barrel pointed out. Raiden was smiling, white teeth, eyes crinkled, dark wraparound shades pushed back on his head.

Mouthwatering.

Heartbreaking.

I just got the chance, and pulled up enough courage, to take in the faces of the two men on either side of him before I heard the toilet flush.

I put the frame back where it was, raced across the room to the kitchenish area, anxiously searched it and found a coffeepot nearly hidden by boxes and dishes. At the bottom was a thick, black crust.

The hinges screamed right before I snatched the handle of the pot and yanked it out making boxes and bowls teeter dangerously. I turned and saw Raiden exit the bathroom buck naked.

I lifted the pot and asked, "Seriously?"

A smile spread across his face as his feet brought him to me. He pulled the pot out of my hand and tossed it on the mess on his counter where it miraculously found purchase between a box of Fruit Loops and a stack of bowls. His hands then went right to my booty, he lifted me up and I wrapped my limbs around him.

He walked us to the bed, turned his back to it and we went down, me on top.

After we bounced, I lifted up to forearms light in his chest and he announced, "We'll shower, go to Rachelle's, get breakfast and coffee."

"Affirmative," I agreed and his lips curled up then I declared. "I get battle pay for doing it, but I'm taking an afternoon this week in this crazy den of yours to sort it out so it's livable. By that I mean you can make a pot of coffee and close your drawers since the rest is beyond my capabilities, unless you rent me a sandblaster and give me a credit card at Sears."

His body was lightly shaking under mine when he asked, "What does battle pay consist of?"

"I'll decide later."

"Babe, you make this place livable, whatever it is, I'll pay it."

I grinned at him.

He was already smiling and he kept doing it.

It hit me suddenly that in all the time I spent waiting for him, watching for him at Rachelle's, when I saw him he would grin at his sister, and maybe if he was in a good mood he would smile, but other than that never did he walk in or move through smiling.

And I'd never heard or seen him laughing.

But he used to do it all the time before he left. I'd watched avidly in the corridors and cafeteria at the high school when he did it. Even if things at home were tight and he lived with the knowledge that his dad was a massive dick, he had a good life back then and he demonstrated that frequently.

And now, again, he did both a lot with me.

"I like to see you smile," I told him softly, sliding one hand up his chest, his neck, fingers in his lush hair but I moved my thumb out to stroke his jaw.

"I know, honey, since you find ways to make me do it and you find them often."

I was thrilled he noticed.

So thrilled, I swept my thumb down his jaw then bent to touch my lips there.

When I lifted up again, his arms wrapped tighter around me and he asked, "Plans for the day?"

"Shipments piling up. I have to spend the day in town sorting that out and hauling them to the Post Office. This doesn't make me happy because I like making afghans, not packing and shipping them, but life happens, you deal. You?"

"Meet in Denver," he answered.

I pressed my lips together, his eyes dropped to my mouth and one of his hands slid up and into my hair.

"Hanna—" he started, but I interrupted him.

"I didn't get a chance to ask. Did everything go okay while you were away? I mean, an indication of the success of your endeavors is that you returned unscathed but did you, uh…get your man or whatever?"

His eyes were warm and amused at my question, but they grew serious which made me mentally brace.

"Business went good," he answered. "And it sucks we're on this topic, but the time was gonna come and this is that time, so you gotta know, with my business, I'm gonna be away like that a lot."

I had a feeling. My guess was that fugitives did not hang around Willow (or I hoped not) just so he would be able to be home for dinner every night.

Although I had that feeling, I didn't like that feeling. I also didn't explore it and was not going to ask about it.

Now I had it confirmed.

Unfortunately.

"Right," I mumbled.

"The look on your face states plain you like that about as much as me, babe, but that's the way it is and I hate to pile shit on top of shit for you, but it's rare I can take care of business in a couple of days. It usually takes longer and sometimes it takes weeks."

Fabulous, I thought.

I said nothing.

He rolled me to my back, got up on a forearm in the mattress but bent close to me.

"Hanna, my crew, I send them on assignments and I take a cut. It's a low percentage that covers admin only. They do the work, they get the fee. That's not gonna change. I don't live good off their backs and I'm never gonna do that. That means to work toward my retirement plan I gotta take jobs."

"Okay," I agreed, but did it unhappily.

Seeing as Raiden didn't miss much, he didn't miss this.

Therefore his eyes got soft and he threw me a bone. "While I'm gone, I'll touch base frequently."

That mollified me, but only slightly.

"Okay," I repeated.

He dipped closer and informed me, "My retirement plan is a good one, baby. Done at forty."

That was better, but it was also eight years away.

Eight years of criminal activity.

Clearly, my face said what I was thinking because Raiden kept talking.

"Hanna, stop listening to me and start hearing me. I'm tellin' you, my retirement plan means I'm done at forty."

"I heard you."

"Okay, now think about why I'd be tellin' you that."

My brows went up and I guessed, "It's an interesting tidbit to share?"

"No, it's because I expect you to be in my bed when I'm forty."

I blinked as my heart swelled so big, it was a wonder I didn't start choking.

Therefore my voice was wheezy when I forced out, "We've been seeing each other just over a week."

"You crawled across a floor just because you thought it would get me off. I'm pointing that out, not because watchin' you do that was so hot it made me so fuckin' hard I thought I'd come before you got halfway across the room, which, incidentally, is true, but because that's just one indication of the immensity of what you give me. And you drop to your hands and knees to give it to me, trustin' me with that when we've been together just over a week. You think I'm a man who's got a thing that good, he'll let it go?"

"No," I whispered.

"That would be fuck no," he corrected.

Holy Moses.

"Raiden—"

"Touchin' base frequently, takin' jobs that'll get me where I wanna be, comin' home and lookin' forward to it for the first time in years, to an actual home, and it's a home I look forward to getting back to because my woman is there. I know it's gonna suck, and it will for years, but that's what I gotta give. Will that work for you?"

A home I look forward to getting back to because my woman is there.

Totally. That would totally work for me.

I left out the "totally" as well as all the rest and just breathed, "Yes."

I watched his eyes flash then heat.

"Fuck me, I knew it would," he growled before he repeated, "Fuck me."

We were there. We were new but we were what we were and we both under-stood it, new or not.

So it was time for more than just this. I knew it by just how much all that meant to him and that he would let that show. Therefore, I pushed up and in and managed to roll him with me on top.

I straddled him, planted my hands in his chest and leaned toward him.

"I'm not going to ask if I can tell you something, but I am going to tell you that I have something to tell you," I announced.

Raiden stared at me a second before the intensity left his eyes. His mouth twitched, his hands came to my hips, dipped down under his shirt that I was still wearing, then back up, spanning them, skin against skin.

"Have at it, honey," he invited.

"I've seen the picture," I shared and his head tilted slightly against the mattress.

"Come again?"

"Of you and your buddies in desert fatigues."

Just as I suspected, the pads of his fingers dug in. His lips stopped twitching, his face went blank and his lips started to say, "Han—"

I pressed lightly into his chest and got closer. "You talk straight, I'm going to try that and hope it works, but if it doesn't, we'll go back and try something different. But, Raiden, it isn't unusual when soldiers see stuff, do stuff and come home feeling disenfranchised and —"

I said no more because I was flying through the air.

I landed on the bed near the edge, and by the time I pulled myself up Raiden was yanking on a pair of cargo pants.

Okay, that did not go well.

"Raid—"

"Goin', you be gone when I get back."

My breath froze in my throat.

I swallowed to clear it, got up to my knees and sallied forth a lot more cau-tiously. "Okay, that didn't work, honey. Maybe—"

He viciously yanked a tee down his chest then bent toward me so fast, he was a blur.

Hand in the mattress, other hand pointing an inch from my face, he growled, "Do not think you know shit. You do not know shit."

Motionless with fear, I forced my lips around the word, "Raiden—"

"I'm goin' and you be gone when I get back."

It took a lot but I lifted my hand, curled it around his wrist and started, "Sweet—"

Savagely, he yanked his wrist free and I went flying into both hands catching myself on the bed. I pushed myself up just in time to see him, boots in one hand, stalking to the door.

I started to scramble off the bed, calling, "Raiden! Please. I screwed up, honey. Please, let's talk."

Before I got to the door, he'd slammed it behind him.

Which meant before I could get it open, he was already yanking open the door of his Jeep.

And this meant, before I got to the bottom of the stairs, he was reversing then he was gone.

Four Hours Later

I DID NOT go into town to sort my shipments.

No. I'd walked too close to the fire and got singed by the flames. I needed to do what I could to try to bank that fire and retreat.

So I stayed at Raiden's house. I cleaned his coffeepot. I did his dishes. With what I had to work with, I made minimal sense of the mess on his kitchen-ish countertop. I folded the clothes in his dresser so the drawers shut. I found a scary-looking but functional washer and dryer in a small room in the back corner of the bottom level and did three loads of laundry, including his sheets, which meant I cleared most of the floor, hung his clothes and made his bed.

Once I'd cleaned the coffeepot (my first priority), I'd made coffee.

I'd also opened the fridge. The wave of scent that assailed me was so strong I was certain my hair wafted back with it and the visions that assaulted my eyes didn't bear thinking about, so I erased my memory of them and shut the door as fast as I could.

Therefore, I'd eaten nothing.

I wasn't hungry, but I figured I needed to keep my strength up for the battle that lay ahead.

But after what I encountered in the fridge, caffeine was just going to have to do.

When I heard the Jeep return, my nerves, already frayed, unraveled completely. I was so rattled it was a wonder I wasn't a trembling mess, incapable of movement.

But this was important.

People were counting on me, and two of those people included Raiden and me.

So I held the good times close, like Raiden Miller telling me he was going to retire at forty and he expected me to be around when that happened, pulled myself together and faced the door, not having any idea that I was about to get scorched.

The door opened and a lick of white-hot flame surged through instantly when Raiden's eyes fell on me.

"I told you to be gone," he growled.

I beat back the blisters and told him, "We need to talk."

"You need to be gone," he returned.

"I need to apologize. That was—"

He leaned toward me.

"Bitch, get *the fuck outta my sight*!" he roared and all my skin boiled away.

I braced against the pain. "Raiden, please—"

"Hanna, trust me, you stand there two more seconds, I'll make you gone, and babe, you do *not* want me to do that."

He'd do that. He would. He'd been physical with me before when he had a point to make. And his face told me he was not making threats.

Thus I didn't wait two seconds.

Not even one.

I ran to the door, even though he was still in it, and my heart splintered when he got right out of my way.

He didn't call after me. He didn't even come out to the landing at the top of the stairs. I knew because, stupidly, when I was in my Z, I looked up.

The door was closed.

I hit the button. My baby purred, I reversed and tested her speed and maneuverability on the way home.

She did not fail me.

I did this crying.

Because a Boudreaux didn't cry unless she was in a place she could do it.

And my baby was that place for me.

Eleven Fifteen That Night

I WAS DRIVING home from my warehouse in town. The afternoon slid by without me able to take my mind off Raiden, so I piled my SUV with finished afghans and went into town, thinking that work would keep my thoughts occupied, so I'd done it for hours.

This, incidentally, was an unsuccessful endeavor, but at least all my shipments were ready for the post.

I cleared the woods around my house and my heart started thumping when my headlights fell on Raiden's Jeep parked in front of it.

As I drove down the side drive, I saw him illuminated by the porch light, standing on the porch, leaning against the post he'd leaned against when, just days before, he said beautiful things to me.

I looked away, rounded the house and hit the garage door opener.

I parked my SUV next to my Z and shut down the ignition. I hurried out, hit the garage door button and hustled out the side door of the garage and across the yard toward the house.

I saw Raiden's shadowed frame rounding the house.

I stopped myself from running, but hurried up the back steps, keys in hand. I now had two locks on the back door (there were two on the front door too; Raiden put them in as he said he would on the day he said he would) and I had the key ready that luckily unlocked all of the new locks on my house, so no fiddling with switching keys.

Just unlock and in, and maybe, if I was lucky, I'd get in and keep him out.

The outside light lighting my way, I yanked open the screen door and got both locks unlocked, but not before I heard Raiden's boots on the steps behind me.

I didn't look back. I pushed in and let the screen door fall behind me.

Except it didn't shut for two beats.

He was in.

Since any further efforts to keep him out would be futile, I left the interior door where it was, tossed the keys on my kitchen table and moved through the kitchen like he wasn't there.

I didn't make it even halfway.

Two arms closed around me from behind and my back slammed into Raiden's front.

My body went stiff.

I felt his face in my neck.

"I'm a dick," he whispered into my skin.

Men thought they could get away with a lot if they admitted that.

Sometimes it worked.

Sometimes, like this time, it didn't.

"You need to leave," I stated.

His face came out of my neck, but his lips went to my ear, "Hanna—"

"You need to leave," I repeated firmly.

"Baby—"

"I crawled across a floor for you and I said one thing out of kindness and concern and you walked out on me, came back, called me a bitch and kicked me out."

"Honey—"

"No one calls me a bitch, Raiden."

"Give me one second—"

"No one makes me crawl across a floor."

His arms got tight and his voice went low. "You dropped to your hands and knees yourself, honey."

"Because I trusted you then. I don't trust you now."

One of his arms shifted up, his hand curling around the side of neck and he whispered, his voice thick, "Listen to me."

With a mighty heave, I tore from his arms. I whirled, lifted a hand and shoved him in the chest, all the while shouting, "You need *to go*!"

His hand caught my raised one and held it firm.

"Baby, *listen to me*."

I ripped my hand from his and took two quick steps back.

"No. I was wrong. I thought I could withstand the heat, but I can't. I wanted to go slow. You pushed us to go fast and I didn't have enough good times stored up. Your smiles, your laughter, there wasn't enough to take the heat. You're a *criminal*, Raid, and I accepted that. This, I can't accept. I don't know what hideous thing happened to you over there except I know it was hideous. But there weren't enough good times when you were the Raiden I know you are to beat back the Raiden that fucked-up shit that happened to you forces you to be that gives me the times I need to endure the inferno within. You lose control of that and I'm close, it doesn't just consume you. It consumes me."

"I don't want you to know what happened in that hellhole, Hanna," he returned.

"You think that hasn't escaped me?" I shot back. "The subject barely comes up before you shut it down, but Raid, if you think I don't feel the squeeze of the elephant always in the room, you clearly think I'm a bigger idiot than I actually am."

"You feel that squeeze, babe, and you can still breathe. If you actually knew, you wouldn't be able to live with that shit. You wouldn't be able to sleep. Your mind would go over it and over it, and since you weren't there, you'd make shit up that would torture you, but I promise you, none of it would be as bad as it actually was."

"I believe you," I retorted. "What you don't understand since you won't let me *talk about it* is that I'd rather live with that torture, the pain of which I would eventually be able to control, than let you hold on to that pain without even a little release so *you* can learn to live with it."

He went silent but the air in the room got heavy.

I ignored that and declared, "You need to leave."

"Hanna—"

"*Leave!*" I shrieked, losing it, hands straight down at my sides in fists.

Then I was going backwards, tripping over my feet, and I would have gone down if Raiden's arm wasn't around my waist.

Then I couldn't go down because my back was flat to the wall and Raiden's front was pressed to me.

Not this again.

I couldn't help it. It freaked me out when he did this so I started panting.

"You know why we do that shit?" he asked.

I didn't answer. I didn't even know what shit he was referring to, but that wasn't the only reason I didn't answer. I didn't answer because he was scaring the pants off me.

He didn't need me to answer.

He kept going.

"It's not for God, babe. And it's not for country."

My chest pressed repeatedly against his with each breath.

Raiden went on.

"It's for pretty girls with tanned legs that go up to her goddamned throat who ride asinine bikes and who'll drop to their hands and knees, crawl to you and take your cock, moaning against it, making you so fuckin' crazy you think your dick's gonna explode in her mouth."

Oh God.

"Raid—"

"You might think that's jacked, but it's not. It's the goddamned fuckin' truth. Whether you got that in your bed before you go or hope to find it when you get back, that's why you do it. You do it for her. You do it to keep her safe. You planted kids inside her, or you hope to, you do it for them. You get home in one piece, she's your reward." His body pressed into mine and his face, partly shadowed, came to within an inch of mine. "*You're* my reward, Hanna."

My reward.

Oh.

My.

God.

Raiden wasn't done.

"I didn't know it. When I was over there doin' what I had to do, I didn't have any fuckin' clue. I didn't know until I saw you laughin' with Paul Moyer. Jumpin' up and down with Bodhi, all excited about shiny ribbons on your goddamned bike. So into me you could barely talk when you ran into me. Sittin' outside on your goddamned fuckin' *porch swing* of all fuckin' things, lookin' right out of a fuckin' movie. So cute. Christ, no joke, it hurts even to look at you and believe you're real. So fuckin' sweet, I remembered there's a God and He actually likes me. You go over there, far fuckin' away, you see shit, you do shit, you get through it knowin' that's home. That girl in the porch swing, knittin' a goddamned afghan and drinkin' wine, carefree because you sweat and bleed so that's what she can be."

Listening to his words, the tears didn't bite the backs of my eyes.

They spilled over in streams.

"Sweetheart——" I whispered brokenly.

"And you know what gets me?" he asked, but didn't wait for an answer. "What gets me now is the guys who bled out in the sand and they didn't have that. They died never understanding. They died not gettin' even a taste of their reward. They thought they were protecting home and country, but they didn't even know what home was. I feel for the women who lost their men in that sand, Hanna, it guts me. But their men died havin' that. Knowin' why they died. Knowin' exactly what home means and knowin' it's worth it. Those guys who didn't have it, they died without a fuckin' clue. And every day since I clapped eyes on you, finally under-standing, it fuckin' *destroys* me."

His words destroying me, I wrapped my hands around the sides of his neck and held on. "Raid, sweetheart, please——"

He talked right over me.

"So I'm not leavin', Hanna. I was a dick and I hurt you and I cannot promise it won't happen again, so I won't. And you are not wrong. This shit burns in me, what happened, what I saw, what I did. But most of all who *I lost*. Every one of those guys deserves to have their reward sittin' in a porch swing or however that shit comes about. When I say those men were good men, there isn't a word in the fuckin' dictionary that describes how good those men were. And there are only four of us left who know exactly what that means. They died and I'm here and I found my reward and I'm not letting it go. Because if they were alive and they knew I let something that important slip through my fingers, they'd be pissed at me. And if they can sacrifice everything so you can have your porch swing and I can come home and have everything they lost, *you* can fuckin' learn how to take the heat and give it to me."

"Okay," I agreed immediately.

I agreed so immediately, Raiden's, "Come again?" was clipped and short with surprise.

"Okay, honey. I'll learn how to take the heat."

The room went completely still. Everything suspended. It felt like time stopped.

I gasped as, unexpectedly, I wasn't against the wall anymore.

Raiden chanting, "Jesus, fuck, Jesus, fuck," he had an arm around me and I was sailing across the room. I landed on my back on the kitchen table with Raiden bent over me.

His hands started to move on me, his mouth came to my neck and I wrapped him in my arms, turned my head and invited in his ear, "Take what you need."

At my words, his body stilled. Then abruptly he stood up, taking me with him so I was seated on the edge of the table, Raiden standing between my spread legs. With a hand cupping the back of my head, he pressed my cheek to chest, his other arm around me. His body bowed so it formed a hard, strong shield around me, protecting me from nothing, but, Raiden being Raiden, instinctively still protecting me.

I kept my arms around him, pressed deep and held tight.

"Jesus, fuck," he murmured.

I was silent.

Raiden fell silent too.

I gave it time.

Raid took it.

Then I asked gently, "You never talked about that with anybody, have you?"

"No."

He only gave that to me.

I shut my eyes and held on tighter.

I said no more and gave it more time.

Raiden took it.

I opened my eyes and promised him, "Like the rest, that gift is just for me and I'm never going to share it with anybody."

"Jesus, fuck," he whispered.

I again went silent, but I held him closer.

It was Raid that broke it this time.

"That 'okay' you gave me, does that mean you're still with me?"

"Yes, honey."

I heard him draw in a deep breath.

"Right," he stated. "Then I need you to promise me something."

"Okay," I replied.

He pulled away, cupped my jaw in both hands and tipped my head back so he could catch my eyes in the dim light.

"I give you shit, you do not eat it. Like today, you give it back to me. We'll work it out, Hanna, but we'll do it like we did it tonight. Not you getting where my head is at and bowin' to that in hopes you takin' my shit eventually turns something in me. Today, I stepped far over the line and that is not cool. After I calmed my ass down, I spent the last two hours standing on your porch, thinkin' if I put a little more strength in that throw you wouldn't have landed on the bed, and the thoughts of what I could have done to you have been brutalizing me. That, babe, I promise I'll check. The other shit, if it overwhelms me and I try to force it down your throat, you force it right back."

"Agreed," I replied.

He dug the pads of his fingers in slightly before they relaxed.

"Okay," he murmured.

I lifted my hands to wrap them around his wrists and took a deep breath.

Cautiously, I said, "Honey, I hesitate to mention this, but I think today proves you've got some issues to work through."

Both his hands slid back into my hair. He stuffed my face in his chest and burst out laughing.

I found this reaction both a relief and a little weird, but even so, as usual I wanted to watch him laugh, but couldn't because it was dark and my face was smushed to his chest. He didn't stop laughing before he let me go, but bent at the waist, put a shoulder in my belly and hefted me up.

This action was more than a little weird *and* a surprise, so much so I straight up girlie shrieked, "*Raid!*"

He turned and walked out of the kitchen, ordering, "Quiet, babe, I got some issues to work through."

Oh boy.

I knew what that meant.

"Um…maybe we should find alternate outlets to battle that burn," I suggested to his back, my hands gripping his tee at his sides.

I became perplexed when he didn't head up the stairs, but unlocked and opened the front door and strode out to the porch. He turned right as he swung me around. He was still holding me, but we were front to front and I frantically grabbed hold of his shoulders so I wouldn't go flying when his hands slid down and yanked my knees up at his sides.

Then he sat in the porch swing with me astride him and tipped his head back to look at me.

"Think, my girl fucks me in her porch swing, that'll beat back the heat."

"Raid——"

"Or at least *that* heat. She'll be building a better kind of fire."

I needed to get a handle on this situation.

Therefore, I slid my hands up to his neck and dipped my face closer. "Sweetheart, I like this idea but I'm being serious."

"Baby, bein' seriously serious, you are the only thing in four years that has come close to getting me to a place where I can even begin to think I might be able to bear those flames."

Automatically my hands shifted to his face, palms to his cheeks, fingers wrapped around his ears and my forehead dropped to his as my eyes closed.

"I want to be that for you," I whispered.

I was both alarmed and pleased that each one of those seven words was weighted with precisely just how much I wanted what I said.

"Good, honey, 'cause you already are."

Oh God.

I *loved* that.

I pressed my forehead into his tight before I angled my head and touched my lips to his.

I moved back slightly, opened my eyes and gave in. "All right, then I suppose I'll fuck you in my porch swing."

I watched him grin. "My own personal firefighter with pretty blue eyes, fantastic tits and a sweet pussy."

His words were sweet (well, most of them) and it was good he was breaking the heavy mood, but I still pulled back a bit and slid my hands down to his neck. "Uh…just to say, I'm not comfortable with you always talking about my sweet, uh…you know."

His brows shot up. "You crawl on the floor for me and you don't like me talkin' about your pussy?"

That sounded ridiculous.

"Well—"

"Hanna, I love my sister's cooking so I'm gonna talk about it. Mostly I talk about that to her so she knows what she does is good and people appreciate it. I love Broncos football, so when they're playin', I'm gonna watch it. I'll probably talk about it, though it's unlikely I'll talk about it to you. You're a girl, so even if you like the Broncs, women can't talk football. And don't get uppity, that shit is just plain true. And I love my baby's pussy, so I'm gonna talk about that too. If you want me to share that with my crew and not you, I'll fill them in on the goodness I got in my bed, but just sayin', I'd rather talk about it to you."

I would rather that too.

"Fair enough," I conceded.

"Now, are you gonna fuck me or spend the next hour talkin' to me?" he asked.

"I suppose I'll fuck you," I muttered.

His voice held humor when he returned, "Obliged you'd make that sacrifice for me."

I glanced at the swing then at him. "Uh…how *do* I fuck you?"

"Babe, you've ridden my lap before."

This was true.

I looked to the porch ceiling at the hooks holding up the swing then down to Raiden. "Do you think the swing can withstand this activity?"

"I don't know. What I do know is I wanna find out."

I bit my lip and looked back at the hooks.

I then stopped biting my lip and surveying the hooks because I was up, and then I was *up*, again being hefted on Raiden's shoulder.

"*Raid!*" I shrieked.

"We'll break the swing in another time, maybe when you're drunk," he muttered, walking to the front door.

"I was good," I told his back. "I was just strategizing."

"You don't have to strategize a mattress."

This was true.

We were inside and he'd started up the steps when I informed him, "You can put me down. I can walk."

"Waste of time," he replied. He turned on the landing, kept ascending and asked conversationally, "So, clue me in. When am I Raiden and when am I Raid?"

I held on to his tee and stared at his back a second before I asked, "Sorry?"

We entered my room and he made for the bed. Five strides (I counted) and I was on it and he was on me.

Only then did he explain, "In the beginning all you did was call me Raiden. The first time I seriously tested you and that sweet pussy of yours," he grinned when I frowned and went on, "you let Raid slip. No one calls me Raiden. Not even my mom. Now you're usin' 'em both, and I'm tryin' to sort out where your head is at with which is which."

I thought about this and shared, "I'm not certain there's rhyme or reason to when I use one or the other."

"Is there rhyme or reason to anything you do?"

For a second I contemplated my eyebrows (which I couldn't see, but I tried) before I looked back at him. "Not really."

He'd been smiling when my eyes came back to him, but after I spoke, his smile faded. He cupped the side of my face with his hand, thumb sweeping my cheek then my lips before he said quietly, "My reward."

I let that slide through me as I turned my face and kissed the palm of his hand.

After I kissed his palm, I said there, "I love it that you think that."

"Know it," he corrected and I looked back at him.

"Sorry?"

"Don't think it, Hanna. Know it."

That slid through me too, and I melted (more) underneath him.

"One more thing before we tear each other up," he said.

"What?" I asked.

Then, even with all that had happened that day, and especially all that had gone on the last twenty minutes, as usual, Raiden Miller still managed to rock my world.

He did this by saying straight out, with feeling, "Thank you, baby, for forgiving me."

Slowly, I closed my eyes.

I opened them, planted a foot in the bed, rolled him and straddled him, closed them again and kissed him.

Raid kissed me back.

15

BIG DICK

Six Weeks Later

I WAS CARRYING Spot out of the vet to my bike, or more like struggling to keep upright under the burden of his weight, when my phone rang. I put him in the basket. He sat on his ample behind, said, "Meow" and faced forward, telling me he was ready to roll.

You could have colored me stunned when Grams and I (well, mostly me, Grams just sat there offering suggestions) grappled for a half an hour trying to get Spot in his kitty carrier. This didn't work and ended with Spot desperately shoving his kitty face into the corner of the latched screen door and pushing it open enough to force his fat cat body through it. As I chased after him, he heaved his big body onto a porch chair then the porch railing where he jumped into the basket of my bike, making the bike sway precariously. By a miracle, it held. Spot sat down, turned his head and stared at me.

We'd already learned the hard way through earlier tussles pre-visit to the vet that, for reasons only known to Spot, he only accepted rides in Grams's Buick. So even though Grams never drove it anymore, it was Spot's checkup day. Therefore I rode to Grams's house and was going to take the Buick and Spot into town.

Shockingly, Spot seemed absolutely fine in my basket. I tested this theory, rode around in Grams's driveway awhile, then into town. He rode with me, happy as a clam, kitty nose pointed to the wind rushing through his fur. The vet receptionist wasn't pleased we showed with no carrier, but she was no stranger to Spot and had learned herself prior to kitty claw laser therapy it was best just to let him have his way, so she didn't say a word.

Spot behaved himself the entire time.

Seemed the cat liked bicycles.

Go figure.

"Crazy cat," I muttered, grinning.

I pulled my phone out of the back pocket of my shorts and saw the display.

My grin turned into a huge smile, I took the call and put it to my ear.

"Hey, honey," I greeted Raid.

"Baby, where are you?" he replied.

"In town outside the vet. Spot's annual checkup."

Silence then, "Drop him off and get home. I'm five minutes out of town. I'll meet you at your place."

A happy thrill raced through me followed by an excited one.

"No. I'm jumping on my bike now and I'll meet you at yours," I told him.

"Hanna—"

"Raiden," I cut him off. "I'll meet you at your place, but you have to promise me you'll go there but won't go inside. Wait for me."

More silence then, softer, "Hanna."

Then nothing but that soft "Hanna" sent another thrill racing through me.

"I'll pedal fast and me and Spot will be there in ten minutes," I said.

"You and Spot?"

"He's in my basket."

Another period of silence then, shaking with hilarity, "All right."

"No going inside," I warned.

"No going inside, baby."

I mounted my bike. "Right. See you soon. Missed you, honey."

"Yeah, me too."

Another thrill.

"'Bye."

"Ten, babe."

He hung up.

I tossed my phone in the basket with Spot.

He looked down at it, turned his kitty face to me and said, "Meow."

"You can share with the phone, buddy," I told him.

"Meow." He didn't agree.

"Suck it up," I ordered.

He glared at me an annoyed kitty moment before he turned to face forward.

I threw back the kickstand, put my feet to the pedals and motored.

THE LAST SIX weeks, Raid was out of town on jobs for three.

This didn't stink as much as I thought it would (though it still stunk) because he did what he said he would do.

He touched base with me. Frequently.

This included him calling during the day at random times. It also included him calling every night right before he went to sleep.

The first time he'd woken me when he did this, which was the third time he called me at night.

He'd been upset he'd woken me and murmured, "I'll call earlier next time."

"No," I'd replied sleepily. "I want to know you made it through the day and you're going to sleep so you'll wake to face another day. Don't worry about waking me."

He'd hesitated and his deep voice was warm and sweet when he agreed, "All right, honey."

Then he did as I asked, calling every night before he went to sleep.

But when I said he touched base, I meant we talked as in *talked*.

Surprisingly, even though we'd been through a lot, but still were relatively new thus didn't know each other all that well and he was a *man*, he was also a man who could have conversations on the phone. It helped we knew a lot of the same people and he cared about what was happening.

He asked me about my day, my business, what was going on in Willow, what I had planned for the next day and he shared about his. Where he was. What he ate. When he thought he'd be home. Nothing deep about his work but he didn't keep things from me, including if he was frustrated, leads had dried up, informants were jacking him around or things were taking longer than he thought.

Weirdly, these conversations were getting-to-know-you conversations that, if we were normal, we would have had during dates. He learned about the vacation

I took last winter. He learned I loved snowboarding. I learned he hated onions and thought Jerry Seinfeld's standup routines were funny. And we planned to go to Crested Butte when the snow started falling and to find a beach when winter turned bitter and we needed to escape to the sun.

Needless to say, learning about Raiden and planning getaways and vacations was *awesome*.

When he was home, life fell into a rhythm. I knitted. I did my thing with Grams. We all went to church and ate breakfast together at the Pancake House. I saw to my business. Raiden saw to his in Denver and in the back room of Rachelle's Café, where I learned he met with his "crew," who I did not, however, meet…*yet*. This last was Raiden's word when he told me he would introduce me to them when "shit slowed down." He was also a good neighbor, and at his sister or mother's request, would go off to do things like the yard work for Grams.

This meant between jobs he wasn't idle. It also meant we had our own things to do, but ended our days together like we would if we were normal.

That was awesome too.

In fact, everything was awesome and had settled in a good way without anything rocking my world.

Except one thing.

Deep into the night one night at my house, the bed moved with such force I woke, sensed Raiden awake and I pressed my hand resting on his chest into his skin.

He shifted swiftly, taking me to my back and reared back a fist like he was going to strike me.

I gasped and tried to scuttle out from under him but got nowhere, because his arms closed around me and he tucked me under his big body.

"Fuck," he muttered.

"What's happening?" I asked anxiously, my entire body tense, but I felt the tension in his and it wasn't like mine.

I was freaked out.

He was strung tight.

"Fuck," he repeated.

"Raid—"

He let me go, rolled to his back, lifted both hands to his face and rubbed.

I got up on an elbow and watched.

"Talk to me. What just happened?" I urged.

I half-expected him to evade my question, but he didn't.

He dropped his hands.

I felt his eyes on me in the dark and he shared, "I dream."

Oh boy.

"Dream?" I pressed gently.

"Snippets of memories. Sometimes shit is warped and not what happened at all. But I dream."

"About——?" I didn't get it out, but he knew what I was asking.

"Yeah."

He dreamed about what happened with his unit.

God.

Worry suffusing me, or, it should be said, *more* worry, I placed my hand light on his chest and asked carefully, "Does this happen often?"

"Not anymore. Not since you. But it happens."

That felt good, but it was also bad.

"Have you talked to anyone about it?" I asked.

"Yeah. Just now. You."

I was his "reward." I gave him whatever it was he needed to feel like he might begin to battle the burn.

I loved that. I loved it a lot.

But I was no miracle worker.

"I was thinking more like one of your buddies," I suggested.

"That's not gonna fuckin' happen."

I went silent.

Macho man, too strong to share, to release, to let go.

Darn.

"I'll get a handle on it," he told me.

I stayed silent.

He lifted up, his arms closed around me and he moved us to our sides, face to face.

"With you, it's goin' away," he assured me.

"Okay," I replied.

"Give it time, they'll be gone."

"Okay, honey."

His lips found mine in the dark for a touch before he rolled to his back taking me with him so I was tucked to his side. Then he lifted a hand and sifted it through my hair again and again, and as he did this, I felt the tension ebb from his body. So I lay there with him, cuddled close, holding him tight.

Eventually, his hand stopped sifting through my hair and his arm wrapped around me. Minutes later, it went slack and I knew he was asleep.

I didn't sleep.

I prayed Raiden Miller found it in himself to get a handle on his dreams.

Because if he hadn't come to after he reared back to strike me it would absolutely not be good.

It was a useful reminder to me that hellfires burned all the time.

Even in sleep.

And I was no miracle worker, but if Raid didn't get a handle on these dreams I was going to have to find a way to learn to be.

For him *and* for me.

———

IN THE LAST six weeks I also had time to check in with KC and fill her in. I didn't go for the gusto, but I did share that things were good in a way they'd be that way for what could be ever.

She was beside herself with glee.

But I waited until Raid was away on a job before I went to her house for dinner and laid it out.

KC had been at her stove, stirring while I sat at her kitchen table with her baby girl, Samantha. Samantha's feet were planted in my thighs, her chubby fingers gripping mine and her plump legs were bouncing when I shared what I could. That was to say, not much of anything, including Raid's dreams, but I shared my concerns about Raiden being scary bossy, and adding getting physical to that scary.

This got me a weird response.

KC burst out laughing.

I turned to look at my friend with her shining, to-the-shoulder light brown hair, her bright, wide hazel eyes and seven months pregnant belly and I said quietly but with meaning, "KC, seriously. It freaks me."

She trained those hazel eyes on me, still smiling. "Okay, babe. But get over that."

"Sorry?" I asked.

"Uh…with your, mine and the female half of Willow's citizenry avid contemplation, I don't think it's lost on any of us that Raiden Ulysses Miller has got a big dick."

He did, this was true. I had seen the physical evidence up close (and felt it, sucked it, stroked it, etc.), but I was hoping the female half of Willow's citizenry had not.

"You might want to explain that," I suggested as Sam lunged forward and giggled, so I wrapped my arms around her and took over the bouncing.

KC's eyes moved to her daughter then took in her daughter with me and her face got soft.

Then she spoke.

"Right. The dudes you picked in the past," she shook her head, "not all that. Except Pete was okay, but he was no Raiden Miller."

"You're telling me something I know already," I pointed out.

She put the spoon in a spoon holder, turned down the burner on the stove and her attention to me.

"What I'm saying is, you don't have experience of men who are *men*. I know you have issues with Mark, and I love you more than I already loved you that you've kept those to yourself. I hope it's because you understand I'm not an idiot and I wouldn't put up with his shit if it wasn't worth putting up with. And he gives me shit, Hanna. He's arrogant, and that can sometimes, not often, lean toward him being a jackass. But he loves me. He loves Sam. He finds ways to show us that every day. No, that isn't right. He doesn't *find* them. He just *does* it, no effort. He gives it naturally. And I know he'd die before he let anything harm either of us," she put a hand to her protruding belly, "*any* of us."

That was huge.

And beautiful.

And something I never knew because I never brought it up.

"Holy Moses, KC," was all I could think to reply.

"So," she went on brightly, grinning at me, "when he's an arrogant ass, tells me what to do or whatever, acting totally like we'd been hurtled back to the 1500's and I was his chattel, I smile, nod and do whatever I want."

I thought about doing this with Raiden and it didn't give me the warm fuzzies.

KC read my face, wagged a finger at me and kept talking.

"This is what you have to learn. Don't backtalk. Don't explain. Don't protest. Don't fight it out. Just say, 'All right, honey,' and do whatever the hell you want. For example, just this morning, Mark said, 'Make tacos tonight, babe,' before he kissed me good-bye. No 'please'. No, 'are you feeling like tacos?' Just 'make them.'" She tipped her head to the side. "Now, are we having tacos?" She shook her head. "Hell no. We had tacos two days ago. I get he loves my tacos, but eff that. My friend is coming over and I just had tacos. Furthermore, I have to make the damn things. So we're having a roast. You serve company a good roast. Not freaking tacos."

She moved to the fridge while I asked, "Isn't he going to be ticked?"

She yanked something out of the fridge as Sam slurped at my neck and I cuddled her closer.

KC turned to me and closed the fridge. "Do I care? If he wants tacos, he can come home and make them."

"So he doesn't get ticked?" I pushed.

"If he does, he keeps it to himself. Usually he just shakes his head and grins at me then gets a beer. I've decided to take that as him accepting the woman whose ring he slid his finger on. If he's storing this shit up to list it out in the divorce papers, so be it. His loss."

If Mark was doing that, it *would* be his loss.

Absolutely.

But I was getting the feeling Mark would never do that.

KC moved back to the stove as I asked cautiously, "But does he get physical?"

She poured something in a pan and turned to me. "No. That said, when he says something like he's going to change locks to keep me safe, I don't argue with him. That's his job. I give him the freedom to do that."

"So you think it's okay that Raiden did what he did?" I pushed.

"I think he didn't hurt you and I think he could, easily. I think what that said was, you were standing in the way of him doing something he thought was important, that something was looking out for you, so it actually *was* important and he did what he said he was doing. He got you to shut up and pay attention. It isn't me, babe, who can say if that's right or wrong. I wasn't there. You gave me what you gave me, so I only have that to go on, and this is my opinion. It doesn't have to be yours. But if he doesn't hurt you, hit you, smack you, shake you but simply moves to make a point that you need to shut up and listen to him because he's relaying something important, honestly, Hanna, I cannot think that's wrong."

"He backs me into walls," I blurted.

She blinked before she whispered, "What?"

"Well, we've had some kind of...*intense* conversations," I thought it safe to share. "One, well, I mistook his intentions about me and accused him of using me..." Her eyes got big and I held on to Sam with one arm but waved my other hand in front of my face. "Long story, and not for now, but he kind of lost it when I wouldn't listen to him. He backed me into a wall, caging me in, got in my face and explained he is most definitely into me."

When I was done speaking, her lips were parted and her eyes were glazed.

"KC?" I called when she didn't say anything.

"Shh," she shushed me. "I'm having an orgasm."

It was my turn to blink.

"What?" I asked.

KC came back into the room and focused on me.

"Honey, in the bedroom department, Mark rocks my world, every time. *Every time*. He does not mess around and has made it clear from the very beginning he has two priorities when we hit the sheets, and the first one is me. No joke. And my man is *hot*. Yum...mee. Four years of marriage, a kid and one on the way and I still get a shiver just hearing his car pull up the drive. And still, the thought of Raiden Ulysses Miller backing me into the wall and telling me he's into me. Instant orgasm."

"But...it scares me," I told her.

"Then start paying more attention to him and less to whatever it is mucking up your head," she returned. "Honestly, Hanna, with how cute, pretty, funny and sweet you are, plus those legs, which I would murder for, I do not get and never have, and I've told you that a million times, why you're so damned shy and don't know down to your bones you deserve a guy like Raiden Miller. But that's you and I love you, so..." she shrugged, "whatever. I'm assuming that he again didn't hurt you. He just wanted your attention, and babe, he's got a fine way of doing that, which a lot of women would *pay* him to do with them."

"Maybe I should explain more around how that came about and you'd under-stand," I suggested.

"No," she shook her head. "Maybe you should stop trying so damned hard to find fault in him or yourself or how you both are together and just accept him for who he is and how he is as he's obviously doing with you. I get you wouldn't quite believe, after years of crushing on that guy, that this can be real and it's all going to go up in a puff of smoke, but girl, the time is nigh *to believe*."

My breath caught at what she said, all it meant and just how true it was.

KC wasn't done.

"Hanna, babe, I haven't seen it, but word on the street is that you've got that man caught so tight in your snare he's never going to get loose. But the thing is, he has no intention of trying. The whole town *knows this*. The only one who doesn't *is you*."

Oh my *God*.

She was right about that, too!

KC kept on talking.

"Now, what you have to get is that he is who he is and he does what he does, and none of it, girl, with the *way* he is, is a surprise. This would be a different conversation if he took his hands to you, caused you pain, said shit that made you feel like dirt, but what you've said, he does the opposite. I'm not saying you need to be a timid little mouse and let him walk all over you. Get in his face. Make him back you in a corner. But then see it for what it is. Babe, if he cares about you and what you two are talking about so much he cages you in and gets in your face, that says *volumes*. Intense discussions, hell, even fights mean there's *feeling*. It means that what you two are building is worth it to him. If he didn't give a shit, if he thought you were a pain in the ass, he knows he can get it good elsewhere, so he wouldn't put any effort into it and he'd just walk away."

This *totally* made sense.

"I *so* should have talked to you weeks ago," I told her.

KC smiled huge and twirled her hand in her hair.

"This is me. I got an alpha who pisses me off at the same time he rocks my world. Four years, five and a half with all that dating and engagement malarkey, I'm an expert." She again wagged her finger at me as she invited, "Now, seeing as I have years on you, you now should feel free to come and share with Auntie KC *all* there is to Raiden Ulysses Miller. *Everything*. I'll give you insights, girl, set you up to go forth and keep your badass hot guy happy."

I smiled back. "I'll do that, honey."

And I would. Well, I *mostly* would.

She kept smiling at me as she came toward me, stopped, bent and kissed the top of Sam's head loudly. That pretty baby head shot back. Sam let me go and smacked KC's face, giggling.

KC giggled back and moved to the stove.

I thanked the Lord I had a good friend right before Sam turned her attention and I got a baby fist to the face.

This was when I started giggling.

Sam and KC giggled with me.

———

Thus, KC MAKING me feel better about just about everything, when Raiden told me he was off on a job, and, "Babe, this one is gonna last awhile," I'd felt safe to do what I wanted to do.

I wasted no time in doing it.

Therefore, Raiden had been gone for over a week and now he was back. I was pedaling to his den, excited to unveil what I had to unveil, hoping like all heck he liked it so much that maybe he'd back me against a wall to share that with me.

And I was looking forward to him doing it.

16

BOUNTY HUNTER LANGUAGE

I PEDALED UP the lane to Raiden's den and saw him, arms and ankles crossed, leaning against the side of his Jeep.

At the sight, my thrill went wild.

I smiled huge and came to a stop behind his Jeep. He grinned back at me, his shades moving over me, Spot and my bike before he started to shake his head and pushed away from the car.

I shoved down the kickstand and hopped off. I started skipping to him, but stopped, dashed back and wagged my finger an inch from Spot's kitty nose.

"Be good."

He made a kitty face at me, which said clearly he would be whatever the heck he wanted to be.

I ignored him, turned and saw that Raiden had almost made it to me. There wasn't a lot of room, but still, I ran it, took a leap and landed in his arms.

They closed tight around me.

I returned the favor with all four limbs then dropped my head to his that he'd kindly tilted back and laid a hot, heavy, wet one on him.

One of his hands slid to my behind and he let me.

I broke the kiss, smiled down at him and said, "Hi."

"Hi," Raid said back.

I battled a shiver that one syllable, said in his deep voice, shot through me and went on, "Welcome home."

"Yeah, baby. You're absolutely fuckin' right. That was a welcome home."

I didn't bother battling the shiver that time and gave him a four limbed squeeze.

He returned the favor with two arms and a hand tightening on my booty.

"Right. Put me down," I ordered. "We've got to get Spot and go inside."

His mouth twitched before he dropped me to my feet and let me go.

I skipped back to Spot and hoisted him out of the basket.

"Meow," he protested.

"Quiet, we have to show Raid his surprise."

"Meow." Spot, like most cats, wasn't big on surprises.

"Shut it, buddy," I ordered, walking up to Raiden, whereupon Spot made a break for it, a successful one, amassing his considerable kitty bulk and launching it at Raid.

Raiden caught him. Spot shoved his way up Raid's chest, planted his paws in Raid's shoulder and started purring.

"Crazy cat," I muttered.

Raiden chuckled, one arm under Spot. His other hand came out and tagged mine.

"You got a surprise?" he prompted.

"Right," I replied and bounced in my flip-flops. "Let's go."

Up the stairs we went, Raiden in front of me, Spot glaring at me over his shoulder, still purring.

When we got to the top, I shoved onto the landing, took the keys from Raiden's hand and said, "Let me."

I didn't give him a choice.

So excited, I was again bouncing on my flip-flopped feet. I unlocked his door, threw it wide, took a huge step in and cried, "*Voilà!*"

Raiden and Spot followed me. Raid lifting a hand to push his shades back on his head, he shut the door and looked around.

I danced around.

"Right!" I cried. "Starting here!"

I danced to the bed, stopped and looked back at him.

"Your sheets and comforter were nice, honey, but they didn't match my afghan so I got this!" I motioned to his bed on the floor, the box springs now covered in a gray sheet, the mattress and pillowcases too. The comforter on top was black and gray, and there were two more pillows and some (not too many, only three) masculine but cool toss pillows scattered across the top.

I moved to the head of the bed.

"Mrs. Bartholomew was talking and said her grandson needed a project for Wood Shop. I got an idea, got the measurements and he made this!" I exclaimed, touching my hand to the black painted, low wood shelves that now ran the length of the head of the bed. Raiden's paperbacks were shoved in the shelves, two attractive lamps on top at either side.

"I got the lamps," I went on. "And Barry came in and wired an outlet in the floor under the shelves, so no more extension cords."

Still holding Spot and standing just inside the door, Raiden stared at the bed, but I was so wired, I didn't take that in and skipped to the kitchen.

"This, I found in an antique shop up Harborough Road. Killer sale," I shared, running my arm down the front of a tall, wide cupboard against the wall like I was a game show hostess. "Up top, on the shelves, as you can see, cereal, protein powder and foodstuffs." I bent and opened a cabinet door at the bottom of the cupboard. "Dishes down below."

I straightened and sideways skipped to touch the range.

"As you know, Rachelle is redoing her kitchen at home and this is her old stove, but it's only two years old and she's a cook so she only gets the best, so even used it's still *awesome*," I announced.

More sideways skipping to the fridge.

"Same with the fridge, and look!" I pointed at the water and ice dispensers in the front door. "Hugh came around and plumbed it so it *works!*"

I threw open the doors, but turned to him, forcing my face to mock grave.

"Now, I hesitate to share with you that I disposed of the lab experiments you were conducting, but Grams got you all this food and all of it is actually *edible*."

I was so into my show, I didn't notice that he still hadn't moved as I closed the fridge doors, did more skipping toward the table and I threw an arm out to indicate the wardrobe.

"Barry and Hugh fixed that to the wall so it's sturdier and not in danger of collapsing, and I WD-40'ed the hinges *and* the hinges on the bathroom doors so no more haunted house sounds."

Winding it up, I threw my hand wide toward the floors that now had a scattering of rugs.

"More sale items from the antique store," I grinned at him, "from me. They don't cover a lot, but they're better than wood, especially when it starts to get cold."

I leaned a hand onto the back of one of his kitchen table chairs and kept right on babbling.

"They have a kitchen table at the antique shop I hope won't sell, seeing as I kinda ran out of money, but it would be *great* in here, and bonus: no padding on the chairs so none of it can come out. They're also having a furniture sale at this place in Denver that has fabulous stuff. I almost bought you a couch, but I figured a man is usually one with his couch, so you'll have to go with me."

I threw my arms wide and finished.

"What do you think?"

Slowly, Raiden bent, dropped Spot to his feet which caused an audible "*thump*" when the cat's weight hit floor. Spot instantly waddled away to start exploring as Raiden slowly straightened again, put his hands on his hips and locked eyes with me.

"My kids are growin' up in a farmhouse."

That was what he said.

And that was weird.

It was also disappointing.

I felt myself deflating.

"Sorry?" I asked.

"What's this shit telling me?" he asked.

My head jerked.

"This...*shit?*" I asked back.

He threw a hand out to indicate the space. "Yeah. This shit."

My spirits plummeted.

"I...well, I'm not sure what you're asking me, Raiden, but obviously I screwed up again and—"

"Plant my sons in you, babe, they're growin' up in a farmhouse in the woods outside of town."

My hand went back to the chair so I could lean my weight into it, seeing as my legs got suddenly weak.

"What?" I whispered.

"The fridge and stove, that's cool. Gonna rent this place come winter, and decent appliances means we can jack up the rent. The rest, Hanna, total fuckin' waste of money and time, unless you're tellin' me something with this shit."

I was feeling a lot of things. Some of them I thought were good, others didn't feel so great.

"Waste of—?" I began.

He took two steps toward me, stopped and put his hands on his hips again.

"What are we doin' here?" he asked.

"I wanted to show you my surprise," I answered, my voice growing small.

"No, Hanna. That's not what I mean. I'm crashing here. You gotta know that. This is no place to live. It's a necessary evil. I think we both know that Willow is it for us and if I wanted to waste time that at least I *thought* both of us had no desire to waste, I'd get a condo in Jackie's complex or somethin'. Seein' as at least I'd prefer not to waste time, I'm not gonna jack around with a year lease which is the only thing she gives. So what the fuck are we doing here?"

I took a calming breath and stated, "Okay, honey, I think I need a bounty hunter language lesson or you need to revert back to normal people speak because I went all out to make your space livable while you were gone and you aren't being real cool about that."

"No?" Raid fired back. "Well I've been waitin' for you to pull your finger out and ask me to move to your space, so you makin' *my* space, which is shit space, more livable and spendin' money until you got no more tells me *you* don't intend to ask me to move into your space."

My fingers curled deeper into the vinyl of the chair.

Raiden kept talking.

"We're young, we got time and we haven't talked about this, but here it is. I want three sons. My dad was a massive dick and I want to erase that memory by havin' boys and givin' them what I never got. I also love my sister and always wished I had another one, or a brother, so my boys are gonna have a lot of siblings. The way you're settled in that house, babe, you're not leavin' it, and I don't want you to. It's you. It's the perfect place to build a family. Now, my question, in what

I hope is normal people speak, is are you tellin' me with this shit we're gonna dick around, or are we gonna get on with it?"

Was he serious?

"Get on with…get on with making babies?" I pushed out.

"No, babe," he bit out, impatient. "Get on with *us* so we can eventually get on with makin' babies."

"I…uh, you…um, don't really go slow, Raid, but this is a bigger leap than most," I told him. "Normal couples discuss this stuff."

"Clue in, Hanna. I am not normal, neither do I ever fuckin' wanna be."

"I think I got that," I said softly.

"But you're right. Couples discuss this stuff. And I'll point out, we're standing here discussing it."

He was sort of right.

"Okay," I agreed.

"So we dickin' around or what?" he asked.

I ignored my heart hammering and asked, "Breaking all that down, are you saying you want to move in with me?"

"Uh…yeah, Hanna. I decided to have a home again, and after I spend time dealin' with scum, I wanna come *home*. Home to a house with a porch swing where I can wash that scum down the drain and climb into bed with a woman who puts an outrageously fat cat in her ludicrous basket on her ridiculous bike. *My* woman."

"My bike isn't ridiculous," I protested.

"Babe," he leaned in, "*it is*."

I ignored that too, and semi-repeated, "You want to move in?"

His brows snapped together. "Are you sleepwalking?"

I stared at him.

Raiden scowled at me.

I let go of the chair, ran across the room and jumped into his arms.

Again he caught me, but this time he had to plant a foot behind him so we both didn't go down.

I didn't care.

I wrapped my legs around his hips, but I placed my hands at the sides of his head and looked down at him.

"They were on sale so no returns, thus the hunters get to enjoy the rugs, but that cupboard will *kill* in my kitchen," I declared and the surprise in his face cleared, it warmed and he immediately started walking.

Toward the bed.

"I take it I just got myself a porch swing," he remarked.

"You so totally got yourself a porch swing," I replied.

We went down on his mattress, me on my back, Raid on a knee then on me.

"Shame not to break in these sheets," he muttered.

"Upon your return, that was on the top of my to-do list, after introducing you to your new abode, which kind of went sideways in a happy way, so now we can tick that off and move on," I returned, and he grinned.

His grin faded and he announced, "That afghan on your bed is gorgeous, honey, but we're switchin' it out with mine."

I *loved* that.

I trailed my hands up the material of his tee at his back. "Works for me."

"Am I gonna traumatize the fat cat if he sees me fuckin' you?"

"As you know, his name is Spot, and he's immune to trauma. You can't feel it if your life is devoted to dishing it out."

Raiden grinned again, then, finally, he shut up, bent his head and kissed me.

Two hours later he left me in his bed and took Spot back to Grams in his Jeep.

Upon return, he reported Spot nearly broke his neck by draping himself on it while Raid drove.

I snuggled into his big body, giggling and wishing I'd seen that.

At that point Raiden rolled over me and we spent some more time breaking in his sheets.

17

ABSOLUTELY

The Next Morning

THE PHONE RANG. It was Raiden's cell. My eyes opened and I saw gray sheets.

I smiled.

Raiden's body, spooning mine, didn't move.

"Honey, you awake?" I whispered.

"Yep," he replied.

"Your phone is ringing."

"I know. I'm ignoring it."

"Oh."

I fell silent.

So did Raiden's phone.

I snuggled my booty into his lap. His arm around my belly tightened and I drifted into a doze.

His phone started ringing again.

"Fuck," he bit off.

"I'll get it," I offered.

"Babe—"

"I got it," I said.

I shifted out of his arms and instantly, a drowsy, crazy, insane but hopefully hot idea came to me.

He was moving, but I moved too, to my hands and knees, wearing nothing but his tee. The hem slid up over my hips as I crawled to turn around then proceeded to crawl down the bed.

I got there, looked down my body at Raiden who was up on a forearm, his eyes glued to my behind in the air.

They came to my face. I gave him a naughty grin (or what I hoped was a naughty grin) and kept my booty in the air as I turned back and reached for his cargo pants.

His phone had stopped ringing by the time I dug it out of his pocket, but I kept it in my hand as I turned and crawled back.

I stopped close and stayed on all fours, but placed his phone on the bed in front of him.

"I took too much time," I pointed out the obvious.

His eyes burned into mine. "Babe, tell me right now you aren't fuckin' with me."

"I'm *kind of* fucking with you in the hopes that you'll return the favor," I replied.

Even as his eyes flashed, Raiden didn't miss his opportunity.

"Crawl over me and stay on all fours when you get there," he ordered, rolling to his back.

My body did a delicious shiver as I did as I was told until I had my knees and hands in the bed around him, my body suspended over him.

His hand instantly went between my legs. It felt good, my head fell between my shoulders and I let out a little mew.

"Wet. She's not fuckin' with me," he muttered.

My eyes moved to his and I knew what he saw because I could barely focus and he had to see what he was doing to me.

"Stay still, let me play. Can you do that for me, Hanna?" he asked, his fingers still toying between my legs.

I could do that for him.

I could do anything for him.

"Yes, honey," I whispered.

I stayed still. Raid lay under me, his eyes moving on my face, his hand moving between my legs. His other hand glided over my body and he played with me.

And played with me.

And kept doing it until my thighs were trembling and I whimpered.

"Now you're ready to eat," he growled and he disappeared, sliding down the bed, and before I knew it his fingers curled around my hips and he pulled me down to his face.

My head shot back and I moaned.

He pulled me deeper.

"Honey," I gasped.

I was close.

He sucked hard on my clit.

I couldn't help it. I shot up to sitting on his face. His hands pulled me down deeper, and I rocked myself against his mouth, chanting, "Ohmigod, ohmigod."

I was even closer, sliding along the edge when his mouth was gone.

"No," I breathed.

I felt his chest at my back, his arms moving around me with his mouth at my ear. "Do not come without me."

"Raid."

His hand dove between my legs and my hips bucked.

"Raid!"

"Hold on for me, honey."

"Oh God," I whimpered.

His fingers slid back and plunged up.

My head fell back to his shoulder.

His other hand moved under the tee, up, and his fingers closed around my nipple, tugging. My whole body jolted.

"Raiden, I can't hold on."

"Hold on."

My hips rode his fingers desperately. "I can't."

"Fuck, you're wet, so goddamned hot," he growled. "Fuck yourself, baby."

I already was, but I slid my hand down his forearm, wrapping it around his between my legs and did it harder.

"Beautiful," he rumbled. "That's it. Harder, Hanna."

"I'm going to come," I whispered.

"You're gonna wait for me. Ride those wild, honey." I kept at his fingers. His thumb came out and pressed against my clit, I cried out but kept going. "My girl. So fuckin' wild. Give that wild to me."

"Please, honey. I can't hold on any longer," I begged.

"Then get my tee off and position for me. Your choice, baby, show me how you wanna take me."

I instantly pulled his tee off and threw it to the side. I got on my back, opened my legs and he was there, slamming into me.

I rounded him completely with my limbs, lifted up my hips, glided my nails up his back and pleaded, "Harder, Raid."

"Fuck. Wild. Wet. Mine," he groaned, his face in my neck.

I felt his teeth scoring gently up a tendon there. I liked that so much that my nails dug in deep, my legs convulsed and my head pressed back. I felt his teeth sink into the flesh of my shoulder where it met my neck and I came apart at the seams.

Raiden was right there with me.

I came down to feel Raid's lips gliding soft against the flesh his teeth had sunk into, something he did often, branding me, and after, finding a way to soothe my skin with a tenderness that was unreal in its beauty.

I loved it.

I wrapped my arms around him and tightened my legs, and his lips moved up to the skin beneath my ear.

"Pretty sure you broke skin again, wild one," he muttered with deep, throaty approval.

"I can confirm she did," a woman's voice came from the room.

I tensed, blinked, prepared to have a heart attack, but Raiden moved.

He pulled out and rolled off at the same time he yanked the afghan over me and barked, "What the fuck?"

I clutched the afghan to my chest, pushed up, stared at the busty, blonde skank I saw Raiden making out with months before, and my lungs seized.

"Didn't know whether to clap or join you," she remarked.

"Ohmigod, ohmigod," I started chanting for a very, *very* different reason this time.

"Please fuckin' tell me you did not walk in my place and watch me fuck my woman," Raid snarled in a way that anyone in their right minds would say they did *not*.

She seemed immune. She hitched a hip, planted her hand on it and shared, "I caught, '*Harder Raid. Fuck, wild, mine,*' but that was enough. Talk in town is right. You're steppin' out on me."

What?

My mind refused to process that. Actually, it refused to process anything. The only thing it could think of was getting the heck out of there.

Immediately.

I sprang from the bed, holding the afghan around me, and raced to my clothes on the floor.

"Hanna, get back in bed." I heard Raid order, but I had my panties and I was struggling to keep the afghan in place as I pulled them up my legs.

"Hanna?" she sneered. "Jesus, Raid, you do vanilla. This is so disappointing."

"Bitch, advice. Disappear. Right now and I don't see you again," Raiden returned in a warning low that scared the dickens out of me.

I could tell he was moving around, but I was concentrating on yanking up my shorts.

The woman again was immune to Raid's warning.

"Honey, you feel like adventure, Raid likes it wild and I got time. You just gave him good but you and me together? We'll blow his mind."

She was talking to me.

And I couldn't believe what she was *saying* to me.

I ignored her and held the afghan up with my teeth as I wrapped my bra around my ribs.

"Meg, not gonna say it again. Get the fuck out," Raiden growled.

"Talking from experience, sweetie," she kept ignoring Raid and addressing me, "brought him a friend. He likes it like that. I know 'cause he came back for more."

Pain seared through me, but I couldn't focus on it since I heard a terrified squeak. My head shot back and I watched Raiden, in nothing but cargo pants, zipped but not buttoned, dragging her by her upper arm across the room.

He opened the door and bodily tossed her out onto the landing.

"Swear to fuckin' *Christ*, I see your fuckin' face again, I'll devote my life to makin' yours a misery. You feel like testing me, you'll learn real fuckin' quick I do not fuck around. And after that shit in there, Meg, I'll go slow and enjoy every fuckin' minute of flushin' your life right down the toilet." He threatened then finished, "Nod if you get me."

"All bark, no bite, 'cept sweet, vanilla Hanna in there. Now *she* gets your teeth when I thought they were all for me," she jeered.

It might make me weird, and before this I didn't care, but I could make Raid lose it often, lose control enough to sink his teeth into me and, as I mentioned, I loved that.

Actually, to be honest, I *lived* for it.

And it wasn't just mine.

I closed my eyes against the pain, then opened them, dropped the afghan and bent to snatch up my blouse.

"You just tested me," he whispered sinisterly.

"Do your worst," she hissed. "No one steps out on me."

"Clue in, bitch," Raiden shot back. "I haven't spoken to you for months. A man fucks you *and* your friend, no dinners, no movies, there's nothin' but pussy to step out on and pussy that's just pussy is also just nothing."

"You dick!" she yelled.

"Yeah, I'm a dick, but you're a goddamned cunt. Prepare, Meg," he finished on a warning and slammed the door right in her face.

He twisted the lock, turned to me and lifted a hand to drag his fingers through his hair, his blazing eyes landing on me.

"Fuck me, so goddamned hooked on my woman, come home to her in my bed, didn't lock the motherfucking door," he ground out.

"I need to leave," I whispered, and Raid focused on me.

"Come again?"

"I need to go," I told him.

"Hanna, that was jacked. Do not take her shit in," he ordered.

"I need to go," I repeated.

"Babe, again, that was jacked. I was never seein' her. It was casual. You cannot step out on what's not real. I haven't even spoken to her in fuckin' *months*. Way longer than you've been with me. She heard talk about us, woke up feelin' like bein' a bitch and came here to spread that joy."

"You called her a cunt," I reminded him.

He threw out a hand, his brows shooting up. "Were you not just here? She *is* a cunt."

This was not debatable. I didn't even know why I brought it up.

I moved on. "Did you…did you…*bite her* like you do me?"

"Honey, why do you think that shit tripped it for me? That bitch has never had my teeth. Fuck, *no* bitch has ever had my teeth."

Thank God.

At least that was good.

Again, moving on. "Did you sleep with her and her friend?"

His torso swung back, his mouth snapped shut and I knew.

God.

I moved toward him because he was at the door, my head was down, my mouth repeating, "I need to leave."

I didn't make it. He didn't step out of my way this time. He wrapped his hands around both my arms and moved me back five feet into the room.

I tore free and stepped three wide strides to the side, lifting a hand his way.

"Don't touch me!" I hissed, and this time his head jerked.

"Hanna——"

"You had threesomes!" I cried.

"I told you, baby, we do not wanna go over past shit."

I threw out both hands. "Now I understand why," I shared. Then I asked, "Are you going to want to do that with me?"

"Fuck no," he clipped.

"And I'm supposed to believe that?" I pushed.

He leaned toward me and bit out, "Fuck *yes.*"

"How?" I snapped. "She's right, you like it wild. When is vanilla going to wear off, Raid?"

Suddenly he smiled huge, white and amused, and if I wasn't mistaken, he looked like he was fighting laughter.

"This isn't funny!" I yelled because it dang well wasn't!

"Honey, you're wrong. You thinkin' you're even close to vanilla is goddamned hilarious."

"Unh-hunh," I mumbled disbelievingly.

His body started visibly shaking.

Yes.

With laughter.

"*This isn't funny!*" I shrieked.

Raid crossed his arms on his chest, tried to fight back his smile without hiding he was fighting it back and began.

"Hanna, baby, I told you we do not wanna go over past shit and I was right. We really don't. But you've worked yourself up so you give me no choice."

I didn't like this start, but had no chance to share that because Raid kept going.

"Meg spends her days at a shit job she hates and spends most of the rest of her time working out and starving herself, so she's usually in a bitchy mood because she pretty much hates her life, but definitely needs a sandwich. Contradicting that shit, she doesn't have a problem pouring alcohol down her throat and smoking a shitload of grass, which gives her the munchies she refuses to give into, thus the vicious cycle with her bein' a bitch and makin' the mellowing qualities of pot lost on her."

"Raid—" I snapped to get him to shut up because I did not want to know any of this, but he talked over me.

"What I'm saying is she's a party girl, up for anything, and she was up for anything with me. When she was able to tamp down the bitch, we had a good time. Maybe she'll get a guy who's into fake tits, lots of hair and women who care more about having a toned body than they do about having a decent state of mind so he'll put up with the bitch to have her brand of fun, but that guy isn't me."

"Raid!" I yelled this time, but he kept right on going.

"You wanna hear this or not, honest to Christ, if you didn't ignite for me our first time, and you were vanilla—you are fabulous, baby—but you would not be here right now. With you I got the whole package. If I had it with her, she'd be here, not you."

"This isn't making me feel better," I informed him.

His amusement died and he shot back, "Then how's this? You ignite for me, but more, you make me ignite for you. And no woman, not in my whole goddamned life, has made me ignite the way you do."

Wow.

I knew he did that for me, but I had no idea I did it for him.

I shut my mouth.

"You get my teeth, Hanna, 'cause makin' my own personal Peggy Sue go wild for me drives me fuckin' *crazy*. You do it for me like no woman before you. I lose control because you make me and you get my teeth, and what makes that shit better is you love havin' my mark on you."

I fought back the desire to touch my skin, knowing, since it happened before, I'd have to choose my top for that day carefully. Because his mark was always mild, but it was there and he was right.

I loved having Raid's mark on me.

He was far from done and he also saved the best for last.

"She doesn't do it for me, Hanna, because I didn't fall in love with her when I saw her across a street, hair shining in the sun, laughing. You do it for me because you were that girl across the street, your hair shining in the sun, laughing, making me fall in love with you, and I didn't even goddamned fucking *know* you."

Did he just say that?

"Oh my God," I whispered.

"Yeah," he agreed.

He just said that.

"Oh my God," I repeated.

"Yeah, honey," he again agreed.

"I—" I started, but again he spoke over me.

"So thank fuck, my mouth on yours, you explode and let go and latch on to my dick while I'm drivin' your car and dig your nails in my back when you come for me, 'cause, baby, that means you give it all to me. Not one woman in my life gave it all to me and not one man can expect that. Hope for it. Yeah. Get it. No. You give it all, so that means I've got it all."

I stared at him.

He let me for a while then he went on.

"Now, I can share what came before you, and I had fun, Hanna. I make no apologies. But I think it's best we leave it where it lies. 'Cause all you gotta know is it's gonna be you—and only you—until the day I die, because life did not lead me down the wrong path when I fell in love with a girl who had the sun shining in her hair who would eventually not do it for me. You're not just enough for me. You're everything I want. So that works for me."

When he stopped speaking, unfortunately, I started.

"Her breasts are fake?" I blurted.

"Absolutely," Raiden replied.

"You're in love with me?" I kept blurting.

"Absolutely," Raiden replied.

We stared at each other while my heart raced and I fought panting.

Then, not finished blurting, I shared, "I beat you. I fell in love with you when I was six and I didn't know who you were."

I saw the tension flow out of his body. His neck twisted, head dropping forward, eyes closing, and he stood in silent contemplation for a moment before he lifted his head, looked at me and said quietly, "Okay, baby, you win."

"Absolutely," I replied.

It was then Raiden Ulysses Miller scorched me a second time, but I didn't battle this blaze. There was no pain. But that didn't mean I didn't end up branded.

"I told you I didn't dream as a kid of bein' a cop or an astronaut, but I gave a lot of thought to the woman I'd want in my bed. I grew older and gave more thought to that woman, but it was also about the woman I wanted in my life. And she was you. Then I met you. And now, every day I wake up I cannot believe my luck because you're here."

Was he for real?

"How can you take a totally insane situation that should *never* happen, was intense and humiliating, and turn it into something I never want to forget in my whole life?" I asked.

"Because you love me," Raiden answered.

"Oh, right. That's how," I muttered.

His fire burned white-hot.

"Get over here," he growled.

I got over there.

The instant I did he crushed me in his arms, buried his face in my neck and I went up in flames.

It felt great.

Late That Evening

WEARING A TANK and pajama shorts, I lay astride Raiden in my bed, my eyes watching my fingertips exploring his collarbone as I felt his fingertips exploring the skin of my thighs.

"Are you really going to make her life a misery?" I asked his collarbone.

"Meg?" he asked me, and I looked at him.

"Yeah," I replied.

"Yeah," he confirmed, and I tipped my head to the side.

"Really?"

"That situation was intense. It embarrassed you and it should never have happened. She should never have walked in there in the first place, but she did. I gave her a chance to walk away, she didn't. Now she's gotta learn a lesson."

"What are you going to do?" I asked.

"Somethin' that'll make her learn that lesson."

"Raid—" I started, but his hands lifted up and gripped me at my hips.

"You don't fuck with me," he declared firmly. "She fucked with me."

That she did.

I said nothing.

"And she fucked with you," he went on. "She saw you were freaked and she went in for the kill. You don't fuck with me. You absolutely do not fuck with you."

"Okay, but that led to us—"

"No, Hanna. No." He shook his head on my pillow. "Love knowin' you love me, feels good you knowin' I love you, but that was ours to share and we would have eventually done it anyway. But what I share with you in bed is mine. It's yours. It's ours and no one else's. She watched me take you, and I don't give a shit she was only there at the end, that's not hers to have. She doesn't get to hear the words I say to you when I'm inside you and she doesn't get to hear what you whisper to me. And no one, but no one, gets to share in you comin' for me."

I had to admit, he was right. I didn't like that she got that from us either.

"So she pays back," Raiden declared. "She hates her job, she's not gonna have it much longer. She likes to haunt a certain bar, she's gonna find herself not welcome there anymore. She rents, her landlord is suddenly gonna rethink her tenancy. Next time she wakes up and feels like bein' a bitch, she'll think again."

I felt my eyes get big.

"Are you seriously going to do all that?"

"I am seriously gonna do all that."

"Holy Moses. Now I feel sorry for her."

"You should, baby. She's a sad, lonely bitch who needs to eat a sandwich and get a life."

It was mean, but he was funny so I started giggling.

Raiden smiled as he watched, his arms moving to circle me.

When I quit giggling, he remarked, "Speakin' about people fuckin' you. You're gonna be getting a check from Bob."

I was confused. "Bob?"

"Reimbursement for the sports package he sold you on the Z, but didn't tell you he sold you."

I blinked.

Then I shared, "The car came that way."

"Other Z's on that lot that come other ways, honey. You drive that Z like it's your grandmother's Buick. You need sports shocks like you need a hole in the head."

I pushed slightly up, or as up as his arms around me would let me go, and protested, "I do not drive my girl like the Buick!"

"Do you know what sport shocks are?"

I could make a wild stab, but the truth of it was I didn't really know what shocks were.

I decided not to answer.

He grinned at me and ordered, "Cash the check."

"It's not Bob's fault I'm an idiot."

His grin died, his hands slid up my back, pressing down so I was face to face with him.

"Cash. The. Check," he growled, his voice rough and commanding.

I stared in his eyes.

Then I said, "All right, honey."

Raiden looked to the ceiling and cursed under his breath.

I let him and when he looked back at me, I asked, "Do you want a late night sundae?"

His eyes got hot, his hands moved to my behind and he answered, "Absolutely."

Two Days Later

I GOT THE check from Bob.

Then I drove to Bob's.

We sat down and talked.

An hour later, I signed the check over to the local hospice where Bob's mom died.

I walked out to my girl thinking KC was a genius.

Then I called Raiden and asked if he wanted to meet me at Rachelle's for lunch.

Three Days Later, Early Evening

RAIDEN WALKED INTO the kitchen, came up behind me at the stove and kissed my shoulder.

I twisted my neck to grin at him.

He grinned back.

I turned my attention back to the pan thinking it was awesome Raid had a bunch of cargo pants, a trunk, a weight bench and not much else. It took his Jeep and my SUV, two hours that was mostly packing, and he was in.

And this living together business was *the business*.

"Babe?" he called and I turned to him.

"Yeah?"

He was standing at the opposite counter where my opened mail was piled. He had a piece of paper in his hand and was waving it.

"The Hospice?" he asked.

Oh boy.

That paper was a thank you letter from the Hospice for Bob's and my donation.

I said nothing and waited.

"Bob's check," he stated.

Raiden had put it together.

I bit my lip.

He shook his head, dropped the paper to the counter and grinned at the floor as he walked to the fridge, got a beer and walked out of the room.

I turned back to the stove.

Absolutely.

KC was a genius.

18

I WAKE UP HAPPY

Three Weeks Later

I WAS RUSHING around my bedroom, getting ready. I'd spent too much time amongst my perfumes trying to pick one, only to go back to Agent Provocateur, the one Raid liked, so I was running late.

I ran to the closet and was faced with another decision regarding flip-flops when my cell on the bed rang.

I dashed to it, saw the display and put it to my ear.

"Hey, honey, I'm running late," I told Raiden.

"This is good since I am too," he replied. "You wanna save us twenty minutes and I'll meet you at Rache's?"

"Sure, I'll cycle in."

"Babe, drive."

Rough and commanding.

I ignored it. This was my baby. Willow was safe, but my Schwinn spent the night in my garage and nowhere else, except, of course, outside Raid's den. But Raiden didn't sleep at his den anymore, so now it was the garage and the garage only.

"That would mean I'd need to leave my Z in town overnight, and Rachelle will let me keep my bike in her back room."

"We'll leave the Jeep in town and drive your Z home. We can pick it up tomorrow."

This idea was a good one so I agreed to it. "Okay, sweetheart."

"See you there," he told me.

"Right. 'Bye, sweetheart."

"Later, babe."

I stopped dashing around, which meant I had plenty of time to make the perfect flip-flop choice.

I did this, locked up the house and moved to the garage to get my Z.

"Yo!" RACHELLE GREETED on a shout when I walked into her café and the bell over the door rang.

I had failed to note that Rachelle's Café looked like it had been torn off the island of Nantucket and planted in Willow, Colorado. Of course, I'd never been to Nantucket, but I'd seen pictures, and Rachelle's Café was it. It had tables all through and a long counter ran down one side. The rest was all serene colors and breezy décor, and trust me, décor could be "breezy."

It was awesome.

Rachelle was behind the counter with her mom in front of her.

"Hey," I called.

"Hey there, Hanna," Mrs. Miller called back.

I smiled and moved to them.

Needless to say, Raiden and I now living together, and regardless that he was out of town quite a bit, us having actual time together under our belts, we'd been to dinner at Mrs. Miller's house.

I knew her all my life, liked her all that time, and after going to dinner at her place I liked her better. She was as she always was: nice, friendly and easy to talk to, but I discovered she was also a good cook.

I also got to know her boyfriend, Gazza, better. Gazza was English, as in actually from England, but, like he'd been a mountain man his whole life, he incongruously carved logs into totem poles or eagles and the like. He did this for a living, selling them out of the front yard in his house up in the foothills.

He was a good guy that everyone liked. Mrs. Miller and Gazza didn't live together, but they'd been together for years and they somehow made being together in separate places work. It was also known in town that it was Ruthie Miller who wanted her own space and Gazza loved her enough to accept her as she came, which, of course, made everyone like him more.

I thought it was even cooler, knowing now that she was a woman who had a man who was not all that great, so she only accepted life and love on her terms, but put the effort in to make it work.

Then again, I was learning the Millers (notwithstanding Mr. Miller, wherever he was) were cool all around.

I stopped and Rachelle asked, "Dinner or flyby for a coffee à la Rachelle?"

"Raid and I are going to the double feature at the Deluxe tonight, but he's running late so quick dinner, not a flyby."

For some reason, this statement made Rachelle roar with laughter, but Mrs. Miller's face grew bright.

"*Dog Day Afternoon* and *French Connection?*" she asked excitedly.

"Yep," I answered. "Kickass 70's Movie Night at the Deluxe, though they missed a great marketing opportunity by not naming it that and instead calling it 70's Masterpiece Theater at the Deluxe." She smiled big, and having taken in her earlier expression I offered, "Do you want to join us?"

She shook her head. "Love to. Plans with Gazz. Another time."

I nodded, looked at Rachelle and smiled through my hopefully not too nosy question of, "Can I ask why you were laughing?"

"My son," Mrs. Miller started to answer the question I'd asked her daughter, so I looked back at her, "was never a kid who sat around watching TV and playing video games. He also didn't go to movies. He climbed trees. He raced around on that skateboard of his, without a helmet, I'll add, no matter how often I got on him about that. He'd disappear into the woods or the foothills and be gone all day doing God knows what. Him sitting through a double feature is out of character," she explained, but it was not really an explanation for why that would be funny.

Then Rachelle gave me the explanation that Mrs. Miller was too well-mannered to give.

"Not even for his bitches back in the day did he sit his ass in a theater. If they didn't tramp through the woods with him or…" he eyes slid to her mom, "whatever, they were toast. So it's hilarious seeing my big, scary, badass brother so...*totally*...*whipped*."

My mouth dropped open, but Mrs. Miller's snapped loudly, "*Rachelle!*"

She grinned unrepentantly at her mother and made a whiplash noise.

"I'm not sure Raiden is whipped," I shared, and Rachelle looked at me.

Then she laid it out.

Scarily, wonderfully, and as Rachelle had a tendency to do, hilariously.

"Your Honor, exhibit A: the pretty girl calls him Raiden when *no one* calls him Raiden because he fuckin' hates to be called Raiden," she said and I stared.

I didn't know that.

"Rache, don't say the f-word," Mrs. Miller hissed.

Rachelle ignored her mother. "Exhibit B: Raid sits his ass in a movie theater, probably spending those hours not watching the movie but thinking of shit he could blow up, tracks he can race on an ATV or other things he could be using that time getting up to with his girl."

"I'm so sorry, Hanna, when she's on a roll——" Mrs. Miller started to say to me.

"Exhibit C," Rachelle pushed on, but her face changed, her eyes locked on me and she finished, "he lets go and laughs. All the fuckin' time. Finally letting people see he's actually genuinely happy."

I knew what she was saying and my throat instantly clogged.

"I'll get you a white wine," she stated in conclusion.

She ducked her head, hiding her eyes and moved away.

With difficulty, I swallowed and felt my hand taken in Mrs. Miller's.

"Can we sit a bit before Raid gets here?" she requested on a hand squeeze.

I nodded. Still coping with Rachelle's emotional bombs and uncertain about sitting a bit with Raid's mother, I had no choice, so we moved to a table by the window.

She sat opposite me.

I'd learned, seeing as I was dealing with one of the Millers, so I braced.

It was a good thing to do.

"Don't let Rachelle upset you," she said.

"I'm not upset," I assured her, which was kind of a lie. I was upset, but not in a *bad* way.

Actually, I was moved.

"We're just…we're just…" she looked out the window and back at me, "real happy that he's settling down."

I nodded.

Her eyes drifted out the window, and to give her time without my gaze on her, mine did too.

"He talks to you."

It was barely a whisper, but I heard it and I looked at her.

Her eyes were still out the window.

When I didn't have a ready answer, she kept going, aiming her words to me but out the window.

"He came back and he…" I watched her pull in breath, "life changes people. Things happen. It's the way life is, but that was…that wasn't how he was different."

Oh God.

She turned her head and looked right at me.

"He was gone. We tried, Rache and me to…well, he shut us down. He would smile, pretend to be himself, but he wasn't. A mother knows. A sister knows. He wasn't our Raid."

"I know," I replied softly.

"He's back," she declared, and my heart skipped.

"I—"

Her hand shot across the table and closed around mine so hard it caused pain.

"He talks to you." It wasn't a statement but a question.

I couldn't tell her how he did, but he didn't.

I just said, "Yes, Mrs. Miller. He talks to me."

"Ruthie, honey, told you to call me Ruthie."

She did so I nodded again.

Her hand tightened further around mine and I fought back a wince.

"You'll find out, I pray to God, you'll find out that a mother has many nightmares. I know that sounds funny, but don't get me wrong. You're happy to live with them, because to be a mother, you get to create these tiny little living, breathing dreams that grow up to be splendid things. But for a woman with a son, that's the worst. When he's gone. What he's doing. You pray so much he comes back safe, you forget to pray to God to keep him safe from all the ways he could be damaged. My son was damaged."

Her hand lifted mine an inch off the table and her eyes got bright.

Mine did too.

"Thank you for fixing him," she whispered.

I held her hand tight right back, leaned in and said gently, but honestly, "My work isn't done, Ruthie."

"I'm sure. But I have faith in you."

Oh God.

I swallowed back the tears.

"I'll do my best," I promised.

"You already are."

Seriously. This was beautiful, but I could take no more.

"You know," I blurted, "Grams would lose it if she saw me, a Boudreaux, crying in the local café."

"Then pull yourself together, bitch," Rachelle, there with my wine and setting it on the table, declared. "Suck that back." She advised and turned to her mother. "Mom, Raid walks in here and sees you all mushy with his woman, he's gonna lose his mind. Suck it up."

After delivering that, she flounced away.

Ruthie looked at me, her mouth twitching. "She's not wrong."

"You made him so I'm sure you know this a lot better than me, but he can have his macho man fit. It'll blow over, and through it we just do our own thing."

Her eyes lit, her hand let mine go and she replied, "Now I'm seeing how you can wring miracles."

"I give all the credit to Grams and KC. Grams is wise and says it straight. KC lives with an alpha and also says it straight. They're my gurus," I shared.

"If you need another guru, you know where to find me, and do not take that as me asking you to share with me where my son is at. If he wants me to know that, he'll tell me. You're not on the hot seat. Just that I know Raid pretty well and I'm happy to do my bit."

I smiled at her.

She smiled back then shouted, "Rache! I'm off!"

"I'll call Gazz and warn him you're on the emotional warpath and he's up next on your agenda," Rachelle shouted back.

Ruthie had stood through this and she smiled down at me. "Again, she's not wrong."

I giggled.

She reached out and tucked my hair behind my ear.

That was familiar, coming from a Miller.

And sweet.

I stopped giggling.

"Later, Hanna."

"Have a good night with Gazz, Ruthie."

She winked at me and took off.

I sipped wine, looked out the window and dragged in a deep breath to pull myself together.

I sort of accomplished this feat when I felt a presence join me at the table. I jumped in surprise, but turned my head smiling, thinking I'd see Raiden.

It wasn't Raiden.

It was a good-looking, well-dressed man staring at me with eyes that were almost as amazing as Raid's.

Thinking he was going to come onto me, I told him, "Sorry, I'm waiting for someone."

"Yes. And when he gets here, I'm asking you to give Miller a message to give to Knight."

My back went straight, my skin started tingling (and not in a good way) and I stared.

He didn't hesitate.

"Tell him to tell Knight that he's being careful, but not careful enough. Tell him that Nair is not going to give up. Tell him he's going to have to do something in a permanent way to shut Nair down. Do you have that?"

My eyes narrowed even as my hand shifted back toward my cell in my pocket. "Who are you?"

"I'm Nick. Miller will get me. Knight will definitely get me. And you, don't worry. Nair is not focused on Miller. He doesn't even know who Miller is. He's not focused on anybody but Knight. Nair has no clue you exist and doesn't give a fuck. But I needed a way in. You were it."

"If you have something to say to—" I began.

"If you want me to lead them to your man, then yeah, I'll talk direct to him. If you want them to keep their focus on my brother, then you'll tell Miller everything I said."

Before I could reply, he was up and gone.

I blinked after him.

Then I looked around and saw the half-full café, most everyone concentrating on their food or conversation. Rachelle was nowhere to be seen, probably in the kitchen.

I wondered if anyone saw him, but they didn't appear to. No one was paying attention.

I pulled out my phone and had my head down, fingers moving on it to call Raid when the bell over the door went.

I jumped and looked up to see Raiden smiling at me and coming my way.

He rounded the table, bent into me, swept my hair back and kissed my neck. Then he stayed there to run his nose up the skin, which made that skin tingle, but in a good way this time.

He continued to stay there when he whispered in my ear, "Love it when my girl's perfume is fresh. Hey, baby."

"Hey," I replied.

His hand went out of my hair and he rounded the table, shouting, "Rache! Beer and get a move on with two specials. Hanna and I are running late!"

"Keep your pants on!" was shouted from the kitchen.

"Lose some coin if you don't hustle. We can get a slice from down the street!" Raid yelled.

"Two specials coming up!" was returned.

Luckily, Rachelle owned the café, so the Millers acting like, well, what I was coming to know as the Millers worked it.

Raid settled opposite me and he barely got his behind in the chair when I announced, "One minute ago, a well-dressed man I've never seen in my life sat right where you are and told me to tell you to tell Knight that he's not being careful enough. A person named Nair isn't going to give up and Knight has to do something permanent to get him to give up."

Raid, his eyes locked on me, froze. The air around him froze. In fact, the entire café froze as he stared at me.

I felt eyes on me because the menace rolling off Raiden was so immense, we were capturing attention even though no words were being said.

In other words, I wasn't the only one who could feel it, and it was so strong this was not a surprise.

Then he whispered in his sinister way, "Come again?"

I repeated myself.

Raiden leaned slightly toward me. "You're tellin' me that motherfucker walked right up to my woman in my sister's fuckin' place, sat down across from you and gave you a message for me?"

I hesitated due to the rumbling, scary quality of his voice that I had never heard before and the ominous blaze burning in his eyes that I had never seen before, then I leaned in and replied, "Yes."

He sat back. "Jesus Christ. I'm gonna fuckin' kill that guy."

"Dude, what is *up?*" Rachelle asked, hitting our table right before a beer bottle hit the tabletop.

There it was. Other people felt his vibe.

"Lose yourself, Rache," Raid ordered.

"Bro, you look tweaked. I—" she began.

Raiden's head tipped back and he cut his eyes to her.

I wasn't getting his look, but I still shivered.

"Bottom of my heart, but get the fuck outta here, babe."

She bit her lip, gave wide eyes to me and wisely skedaddled.

Raiden looked at me and I wished Rachelle was back.

"You see him again, you tell him that he needs to find an alternate conduit for communication with his brother. It is not you. And you finish with telling him if you see him again after that, I will find him, rip his head off and shove it up his ass."

Cripes!

"Raid—"

"You got that?" he cut me off to ask.

Now was *clearly* not one of those times to backtalk, so I nodded but sallied forth cautiously, "Yes, sweetheart, I got that, but what's going on?"

He sucked in breath then grabbed his beer and sucked some back before he put it back on the table and again leaned into me.

"I told you about my buddy Knight having problems. A man named Drake Nair is that problem. Nair keeps fuckin' with him. First, Nair approached Knight's woman, Anya, sharin' some things it was not his to share. That didn't have the desired effect. Second, Knight has a variety of people under his protection and Nair had some of them hurt. When Knight shut that down, Nair found the guy I'm hunting, who got some of his soldiers to infiltrate some of Knight's dealings, found some weak links, and by that I mean ex-junkies. He reintroduced them to ice, got them hooked so Knight had to clean that shit out of his business and also expend the effort to get the junkies clean again."

Holy Moses.

Drake Nair sounded like a world-class jerk.

I wondered what Knight did to inspire this animosity, but I didn't get a chance to ask. Raiden was still talking.

"Knight is not unaware that Nair was a nuisance that, through demonstrated tenacity, has grown into an enemy who is a genuine threat. Nick is Knight's brother, and Nick is a wildcard."

He quit speaking so I finally had the chance to get a question in.

"If he's Knight's brother, why doesn't he just talk to his brother?"

"Nick Sebring was a pain in the ass that got off on ridin' his brother's coattails, copious amounts of pussy and cocaine. Nick's dad hauled him to Hawaii and supposedly cleaned up his act. He came back to Denver and since then his behavior has been random. Then he dropped off the grid, only to reappear randomly, and in not good ways, with really bad people only to drop straight off again. Although he's thrown time, energy and money at this question, Knight still has no clue what his brother was up to."

"Well, obviously Nick has his brother's back if he goes out of his way to warn him of trouble," I noted.

"Babe, wildcard," Raid replied.

"Sorry?" I asked.

"You play with wildcards, you got one in your hand, golden. Your opponent gets one, you're fucked."

"Oh," I said.

"With the company he's been keeping, Nick warning his brother does not mean we have him in our hand. Since he's a wildcard, it could mean anything."

That made sense, so I said, "Okay."

"Bottom line, you do not give this guy any time except to tell him what I told you. Once you relay that message, you get the fuck away and call me. If you see him again after that, you just get the fuck away, around people and you call me immediately."

This sounded like a good plan I was totally down with.

"Okay."

"Now I need to call Knight. Food comes, start without me."

Instead of repeating my "okay," I nodded.

He got up and moved toward the front door.

I took a sip of wine, but paid attention this time to my surroundings and spent a good amount of effort getting my heartbeat to regulate.

Rachelle came out with the food.

"All okay?" she asked.

I gave her a grin I hoped didn't look fake. "Yep."

Her eyes narrowed on my grin before, with experience dealing with things Raiden Miller, she wisely let it go and said, "After you eat that, you can build shrines to my brilliance. Enjoy the movies with my brother."

Then she was off.

I started eating and at the same time creating shrines to her brilliance in my head.

Raid came back and started eating.

Without another word about it, we went about our evening as if my brief visit from Nick Sebring didn't happen.

"More," Raiden's gruff voice ordered.

On my knees, booty in the air, face in the bed, I gave him more, surging back as he powered in.

Amazing.

"That's it. So fuckin' wild," he growled.

I whimpered as it started to wash over me and when I reared back to find it, he pulled away.

I was about to protest when he commanded, "Back. Spread."

I rolled to my back and spread. He bent over me, gathered me in his arms, lifted me up and rammed me down on his cock.

I cried out, my hands going to his lush hair, both of them fisting as his hips thrust up.

"Hold on," he told me unnecessarily.

We did this a lot. It was always a wild ride.

I knew to hold on.

"Finger to your clit, baby, give it to me," he demanded.

He was ready and he wanted me to be there with him.

I did what he said, and two seconds later I shoved my face into his neck and sunk my teeth into his skin.

He grunted then groaned, surged up so hard and deep, I nearly bucked off and he came with me.

Half a minute later, he murmured, "Give me the glide, honey."

I knew what he wanted and started gliding up and down on his cock, my lips and tongue moving over his skin.

"Taste blood?" he asked quietly.

"No," I whispered into his neck.

"Next time."

I smiled then slid my lips to under his ear. "Talked to your mom at the café today."

"Her pussy's workin' my dick and she talks to me about my mom," he muttered, I slid down, lifted my head and looked at him, grinning.

"And Rachelle'" I added. "So," I started conversationally, "no one has ever called you Raiden but me?"

"Raiden is a silly-ass romance novel hero's name my mom came up with to torture me," he replied.

I stifled a giggle and remarked, "And Raid isn't silly?"

He smiled. "Raid's a badass's name."

He was not wrong.

I brushed my lips against his and mumbled, "I see."

"Love you, Hanna."

He said that to me now. Not frequently, but he said it.

But the way he said it right then made my head come up an inch and I glued my eyes to his.

"I love you too, honey," I whispered.

"Nothin' ever touches you," he declared and I knew.

He was still thinking about Nick Sebring.

"I'm okay," I assured him.

"My work doesn't touch you."

"Honey," I wound my arms and him. "I'm okay."

"Knight was about as unhappy as I was you were approached. He's got a woman, she's his world. He gets where I'm at. You won't see Nick again."

I nodded, but my belly fluttered.

I was his world.

He bent his head and kissed my chest before he tipped it back again. "You want me to clean you up or are you feelin' energetic?"

Since it was just him and me and always would be, plus the fact I was on birth control, we'd discussed it and he'd dispensed with the condoms.

Gratifyingly.

"I'm feeling energetic," I told him.

"Then climb off, but I'm feeling energetic too, so we go to bed naked. If I want you in the night, all-access."

I slid off but I did it shivering.

I started to move, but Raiden brought me back with an arm around my waist so I was pressed to his front. His other hand slid between my legs. Sensitive, my body melted into his, my hands settled on his shoulders, my eyes slid half-shut and my lips parted.

"Fuck me," he murmured, his beautiful eyes moving over my face. "Just wanted a quick reminder of that sweet pussy, and one look at your face, now I gotta finger fuck it to make you come again."

He most certainly did.

I started breathing heavily and my fingers clutched his shoulders.

"Face in my neck, hold on and let me give it to you, baby," he ordered. "And this time, I'm gonna make you mark me."

His words made my hips twitch. I held on, pressed close and let him give it to me.

In the end, I wasn't feeling as energetic as I thought, so Raid ended up out of bed to get a washcloth to clean the remnants of him away me.

I fell asleep moments after I felt Raiden's arm move, my eyes drifting open and closed, watching his fingertips move over the skin of his neck then the skin of my lips.

And the last thing I heard before I floated off was his muttered, "Love my wild one."

THE BED MOVED violently. My eyes flew open, then my body rolled over Raiden's and I was flying through the air.

I landed on my back on the floor beside the bed with a pained cry as the jolt of landing raced along my spine, radiated over my scalp and along the small of my back.

I blinked, trying to understand what was happening, at the same time concentrating on the thankfully receding pain, when suddenly Raid was kneeling beside me.

"Jesus, fuck, Hanna. Fuck. *Fuck*." He ended on a snarl as I pushed up to my elbows.

"I'm okay."

"Move your legs for me," he ordered.

I pushed up fully and bent my legs, repeating, "Honey, I'm okay."

A moment of silence slid by before I was cradled in his arms. He picked me up, turned, sat on the side of the bed and held me close, my behind in his lap, his face in my neck.

"Goddamn it," he muttered there.

"A dream?" I asked.

He didn't answer, but it was then I noticed his big, strong body was shaking.

I closed my eyes, pressed close and wound my arms around him. "I'm okay. It's okay. Okay?" I asked stupidly.

"Coulda hurt you," he said.

"You didn't."

"I could have."

I held tight and stated firmly. "You didn't."

"Fuck," he clipped and his arms went tight around me too.

He went silent and I just held on for a while, then I moved my hand and sifted my fingers through his thick, silky hair before curling it around the back of his neck.

His body stopped shaking, but he didn't let me go, so I returned the favor.

He lifted his head and I tipped mine back to look at him.

"Goin' to the guest room, honey. I'll sleep there until I get a lock on these dreams," he declared.

At his words, I automatically put a lock on him, one arm going tight, the other one sliding into his hair and fisting.

"Sorry?" I asked.

"We fuck, we kiss, I'll leave you safe in here, sleep in the other room 'til I'm good, know I got them under control, then I'll come back," he replied.

My back shot straight and my lips, rough and commanding, stated, "No. You. Will. Not."

I felt his body jolt around me.

"Hanna—"

"They do not get to take you away from me," I snapped, and at that I felt his frame string tight.

I didn't care.

I moved my hands to either side of his head and brought my face close.

"They tore huge chunks of you away and they can have those. I can't get those back, but they are not taking the you that's mine away from me."

"Babe—"

"No," I bit off. "I waited for you for almost a lifetime. I'm not going to get you and have any of the good parts torn away, like you sleeping somewhere else. I *like* sleeping with you. I feel safe with you beside me. I wake up happy. They don't get to take that from me, and further, they don't get it *from you*."

He gave me a light shake. "Babe, tonight, no clue what I was doin', I threw you across the room."

"Throw me out the window, I don't care. Just don't make me sleep without you."

His arms convulsed and his voice was hoarse when Raiden began, "Love that, baby, but—"

I cut him off. "Not to throw your words in your face but did your buddies die so you can sleep without your woman?"

He went completely still.

I didn't give up.

"Talk to one of the guys," I ordered.

"Babe—"

I pressed my hands into his head. "Raid. Talk. To. One. Of. The. Guys." I didn't give him a chance to respond. I took my hands from his head, slapped them on his chest and cried, "God! Don't you think the same thing is happening to them that's happening to you? So much testosterone, sucking it up and not wanting to appear weak. Don't you think that they're waiting for the strongest one of you to step up, get it out and give them that outlet so you can all find ways to move the heck on?"

I stopped talking and braced for his reaction, which could be anything, but was stunned with what I got.

His head dropped forward so his forehead rested on my shoulder. He turned it, tipped his chin, and, lips at my ear, whispered, "Hal was with me. Hal was…I'll talk to Hal."

I had no clue who Hal was. I just knew I was thanking God the unknown Hal existed and my man trusted him enough to talk to him about this.

I also closed my eyes and clutched him to me.

"Thank you," I breathed.

"And I'll sleep here. With you."

I clutched him closer and repeated my relieved, "Thank you."

His head came up and he caught my eyes in the dark. "You got that, honey. But you got it understanding right now we make a deal that if that happens again, no matter how it happens, I hurt you, I almost hurt you, we're done and I move to the other room until I get a lock on it."

"Raid—"

"No, babe, that's your compromise and as far as I'm willin' to go. I love you'd take the risk. I love you don't want to lose me. But see it from my perspective. If I actually hurt you, I'd have to live with that. Don't make me."

I got that, and while I didn't like it, I got it, so I'd give it to him.

"Okay. I won't make you."

"Thank you."

Even though I didn't like giving him what I had to give him, I was glad I gave it to him because his thank you was so darn sweet.

I pulled in a deep breath, let it go, moved into him and cuddled close.

Raiden held me for a good long while then he shifted us so we were in bed, him on his back me tucked to his side.

His hand sifted through my hair then his arm stopped and curved round me.

It didn't go slack.

He didn't go to sleep.

Neither did I.

He was torturing himself because of what he did to me, and maybe scared of hurting me through another dream.

I was heartbroken he was sleepless for these reason.

Dawn touched the sky, and finally his arm went slack.

I finally allowed myself to drift to sleep.

19

NOTHING SWEETER

Three Weeks Later, Labor Day

I watched as I wandered across Grams's lawn. It was filled with people and tables groaning with food that she helped prepare, but these days the existence of the food had more to do with me, KC, Eunice, and this year Rachelle and Ruthie.

I folded myself in the chair next to Grams, feeling the sun beating on me, as well as a variety of other things.

Raiden was at the end of the yard, bent in, his hand curled around the red flag dangling from the middle of a long length of rope.

Kids were on either side, hands to the rope, ready.

"On three!" I heard him shout and my heart started beating harder, my belly getting warm, my skin tingling. "One!" He looked to his left. "Two!" He looked to his right. "Three!" he yelled.

He let go of the rope, stepped back and the kids started straining.

Grams's annual picnic.

Tug of war.

His eyes came right to me.

My breath caught.

Then Raiden Ulysses Miller smiled at me.

The sun was warm and bright, but the heat that engulfed me had nothing to do with it.

I smiled back.

Grams's hand curled around mine.

"Proud of you, *chère*." I heard her say, but I didn't take my eyes off Raid as he monitored the game.

I turned my hand and curved my fingers around hers.

"Battled the blaze," she went on.

"It's still burning."

"Yes, I see. But I believe in you, precious girl. You'll get it so it's warm and cozy."

I hoped she was right.

I didn't share that. I just tightened my hand around hers as much as I dared.

"How's it feel?" she asked.

"Nothing sweeter nor will there ever be," I answered.

"Your old biddy of a Grams is right," she murmured.

"Always."

She held on to my hand.

I didn't let go.

One Month Later

I RODE UP to my house on my bike and saw Raiden sitting on the porch in one of my wicker chairs, hand curled around a beer.

He'd never done that, so I didn't know if it was a good thing.

I rode up to the steps, pushed my kickstand down and dismounted. I walked up to the porch, appreciating his fall action man gear. This consisted of everything being the same, but instead of a tee, he was wearing a skintight thermal.

Indian summer long gone, a nip in the mountain air, I was wearing jeans, a cute pink sweater and low heeled boots.

I approached and his eyes moved over me before they shifted to my bike then back at me.

When he said, "Gonna have to put her up for the winter soon, babe," I decided not to move into him and give him a kiss, and instead headed to the swing.

Shifting onto it with practiced ease, I lifted my legs and crossed them under me, looking back at him to see, through my movements, I had never lost those beautiful, unusual green eyes I hoped he gave our babies.

"I know," I agreed.

"You keep ridin' it, need to get a clip for your jeans or you're gonna catch them in the chain."

He was right, so I nodded.

Raiden looked away and took a tug off his beer, his attention going to the front yard.

I gave him some time then asked, "Is everything okay, sweetheart?"

To which, straight out, he answered, "Talked to Hal today."

I knew what he meant. I was surprised he told me. I was also surprised he took this much time to do it. He hadn't had any dreams since he threw me off the bed. I thought he'd already done it and things were good. But I hadn't asked because I felt it was his to tell.

He must have felt my surprise because his eyes cut to me.

"Last night, I dreamed."

My lips parted, his eyes watched then they came back to mine.

"Just woke up, knew right where I was, you didn't wake. Thought it's been so long they were gone. Thought the last scene was so intense it worked them outta me. I was wrong."

"Okay," I said when he stopped talking and didn't start again.

He took another drag off his beer and looked back at the yard. "You were right. Brought it up to Hal, he told me he's havin' issues too."

"Dreams?" I asked.

Raid looked back at me and shook his head. "Goes out, picks a fight, beats the shit outta somebody. Next morning, feels like an asshole, knows exactly why he's doin' it, can't seem to stop."

Oh God.

Raiden looked away and took another pull of his beer.

He said nothing.

I didn't either.

Then I had to ask, "Did it, uh…help do you think?"

"Felt shit, goin' over that, knowin' Hal's fucked up. Felt shit," he told the yard, and I held my breath.

His eyes moved to me and my lungs started burning.

"Fucked up, totally, but it also felt good knowin' I wasn't the only one."

I let my breath go and nodded.

"Could tell, he felt that too," he added.

I said nothing.

He tugged back more beer, dropped the bottle to his thigh and announced to the yard, "Gonna sleep in the guest room tonight."

I pulled in my lips.

His eyes came back to me.

"Just tonight, baby," he said gently. "We dredged up shit, it's on the surface, too close. I want you safe just in case."

I let my lips go and nodded.

"I'll come back tomorrow," he told me.

"Okay," I agreed quietly.

"Nothin' hurts you, especially not me."

"Okay, sweetheart."

He held my eyes a moment before he looked back to the yard.

I sat in the swing wanting to touch him, move to him, say exactly the right thing, develop a magic touch that would erase this for him.

I didn't do any of that, and not just because some of it I didn't have the power to do.

I just sat in my swing.

His eyes came back to me. "What's for dinner?"

"Why don't we go into town and see your sister?"

His head cocked to the side, and I remembered that from when I first ran into him, how hot I thought that was, how beautiful I thought he was doing it.

He was no less so now.

Knowing him, him being mine, it was more.

His eyes moved over me, my swing and his face got soft.

He knew what I was doing, sitting in my swing, suggesting we go see his sister.

There was nothing that would give him back what he lost.

But that didn't mean a reminder of what he had wasn't welcome.

"Works for me, baby."

I smiled at him and I knew it was shaky.

He pushed up from his chair and came to me. He bent and tucked my hair behind my ear before he wrapped a hand around the side of my head and swept his thumb over my cheek, his eyes locked to mine.

"My girl and her swing," he murmured.

"That's me."

"I love you, Hanna."

My heart skipped a beat.

"I love you too, Raiden."

He held my eyes long moments before he dipped his head, brushed his mouth against mine then moved away but caught my hand, pulling me out of the swing, saying, "Let's go to town."

I followed him into the house so he could get rid of his beer.

Then we went into town.

We took the Z.

Raiden driving.

Me sitting beside him.

Touched.

Hopeful.

Happy.

20

CLEAN

Raid

Two Weeks Later

RAID WALKED AHEAD of Marcus Sloan's two men who had met him outside and were pushing the cuffed fugitive Raid captured into the warehouse.

As Raid and the men moved, Sloan stood in the warehouse, watching.

Sloan was a dark-haired, good-looking, very dangerous man wearing an expensive, well-cut suit.

Sloan was also a new client.

His eyes moved from Raid to the men behind him.

"Jesus," he murmured and looked back at Raid. "What happened?"

Raid knew what he was asking. The fugitive didn't look too good. This was due to two black eyes, a fat lip and a swollen, broken nose.

"It took two days longer than I wanted it to take to find him. He became a bigger pain in my ass when I found him by attempting to evade capture, so he learned what it feels like to have his face slammed into a dresser," Raid answered matter-of-factly.

Marcus Sloan didn't even wince.

"Not a pleasant lesson," he stated quietly then jerked his chin to the men behind Raid.

They dragged the fugitive to a door off to the side and Raid knew the fugitive was about to learn another unpleasant lesson.

"I'll want those cuffs back," Raid called after them and he got a curt nod from one before the three disappeared behind the door. He looked back at Sloan. "Got somewhere to be. You got something for me?"

"Of course," Sloan answered and moved to a table on which a black duffel was sitting.

Raid moved there, too. He grabbed the handles and hefted up the bag.

"Nuisance," Sloan stated and Raid's eyes went to him. "Acquiring that amount of cash," he explained, tipping his head to the duffel. "We could do direct deposit."

"No offense, Marcus, but your shit isn't exactly tight," Raid replied. "I run a cash only business. You know I gotta be careful what line items I got on my accounts."

"And you know my business is tight," Sloan returned.

"Not as tight as mine," Raid said.

Sloan's lips quirked before he murmured, "This is true."

Raid didn't have time for this. If he left now, in an hour and a half he could be home with Hanna.

Still, when he pulled the handles of the duffel over his shoulder, he studied Sloan, and in case things he should know but didn't made things messy, he was forced to ask, "Not my business, but you wanna tell me why you're contacting me and not Nightingale to do this shit for you?"

"Things with Lee have become complicated," Sloan answered.

Raid kept studying him, suspecting that was true.

Lee Nightingale and the boys of Nightingale Investigations were on retainer to Marcus Sloan for a variety of purposes.

Unfortunately for Sloan, his wife became tight with not only Nightingale's wife, but all the women who belonged to his crew. And if that wasn't enough, part of that crew included two cops and *their* women.

Something a man like Sloan would wish to avoid.

And, considering how Sloan felt about his wife, Raid could see him adjusting business practices in order to keep her relationship with her posse healthy.

Messy for Sloan, not messy for Raid.

Therefore acceptable.

<del></del>
— 233 —

"Right," Raid muttered before he cocked his head to the side and finished, "Appreciate the business."

He was about to turn to leave when Sloan locked eyes with him and remarked, "Enjoy your welcome home from Hanna."

Raid's body strung tight.

"Come again?" he asked low, and Sloan shook his head.

"Don't mistake me," he said quietly.

"You want me to ask after Daisy?" Raid queried, returning the perceived threat and referring to Sloan's wife, a woman Raid did not know personally, but a woman Raid and everyone in Denver did know Marcus Sloan would not only change business practices for, but he'd also kill and die for.

"That was not my point," Sloan told him.

"I suggest you make your point," Raid demanded.

"It's a lovely town you live in, Miller, but you don't get there through your personal magical door no one else can get through," Sloan replied.

"You think I don't know this?" Raid returned.

Marcus Sloan held his eyes then stated, "I'm happy for you. It would be easy for you to go the way of Deacon. Lose yourself in the job, feel nothing, want nothing, get up and exist through the day doing what you have to do then go to bed with nothing to look forward to when you wake up in the morning. The walking dead with handcuffs and brass knuckles, existing until your luck ended or your skills dulled and the hunter became the hunted. Instead, you found something better. Now you have something in your life that's important, something you didn't have before. My point is, take advice from someone who's lived the life much longer than you. Take measures to ensure her protection."

Since Nick Sebring's visit, this was something that had been weighing heavily on Raid's mind.

His crew, however, were constantly out on jobs.

He needed to make a priority of getting them all free for long enough for a sit down. The longer he stayed in the job, the more enemies he could make. He needed a man in Willow at all times to keep an eye on things.

It wasn't only Hanna. It was his mother, Rachelle and Miss Mildred.

The time had come.

"Point taken," Raid muttered.

The door opened and one of Sloan's men came out. He walked close enough to toss Raid's cuffs to him. Raid caught them and the man moved back to the room, shutting the door behind him.

Raid shoved the cuffs in his belt at the back of his cargoes and looked at Sloan. "We done with our counseling session?"

Sloan gave him an amused smile and nodded.

Raid moved toward the exit.

"No, actually, I'm not," Sloan called after him.

Raid stopped and looked back, brows raised.

"Hopefully, it won't happen. If it does, more advice. Make a statement, Raid. Make a statement no one can miss. Am I being clear?" Sloan asked.

He was, and Raid didn't like what he was being clear about.

"Nothing's gonna happen to Hanna," Raid rumbled.

"No, likely not, but if it does, pray for her strength. But make *your* statement clear," Sloan shot back.

Raid's blood ran cold.

"You know something I don't know?" he asked sharply.

"I know this life. You're the man I think you are, you now have a new number one priority. See to making sure everyone knows exactly what that is and what you'd do if they don't take that seriously."

Jesus, the man had another point.

Raid didn't concede it this time.

He clipped, "Now are we done?"

Sloan nodded.

Raid moved again toward the door, and while he did he heard a man's chilling, agonized cry.

As he always did, Raid just kept walking.

Hanna

"I'M GOING, GRAMS!" I shouted as I hustled down the hall.

I went through the back door, pushing back the screen door that Raiden had put the storm window in the week before, the day before he left on a job, and saw her sitting outside under one of my afghans.

She turned to me.

"When does he get home, child?" she asked and I smiled at her.

"He called an hour ago saying he'd be home in an hour and a half."

"Then you get home to your man, *chère*. Tell him I said, 'hey'."

"I'll tell him," I assured her then asked, "Do you want me to help you inside?"

She looked to the waning sun. "Gonna stay out a while longer."

"Grams—"

She looked to me. "Just a while longer, precious. I'll be okay. Eunice is coming over later." She waved her hand at me. "Shoo. Get on that bike of yours and go home."

I smiled again, dashed to her, gave her a kiss on her wrinkled cheek then dashed back to the house calling, "See you later!"

"Tell that boy I expect to see him for church on Sunday!" she called back.

"Will do!" I yelled.

I threw open the front door, the storm door that again Raiden had put the storm windows in and then I felt a whiz at my feet. I looked down and saw Spot run-waddling out.

"What the—?" I snapped, following him only to see him jump on a chair, the railing and into the basket of my bike that I really needed to put up for the winter.

Crazy cat.

"Inside, Spot," I ordered.

"Meow," he defied me, settling his fat booty in my basket, demanding a ride.

I hurried down the stairs, picked him up and he lost it, writhing and hissing until I could hold him no longer. I dropped him back in the basket, having to grab onto the bike to hold it steady when he went in.

He sat on his behind, looked up at me and said, "Meow."

"I need to get home, buddy."

"Meow."

"My man's coming home."

He pointed his face to the driveway.

Gah!

I didn't have time for this!

I ran back to the house, threw open the door and shouted, "Spot feels like a ride! Raid will bring him back later!"

"Righty ho!" Grams shouted back.

So *that* was where I got it.

I grinned to myself, raced back to my bike, mounted and threw back the kickstand. Putting my feet to the pedals, we were off.

"You're going to have to explain to Raiden why he has to leave our bed and bring you home," I informed Spot.

"Meow," he replied to the wind blowing in his face, unafraid of badass Raiden Miller as only Spot would be.

We rode home. I stopped at the front and hefted him out of the basket. He crawled up to get paws on my shoulder and started purring as I walked up the steps.

I grinned.

Totally a crazy cat.

I pulled out my keys, opened my screen door that had storm windows too, ditto with Raid putting them in. A fat cat in my arm, the storm door resting on my behind, I inserted the key in lock one, turned it and it didn't do anything.

It was unlocked.

"Didn't I—?" I started to ask the doorknob when it turned.

The door was thrown open, my hand was caught in a vice-like grip, and on a terrified scream Spot and I were pulled inside.

For the next ten minutes I felt a lot of terror.

And a lot of pain.

This was because in the foyer of my childhood home I got the shit beaten out of me by three men with one man watching.

The only thing that I processed outside the fear and pain was Spot hissing then his agonized, "*Muuuuurrrrroooowww!*" when he was kicked into the living room.

Finally down and almost out, on my belly, unable to move, pain searing through my insides as I coughed up blood, my arm useless and broken under me, my head was pulled back by my hair.

I gave out a tortured whimper at the additional pain and tried to force myself to focus on the man who was in my face.

"Just so you know, Heather gave you up after she watched us put a bullet in Bodhi's brain," he told me.

Oh God.

Oh *God*.

Banana, I heard Bodhi's voice in my head.

The pain so immense, physical and now emotional, my head swimming, my eyes drifting open and shut, I was going to pass out. I wanted it. I needed it.

But he wasn't done.

"I don't like to lose money. You made me lose money. Now we're square."

He slammed my head into the rug.

And when he did, thankfully, I lost consciousness.

My EYES DRIFTED open.

Something was happening.

I was in agony, head to toes.

I needed to get to a phone.

I needed the black back.

Something shifted at my side as I heard the back door open.

I tensed, my mouth opening to call out, then closing.

They wouldn't come back.

Would they come back?

I scuttled and something scuttled with me.

Spot was pressed to my side.

I could scuttle no more. It hurt too much. Way too much.

I stopped.

"Hanna!" I heard called.

It was Raid. He was probably wondering why I didn't rush to greet him like I usually did.

My mouth opened.

My eyes drifted closed.

"Jesus, *fuck*!" I heard barked.

I felt movement, heard boots on floor, a cat's hiss, another one, a furry body shifting, thumping, striking, more hissing then, "Fuckin' cat! Hanna."

My hair was shifted off my neck.

My eyes fluttered.

"Fuck me, fuck me, fuck me."

A hand moving on me.

"Baby, are you with me?"

My eyes fluttered again.

"Fuck me…yeah, this is Raiden Miller. I'm at 10 Hunter Lane. My woman's been attacked, beaten badly, she's barely conscious. I need an ambulance." Pause then I felt him close. "Hanna, baby, you with me?"

I tried to flutter my eyes.

But it all went black.

⸻

My eyes drifted open.

It was dark, but there was muted light and I didn't understand the smells I was experiencing. I also didn't understand the wooziness I was feeling.

"Baby."

My eyes drifted to the side and I saw Raiden there.

"Hey."

My lips hurt.

Why was that?

Raiden's face got closer which was good. That meant I didn't have to expend so much effort focusing on it.

"You're gonna be okay," he told me.

"Okay."

My voice was strange. It was quiet, weak and hoarse.

I didn't see his hand move, but I felt him tuck my hair behind my ear.

That felt nice.

"You're gonna be all right," he assured me.

"Okay," I whispered again in that voice.

"I'm gonna take care of this," he promised.

I had no idea what he was talking about, but I replied with another, "Okay."

His eyes closed then I could really focus on him when his forehead came to rest gently on mine.

He had great eyelashes.

"I love you, honey," he said, low and fierce.

"I love you, too," I told him, losing focus, my eyes slowly closing and reopening.

"I'm gonna take care of this," he repeated his vow.

"Okay, sweetheart," I replied, my eyes slowly closing and staying that way.

I felt the brush of his lips on mine.

Then I felt nothing.

I OPENED MY eyes to sun then I blinked.

At what I took in, I pushed up the hospital bed, everything hitting me at once.

My arm in a cast. Pain in my ribs. My face. A concentration of pain at my upper lip.

No.

Pain everywhere. Dull pain, but it was there.

Everywhere.

And three big men I'd never seen standing around my bed.

Oh God!

"Told you you'd freak her," a woman's voice stated, and around the big man to my right, who had brown hair and a wicked scar on his face but was nevertheless extremely hot, came a pretty, petite blonde woman holding an adorable baby boy to her hip.

Her eyes hit mine. "Yo, I'm Sylvie Creed."

This meant nothing to me and my hand inched toward the call button.

Her eyes didn't miss this so she kept talking, jerking her head to the dark-haired man with unusual blue eyes standing to my left. "That's Knight Sebring."

Knight.

Knight was Raiden's buddy.

My eyes went to him and my hand stopped.

"Least she knows you," Sylvie muttered toward Knight, and an unbelievably beautiful woman came around his side and looked down at me with a small smile.

"Hi, Hanna. I'm Anya, Knight's woman, and you're safe. Okay?" she said in a soft, calming voice.

Not okay.

Nothing was okay.

Or nothing would be okay until I knew where *my* man was.

Because I remembered. I remembered everything. All of it. And as bad as what happened to me in my foyer was, it was worse with Raiden vowing he was going to take care of it.

I had a feeling with what he did to Meg (and he *did* do what he said he was going to do to Meg, the last thing I heard, she'd moved to Denver, mostly because she had no choice), since this was *way* worse, he was going to *take care of this*.

So I asked Anya, "Where's Raiden?"

"That's what we need to talk to you about," she told me.

I did not take this as good.

"First, as Sylvie said, this is Knight," she motioned to the man at her side and he jerked his chin up at me. "That's Tucker Creed, he's married to Sylvie," Anya went on, motioning to the man with the scar. I looked to him and he gave me a small smile. "And that's Deacon," she concluded.

My eyes flew to the end of the bed to take in the extortionately good-looking, tall, dark-haired, scary man there.

"Looks like she knows you too," Sylvie noted.

"I'm pleased to meet you all," I cut in. "But where's Raiden?"

"Hunting," scary, hot guy at the foot of my bed grunted, and my heart started beating hard.

Or harder.

"Hunting?" I whispered.

"Yesterday," Knight spoke gently and my eyes cut to him, "you were assaulted in your home by a man we're looking for. You have a broken ulna, six broken ribs, a concussion and two stitches in your lip that the doctors say will dissolve and you'll barely notice the scar. You'll be under observation here at least until tomorrow and you'll endure a recuperation period, but the doctors have assured your family that you'll make a complete recovery. There's no lasting damage."

Except for the broken arm, ribs, barely noticeable scar, mild head injury and recuperation period and the news that my "family" was out there, probably worried like crazy about me, my ninety-eight-year-old Grams amongst them, that all sounded a lot better than what happened to me felt.

But I had bigger fish to fry.

"Okay," I said softly. "But what does hunting mean?"

"You know your man, babe." This came from Tucker Creed, and he was also speaking gently. "You know what it means."

He was right. I knew what it meant.

Oh God.

I looked frantically to Knight. "You have to stop him. Stop him from doing something that might get him in trouble. Stop him from doing something he can't live with."

"He'll be able to live with this," Deacon's voice rumbled up from my feet, and my eyes moved to him.

"Don't let him do this," I begged Deacon, his mentor, a man he trusted.

"Woman, we're here to find out how to help him," Deacon told me, and I stared.

"We need to find him, Hanna," Sylvie Creed said, and my eyes moved to her. "Find him, calm him down and find these guys who did his to you. You need to help us."

Okay, calming him down sounded good.

"Tell us everything you know," Tucker Creed ordered.

Darn.

"I don't know anything," I told him.

"No, honey, everything you saw, everything they said, everything you can remember," he clarified.

I shook my head. "I…they set on me fast and I…"

Sylvie (and her cute baby) leaned into me and she wrapped her hand carefully around my cast. "We dig this can't be easy, not this soon after it happened, but as they say, time is of the essence. Anything you remember could help, Hanna. I know it sounds crazy, but even what shoes they were wearing could help. An accent you heard in their voices."

My eyes widened, she saw it and leaned in.

"Talk to me, girl," she urged.

I talked.

They asked questions.

I answered them and talked more.

Then they were done, and I knew this because they all looked at each other and Anya shifted around the bed.

"Give me Jesse, Sylvie," she said.

Sylvie handed Jesse to Anya, leaned in and kissed her son before she ran a finger down his cheek then she turned and looked down at me.

"We'll find your man and it'll all be good. I promise, Hanna."

I nodded. She nodded back, turned, tipped her head back to her man and she started to move. Tucker Creed moved with her.

I lunged, pain shot through me, but my hand clamped onto Knight's.

He stopped and looked down at me.

Really unusual blue eyes. Startling.

"Hanna?" he prompted.

"Don't let him do anything he can't live with," I whispered. "He lives with enough. He doesn't need more. Not because of me."

"What happened to you is because of me," Knight returned, and my brows drew together in confusion. "So Raid won't be takin' care of this sick fuck. That'll be me." He caught my eyebrow movement and finished, "In other words, don't worry."

That seemed pretty firm.

Still.

"I'm trusting you," I told him.

His hand twisted until it was holding mine and he bent close.

"That means something to me," he stated low.

Then he let me go, moved back and he was gone.

That was it.

Seriously?

"If he says it means something, seriously, it means something," Anya told me, and my eyes went to her to see her bouncing Jesse on her hip.

"Did I just get surrounded by a pack of hot guys and a petite woman who is clearly badass who are all off to hunt my man, who's off hunting the man that had three of his goons beat the dickens out of me?"

She grinned and answered, "Yes."

I settled back on a "*humph*" then kept grumbling. "You know, when Raiden entered my life, I knew something huge was happening. I was not wrong, seeing as the foundations of my world have shifted about a dozen times. Most of it was good, but I have to admit, I'm kind of getting sick of it," I shared and she smiled.

"You'll get used to it," she replied.

I stared at her.

Great.

Then she turned her head and cooed at cute, little Jesse.

Watching that, I sighed, thinking that maybe I would.

Then I went straight back to worrying.

⁂

Raid

Three Weeks Later

THEY ALL STOOD in the dark parking lot of the Pancake House to touch base before they disbursed after finally taking care of the guy responsible for attacking Hanna and Knight's girls.

"I want Nair," Raid rumbled.

"Patience, Raid," Knight said quietly.

"I think you get him, man," Creed stated. "He found his woman on the floor of their house with her face in a puddle of blood she coughed up. You need to speed this shit up."

"That fucker we took care of had no idea Hanna had anything to do with Knight 'cause he had no idea Raid was lookin' for him. He doesn't even fuckin' know who Raid is," Deacon put in. "He was just pissed he lost a shitload of dope and it was Hanna who called it in. The operation is still sound."

"When you got a woman or kids or, I don't know, maybe even just a fuckin *home* you give a shit about, Deacon, then you can talk about how sound this operation is," Creed growled.

Deacon's body went dangerously still.

"That blow was low," he clipped.

"But it hit true," Creed bit off.

"I don't want a fuckin' debrief and I don't wanna pull you two out of a goddamned smackdown. I wanna get to my woman," Raid ground out and his eyes cut to Knight. "We bottom line this, this shit is on Nair. I want him."

"I indirectly put your woman in danger, Raid. This shit is on me," Knight stated.

"I don't wanna go over what we've gone over time and a-fuckin'-gain the last three weeks either, but I will repeat what I've said a hundred goddamned times. That's bullshit." Raid's eyes grew sharp on Knight and his voice got rough. "I. Want. Nair."

"We do that, we have to do it in a way that it's permanent," Knight replied. "That requires planning."

"Think we proved about ten hours ago not a one of us has got a problem with a permanent solution to a problem," Deacon reminded them.

The men fell silent.

Knight broke it. "I need to understand what my brother's involvement is, Raid. I know you get that."

"Yeah. I do. So find the fuck out and let me loose on Nair," Raid shot back.

"I'll take care of Nair," Knight returned.

"I get he's fucked with you, and God forbid he reaches out to Anya, Kat or Kasha, then you can have him. But until you come home to find someone you love lyin' unconscious in her own blood, I got dibs."

Knight held Raid's eyes.

Then he jerked up his chin, saying, "Fair enough."

Raid headed to his Jeep.

He swung in, pulled out and didn't look back.

Because he was headed home.

Twenty Minutes Later

RAID DROVE HIS Jeep around the back of the farmhouse.

It was after one o'clock in the morning and all the outside lights were on. The house was dark except a light coming from the kitchen.

She was up.

He parked in the back, angled out, moved swiftly through the yard, up the back steps and tried the handle.

She'd locked up.

He almost smiled his relief when he inserted his key, got the door unlocked, moved in and stopped dead.

Miss Mildred was standing in the kitchen.

Fuck.

He stood silent, but impatient as she made her slow way to him, stopped a foot away and tilted her head way back.

Her shrewd eyes moved over his face.

He let them and it was his mother's deeply ingrained manners that kept him standing there rather than setting her aside and getting to Hanna.

He watched her eyes close.

When she opened them, she whispered, "Wash it away. God gives tools to His earth that He uses, son. He puts men here like you to love girls like her, to protect them." She lifted her hand, rested it on his chest and her sharp eyes flashed with wrath. "And, if necessary, to *avenge* them."

It was then Raid closed his eyes.

She knew.

"But you know that already, don't you, Raiden Miller?" she asked. "You already know God's use for you 'cause He's needed to use you before."

Raid kept his eyes closed and said nothing.

"Wash it away," she kept whispering, the words flowing through him, leaving him clean.

Jesus.

Fucking *clean*.

Raid hadn't felt clean in nearly five years.

He opened his eyes.

She shuffled away, murmuring, "Go to her. I'll call Eunice. It's late but she'll come get me."

"Miss Mildred—"

She slowly turned her head to pin him with her eyes. "Proud of you, son. You do things others can't do and you stay standing. Now get upstairs and reap your rewards."

Jesus, she understood everything.

Raid needed no further prompting. He moved through the kitchen, but stopped and turned when she called, "Boy?"

His eyes hit her.

"Since she got home, Spot won't leave her side. Take your time, but I'll be expectin' you to do somethin' about that. I want my cat back."

Again, Raid nearly smiled.

He didn't.

He jerked up his chin.

She slowly folded herself into a chair and reached for the phone sitting on the kitchen table.

Raid turned, moved through the foyer and took the stairs three at a time.

Their room was dark, but he could see Hanna asleep in bed.

He went directly there, sat on the side and was immediately attacked by a cat.

Raid put a hand to either side of the animal's considerable stomach, hauled up its bulk and put him on the floor.

When he turned back, Hanna was up on an elbow.

"Raiden?"

The cat attacked his ankles.

He ignored it, reached out and tucked his girl's hair behind her ear. "Yeah, honey."

"Raiden," she breathed, then moved and she was in his arms.

Hanna, safe, happy he was home and in his arms.

Thank.

Fuck.

Raid held her close, but he held her carefully.

Hanna held on tight.

Clean.

She pulled back, lifted her hands like she was going for his face, stopped and grumbled, "Stupid cast."

"Baby, let me get my boots off and we'll lie down."

"I want to see your face."

"You can see my face tomorrow. I'll be two seconds."

"I want to see your face *now*," she demanded.

She reached for the light, and he sighed before he reached beyond her to turn on the light.

The cat jumped up on the bed. Raid set him down on the floor again and went back to Hanna.

She lifted her good hand to his face and her eyes moved over it.

He hoped like fuck she didn't see what her grandmother saw.

Her eyes stopped and looked into his. "You okay?"

"Yeah."

"Did you get him?"

She couldn't read him.

Thank.

Fuck.

"Yeah."

"Is everyone safe?"

"Yeah."

Her eyes again moved over his face.

Finally, they stopped on his.

"Next time you go on a path of vengeance, Raiden Ulysses Miller, I expect updates direct from you. I don't care how hilarious Sylvie is, and by the way, you can tell Deacon his grunts of, 'All good. Don't worry. Raid will be home soon,' don't tell me *anything*."

Looking in Hanna's sleepy but annoyed pretty blue eyes, he knew she was okay.

So that was when Raid allowed himself to smile.

Eight Hours Later

R AID OPENED HIS eyes, saw ceiling and realized he couldn't breathe.

This was because he had a fat cat lying on his chest.

He also had his woman's head on his shoulder and her heavy casted arm on his gut.

He didn't move.

Time passed.

He still didn't move.

He knew when she woke because her body shifted minutely before it melted into his.

She gave it time before she whispered, "Honey, you awake?"

"Yeah."

She snuggled closer.

The cat woke and started purring.

"He's going to want food in about five seconds," Hanna warned.

Raid, nor Hanna, were going anywhere.

"He's gonna have to wait," Raid replied.

"Can you breathe?" she asked.

"No," he answered.

He felt her smile against his skin.

She fell silent.

Raid didn't break it.

Eventually, she asked, "Do you want to talk about it?"

He did not.

"It's over," he declared in an effort to communicate that to her.

"I'll take that as you not wanting to talk about it," she mumbled.

She got him.

Since she did, he didn't bother to confirm.

She was silent another long while before she remarked, "Sylvie's a kick in the pants."

Sylvie Creed was a lot more than that.

"Yeah," he agreed.

"It was nice of her and Tucker to go all out for us," she noted. "Especially taking them away from Jesse."

"They were away from Jesse for a day," Raid told her. "They hooked up with me, and Tucker went back to Denver 'cause we were havin' better luck with our informants using Sylvie. Then Sylvie found she couldn't be away from her boys and she took off to join Tucker and Jesse in Denver, but those two worked the case in Denver. Tucker came back, then he left and Sylvie came back. In the end, Tucker came back, Sylvie left to go to Jesse and then it was done."

"Sounds confusing."

"They don't like to be apart and they don't like to be away from their boy. Now they're all together and headin' back to Phoenix."

"Good," she murmured.

"Is it?" he asked, and she lifted her head to aim her still sleepy eyes at him.

"Well, yeah. The family back together, this done."

"That's not what I'm talking about," he returned.

Her head tipped to the side and her sleepy eyes warmed. "You mean you and me?"

"Cuddled close to me, baby, you throwin' yourself in my arms when I got home last night, I'm guessin' we're all right. What I want to know is if you are."

Her eyes drifted to his collarbone before she said quietly, "I should have talked to you at Chilton's after I overheard your conversation on the phone."

That was when he shifted and the cat jumped away, surprisingly without objection, as Raid rolled to his side. He pulled Hanna into his arms.

She rested her casted hand on his chest and tipped her head back to look at him.

"This is not your fault," he stated firmly.

"You were going to take care of it. I jumped the gun."

"This is not your fault."

She looked deep into his eyes before she dipped her chin and pressed her face in his throat.

"They killed Bodhi," she said there.

"Yeah, and they fucked Heather up in a way she's not ever gonna heal," he shared. Her body twitched then her head went back and she caught his eyes again. "Their consequences. Not on you. This is no one's fault except the asshole scumbags who make poor life choices and blame good people doin' the right things for those assholes bearing the consequences of their own fucked-up decisions. They made more, they got more consequences. Now they're done and you're done. Safe."

Hanna studied him a moment before he saw that settle in and settle deep, thank fuck.

She then asked, "I get the sense you don't want to talk about it, but after looking for this guy for ages, how did you find him in three weeks?"

"Phantoms can't be seen in the sun. Men can be phantoms for a while but they make mistakes. He always stood in the shadows." Raid's arms got tight around her. "To do what he did to you, he made a mistake. He came out into the sun."

"Uh...that's kinda bounty hunter speak," she informed him, and Raid felt his lips tip up.

"What I'm sayin' is he never got close to his business. This time he showed. Your neighbors saw the car *and* the Nevada plates. You saw him and told the team about him. This time he left breadcrumbs. We followed them."

"Oh," she replied, and his grin got bigger.

She pressed closer, her eyes grew warm and intense and she asked, "Are *you* good?"

"Absolutely."

He knew she knew he did not lie when he watched her face go soft and she whispered, "I love you, Raiden."

"I know you do, honey. That's why I'm absolutely good."

Hanna smiled.

Raid asked, "You think I can fuck you without you giving me a head injury with that cast when you latch on to my hair?"

Her smile changed as her eyes grew excited.

"I can try, but you should know, my ribs aren't one hundred percent," she warned.

To that, he rolled into her, but he did it carefully. Then he shoved his face in her neck.

"I'll take that into account."

From the floor, they heard an insistent, "Meow."

Raid's hands up her tank, Hanna's fingers drifting over his back, Raid lifted his head, found her mouth and the fat cat had to wait a long time for breakfast.

He survived.

Epilogue

SHE WAS ALWAYS RIGHT

Three Years, Two Months and Two Weeks Later

I MOVED OUT of the kitchen at Grams's place, into the hall and stopped.

Raiden was crouched in the hall, head turned to me, camera in one hand. He lifted his other hand and put a finger to his lips.

I tiptoed his way and peeked around the doorway he was crouched in front of. I took in the scene and smiled.

Grams was in her chair, Raid and my baby boy, Clayton, in her arms. The lights from the Christmas tree we'd only just finished putting up in the window were twinkling into the room. Spot was dozing on the arm of Grams's chair.

"So then, I walked in the back door of Momma and Pop's house, still smoking, mind, and I asked Momma, 'What's for dinner?'" I heard Grams saying to Clay, who, being only three months old and also snoozing, had no clue.

I bit my lip to stop myself from laughing.

The struck by lightning story.

I heard Raiden's camera going.

"I know you're there," Grams stated, not looking our way.

One hundred and one years old, and still the hearing of a German shepherd, and now proof she had eyes in the side of her head.

I bit my lip harder and looked down at my husband.

His head was tipped back to me and he was grinning.

Then he looked back to the sight of his camera and kept clicking.

———

Three Hours Later

I FELT RAID fit his front to my back and his arms come around me.

Then I felt his lips at the skin below my ear.

"You know, he can sleep without your help," he whispered there.

I didn't take my eyes off my baby boy lying asleep in his crib.

"I know," I whispered back. "But I'm sure me standing here watching him helps him to have sweet dreams."

His arms tensed around me and his voice was rumbling when he replied, "I'm sure too."

There was something more in those words. Something that made me melt further into him.

Something I knew had to do with the fact Raiden hadn't had a nightmare for years.

It wasn't me who got rid of them. It was him working through things with Hal.

Still, Raiden gave me the credit.

We stood there for a good long while, our eyes on the tiny little living, breathing dream we created.

Raiden broke the moment.

"Could do this all night with you, honey, but we gotta talk," he told me.

Before I could reply, he moved away, his hand curled around mine and he tugged me out of the nursery to our bedroom. He went direct to the bed, sat on the edge and started to fall back, taking me with him.

I landed on top of him and we stretched out.

I lifted up on a forearm in his chest and smiled down at him.

"How long is this talk going to take?" I asked, my free hand moving down his side.

He grinned up at me and lifted a hand to tuck my hair behind my ear. "Not long."

"Good, because Clay'll be up soon, and it's my turn to feed him so I need some shuteye," I told him, my body shifting so my hand could move over his stomach before it changed directions and started down.

His head on the pillow cocked to the side.

Hot.

Why did I love that?

It didn't matter. I just did.

"You goin' for shuteye, babe, or are you goin' for my dick?"

I dipped my face closer to his and I also dipped my voice quieter. "Me having the latter makes the former better."

My hand slid in his pajama pants and I found him hard.

His eyes flashed.

"Jesus, baby," he growled.

His arms, having been around me, moved so his hands could cup my behind.

I stroked, a rumble hit his chest and I prompted, "You wanted to talk?"

Raiden rolled us, one of his hands slid over my belly and right into my pajama bottoms, under my panties and *in*.

My eyes went half-mast and I bit my lip.

Then I stroked.

Raid whirled.

Oh God.

"You going to talk?" I breathed as I lifted my hips to get more of his fingers.

He whirled again, which made me stroke again at the same time press up, feeling his hips push into my hand.

"Change of plans," he announced.

"No talking?" I asked hopefully.

"No. No retirement at forty."

I blinked and asked, "Sorry?"

He didn't repeat himself. He stated, "And at least one daughter."

"Raid——"

His face got close. His fingers whirled, my hand tensed on his cock and he declared, "Leavin' you has always sucked. Every time, it got harder and harder. Leavin' you when you had my boy growin' in you, torture. Leavin' you *and* our boy, it kills. Two more years then it's done."

I stroked, I stared and my heart did a happy bump.

"And I want a girl," he finished.

Oh my God!

Could you die of happiness?

I certainly hoped not.

"Honey—"

His lips came to mine. "We'll get started on our daughter later. I'll get started on makin' sure I can take care of my family after I quit the job now. Agreed?"

Did he think I'd say no?

"Affirmative."

I felt his mouth smile against mine, then I saw, up close, his eyes start burning at the same time I felt his fingers move then plunge.

I gasped.

"Done talkin'," he announced, his voice rough and commanding.

I was down with that and that was good, seeing as his head slanted and his mouth took mine in a searing kiss so I had no choice but to be.

Raid

Early Afternoon the Next Day

RAID WAS IN his Jeep heading to meet Clay and Hanna for lunch at his sister's café when his cell went.

He didn't know the number on his display and almost didn't take the call.

When he did, he was glad, but only because if he didn't, they would have called his wife.

"Miller," he answered.

"Raid?" a woman asked.

"Yeah," he replied.

"Hi, uh, this is Judy from the visiting nurse's program. Uh…"

She went silent and said no more.

Raid felt his gut instinctively get tight and he concentrated on driving.

When she didn't speak, he asked, "Judy, you got something to say?"

A hesitation, then in a quiet voice, "I'm so sorry. We talked about it and thought it best to try to phone you first. I hate having to be the one to tell you, but when Fran went in to get Miss Mildred ready for the day, she found that Miss Mildred had passed away in her sleep last night."

Raid moved the Jeep to the side of the road, put it in neutral and engaged the parking break.

"Repeat that," he ordered.

"I'm really, *really* sorry, Raid. We didn't want to call Hanna. We thought it would be better coming from you. But Miss Mildred passed last night."

He closed his eyes, leaned forward and rested his forehead against the steering wheel.

"Are you okay?" she called in his ear.

He was not.

He lifted his head and lied, "Yeah."

"Uh…there are things that—"

Raid cut her off, "You communicate with me, not Hanna. I'll be there or my mother will be there. Yeah?"

"Right, okay."

"Wait for our call. Someone will be in touch soon to deal with whatever we gotta deal with," he went on.

"Okay, Raid."

He pulled in a sharp breath through his nose and lied again, "Thank you for your call."

"I'm so, so sorry."

He was too.

Judy went on, "Please give our condolences to Hanna. 'Bye Raid."

He disconnected with no good-bye, went to his contacts and found the number to his sister's café.

"Rachelle's Café, Grand Goddess of Cuisine and All Things Gastronomical, Rachelle speaking. How can I help you?" his sister answered.

Normally this would make him laugh or at least smile.

He did neither.

"Rache, Hanna there yet?" he asked.

"And hello and how are you, too?" she answered.

"Rache. Is. Hanna. There. Yet?" he repeated.

She was silent then, with zero attitude, "Yeah."

He put the car in gear, checked his mirrors then moved back onto the road, ordering, "Call Mom. Get her down there. After you do that, go to Hanna and find a way to get Clay from her. I'll be there in ten."

"What's wrong?"

"I wanna tell my wife first. Call Mom and get my son."

Another silence then, "Okay, Raid."

"Thanks, Rache."

He disconnected and did as promised, parking in the lot at the end of town, jogging across the street and down the block. He was there in ten.

Rachelle had done as asked, not that he questioned she would. She was sitting with Hanna at a table by the window, cuddling Clay close, bent over her nephew, cooing.

His eyes went to Hanna to see her eyes on him, smiling.

"Hey, sweetheart," she called.

Christ, he fucking loved it when she called him sweetheart.

And he fucking hated what he had to do.

He didn't move from the door and crooked a finger at her.

Her brows drew together, her smile got bigger and she looked at Rachelle. Muttering something he couldn't hear that made Rache give her a smile she didn't fully commit to, Hanna got up and moved to him.

The instant she was close enough, he reached out, grabbed her hand and pulled her out the door.

"What on earth? Have you gone loopy?" she asked his back as he dragged her down the street.

"Hush a minute, baby."

"Whatever," she murmured then finished, "Macho man, loopy."

He wanted to smile at that, too.

He didn't.

He looked both ways, led them across the street and to his Jeep. Once there, he turned her, pushed her into its side and closed in.

She blinked and looked around, got the wrong idea and her face changed as her eyes lifted to his.

"You know, we're married now so I think it's okay if you kiss me in public even if you're in the mood to taste me," she informed him. "Though I'll also remind you that even when we weren't married and just living in sin, you had no problem doing that, so this has got me a little confused."

Raid lifted his hands to either side of her neck, bent deep and whispered, "Hold on to me."

Her eyes moved over his face. She finally read it and he knew it when her body tensed. Without further hesitation, she lifted her hands and curled her fingers into his jacket.

"What's happening?" she asked, her eyes now anxious, her voice holding a tremble.

"Honey…" he started then clipped, "*fuck.*"

She jerked his jacket out then in. "Raid—"

He slid his hands up to her jaw, got closer and laid it out fast, "Got a call from the visiting nurses. Fran went there this morning and found Miss Mildred passed away in the night."

Pain seared through him as he watched that same pain blister over his wife's expression leaving it stricken, pale and vulnerable.

And agonized.

Fuck yeah, he hated having to do this to her.

Hanna pushed through his hands and planted her face in his chest, her arms going tight around him.

Raid gathered her closer, bent his neck and whispered into the top her hair, "I'm so sorry, honey. I'm so *fucking* sorry, baby."

She didn't say anything.

But she did hold on tight, even as she started trembling.

"Mom's comin' to the café. We're gonna get Clay and go home. She or I'll stay with you and the other will go deal with shit," he shared.

Hanna said nothing.

"I'll call your folks when we figure out who's doin' what," he continued.

Hanna still said nothing.

"Baby, look at me," he urged.

She didn't move.

Raid lifted a hand to her jaw, trying to force it away so he could see her face, but she pressed deeper into him so he stopped.

"Hanna—"

"He won't remember," she told his chest.

"What, honey?"

"Clay. He's named after a man he'll never meet and he'll grow up and won't remember that she told him the lightning story."

Raid closed his eyes, wrapped his arm around her again and held her tight.

With no room to move, his wife still managed to burrow deeper.

"We can't ever let him forget," she said.

"We won't let him forget," Raid promised.

"We can never let him forget."

"We'll never let him forget."

Hanna held on.

So did Raid.

Silence ensued.

His wife broke it.

"She thought you were the cat's pajamas," Hanna told him.

He fucking loved that.

But Raid said nothing.

"She also told me she thought you were the bee's knees," she continued.

He fucking loved that, too.

Raid again said nothing.

Finally, her voice broke when she whispered, "She was always right."

Raid slid a hand into her hair and held her cheek close to his chest as she poured her grief into his sweater.

Through her tears, she shared, "This is okay. Even Grams would think being in your arms was an okay place for a Boudreaux to cry."

Raid closed his eyes and kept holding tight.

When she quieted, he led his wife to his sister's café and shared the miserable news with his family. His mother took off to deal with things, he got his son and Raid took his family home.

Though, at Hanna's request, they made one stop.

He left his wife and son waiting in the Jeep while he went into Miss Mildred's house to pick up Spot.

<hr />

One Month Later

RAID MOVED THROUGH the house to the front door.

He pulled it open and pushed out the storm door, stepped on the front porch, turned right and stopped dead.

There was Hanna. In a wool sweater, scarf wrapped around her neck, wide flannel headband holding her hair back, but wrapped over her ears keeping them warm. The rest of her was wrapped in his black cashmere afghan that she took off their bed. Their swaddled son, also under the throw, was lying asleep on her chest.

She was in her swing, one leg up and bent, one foot to the porch, swaying them.

His chest burned at the sight.

Her eyes came to his and she smiled.

His chest eased.

He walked her way and sat in the wicker chair closest to them.

"Sick of winter. I want my bike," she informed him once he settled in.

"Time to plan a vacation to a beach," he replied.

"A beach where they have places to rent bikes," she amended, and he grinned.

He'd give her that.

He'd give Hanna Miller anything.

Her eyes dropped to his mouth and her lips tipped up.

That lip tip meant she knew he'd give her anything.

Then she turned her head, bent her neck and touched those smiling lips to the baby beanie covering Clay's head.

After that, her gaze moved to the yard.

Raid stretched out his legs, crossed them at the ankles and didn't take his eyes off his wife and child.

They stayed that way for a while. Silent. Comfortable. Together.

Hanna broke the quiet.

"It was a dare," she announced.

"Come again?" he asked.

She didn't move her eyes from the yard when she answered, "I've been thinking about it and figured it out. She knew what I'd do when she told me you were dangerous."

Raid felt his shoulders tense.

"What?" he asked.

Finally, her eyes came to his. "Grams. She loved you. She respected you. She wanted me to have you. She knew exactly who you were. She knew everything. And she was worried I might not go the distance. So she warned me off you, knowing the minute she did I would not back down. She did this by scaring the pants off me then telling me that if I saw it through, I'd know nothing sweeter in my whole life," she snuggled Clay closer before she rocked his world, "than the love you'd give to me."

Raid held her eyes.

"She was always right," Hanna finished, and that burn came back into his chest.

Fuck.

Fuck, but he loved his wife.

And he missed her great-grandmother.

"Raiden?" she called even though his eyes were locked on her.

"Right here, baby," he answered quietly.

"I figure she thought she knew something else and I have to know if she was right about that too."

"What?" he asked.

"Only you can answer," she told him.

"What is it, honey?"

She gave it to him.

"She knew you'd know nothing sweeter than the love I give to you."

Jesus, fuck.

"Was she right?" Hanna asked.

Raid held her eyes.

Then he unfolded his body from his chair, taking her in swaying on her porch swing with his son held close to her chest, wrapped up in home, warmth, comfort, nurture.

Love.

He got near and bent deep, put his face close to hers, looked into her pretty blue eyes and curled a hand around the side of her head.

Only then did he reply, "Absolutely."

The Unfinished Hero Series will continue with the story of **Deacon**.

Author's Note

Readers of the Unfinished Heroes Series and loyal readers of my books will note that in *Raid*, I revisited a theme I have touched on before in other books, including the first book in this series, *Knight*.

This theme being Hanna's issues with her figure, primarily her stomach.

In the editing phase of this book, my editor, Chas, and I discussed this repetition and I thought long and hard about deleting references to Hanna's "pouch" and the two scenes in Chapter 13, "That Kind of Love," that explored Hanna's hang-ups with her body and Raid's response.

In finalizing this book, I found that, even though I was aware of this repetition and my readers would certainly notice it, I could not delete it.

I'll explain why.

First, I need to go where my characters take me and Hanna had a variety of lingering, though vague, issues regarding Raid's attraction to her after she crushed on him so long. It was important that Raid have the opportunity to sweep these away, one by one.

Second, there was a nuance of difference regarding this theme in this book as it manifests itself during sex when Hanna adjusted Raid's lovemaking unconsciously in order to take his attention away from a part of her body that she disliked.

It's a sad fact of life that many women have hang-ups about their bodies and these can manifest themselves during intimacy in not very good ways. At best, it can inhibit the experience for them *and* their partner. At worst, it can take them out of "the zone" so what is being shared isn't all it could be or even not enjoyed at all.

I have many heart's desires and one of them is the slim chance that my books will guide women to accepting themselves as they are, having confidence in their bodies, brains and beauty and letting all that poison go so they can enjoy their lives, including sexually. I know I'm drilling this home by repeating this theme. But I decided it was important enough to do it. So I left those bits in.

And last, those scenes in Chapter 13 are funny, sweet and *hot*. I liked them. Hanna liked them. Raid liked them. So we left them.

For my loyal readers, I hope this didn't take you out of those moments. They were left in with intent and the intent was good.

Actually, I hope you were so into the book, you didn't notice at all.

But if you did, now you know why I did it.

Printed in Great Britain
by Amazon

77798001R00157